Traces of You

Barry Homan

DEDICATION

To my daughter,
Lynn Homan Radford,
Who has always made me proud
To be her dad.

ALSO BY BARRY HOMAN:

WHISPERS THROUGH TIME

COVER DESIGN BY:

COREY MASTRAPASQUA

TWINCITY-DESIGNS.COM

ACKNOWLEDGMENTS

I would like to thank a few people for their help in bringing this book to fruition.

To my daughter, Lynn Homan Radford, my great thanks for your many readings of this work and your help in the editing of the book.

To Corey Mastrapasqua, a very large thank you for the wonderful work you performed designing the cover of Traces of You. I do believe your talent knows no bounds.

To my fabulous wife, Karen, for the wonderful love and support you always supply and the immense help you give me in solving all of my computer problems. Love you always and forever, my dear.

Finally, to my much appreciated fans who loved Whispers Through Time so much and clamored for a sequel. I hope you will be well pleased, and yes, a third book in the series is planned.

ONE

The sudden frantic knocking on Simon Taylor's office door startled him. The psychologist took off his glasses, rubbed his eyes, and then ran his hands through his hair. He glanced at the digital clock on his desk; almost nine. He had locked his office door over two hours ago. "Go away," he mumbled, not nearly loud enough for the intruder to hear.

The knocking came again, the pounding harder this time, knuckles rapping hard on the glass window.

Annoyed, Simon began massaging his temples. "We're closed," he shouted, not getting up.

The response from beyond the door was female, plaintive. "Please, you must help me." It was the cry of someone in obvious distress.

Simon sighed. He lifted his six foot, two inch frame from the chair as he put his glasses back on, and then he slowly walked to the door. "We open at eight," he informed the intruder. "Come back then."

"No, please," came the reply, the voice now soft but sounding desperate. "I can't stand the nightmares anymore. If you're Doctor Taylor, please help me now."

Nightmares.

Simon's mind went numb for a moment as he stared through the frosted glass at the shadow of the girl. He understood nightmares all too well. He unlocked the door and slowly turned the metal knob, opening the door an inch at a time as he glanced at the disheveled creature standing in the hallway.

She was of average height, perhaps five-foot five, wearing a floral print dress and sea shell flip flops. A backpack lay on the floor next to her. She had been staring down the hall, running her hand through her hair much as he had done a moment ago, but now she turned to face him as he opened the door.

"Are you really Doctor Taylor?"

"I am," he said. "Are you sure this can't wait until morning? I was getting ready to leave." A lie, but perhaps it would make her go away.

"I need a regression," she said. "I don't want to sleep again without one."

The fear on her face spoke volumes to him. He'd seen it in his own mirror many times in the past year. He wondered if her story would be as painful as his. Simon stared at the girl for a moment, and then decided that helping this waif in his doorway might make him feel better.

"Come in," he finally said.

She grabbed her backpack and rushed through the door before he could change his mind, quickly took in the surroundings, and then turned to face him. "Where do I go?"

He gave her just the hint of a smile. "First you take a deep breath and calm down," he said.

She gently put her backpack on the floor, closed her eyes, and did as she was told, taking three deep breaths and letting them out slowly. As she did Simon noticed her hands go out to her sides, palms up, thumb and index finger forming a circle in each hand.

She meditates, he thought. When she finished he said, "Follow me." He led her to his office in the back and pointed to a chair. "You can sit here."

She looked puzzled. "Don't I lie down?"

"Let's talk first," he said.

It was obvious to the girl that the doctor was tired. He had bags under his eyes and weariness seemed to be oozing out of every pore in his body. He looked like a man who had been knocked down and was deciding whether to get back up. She knew why, having read everything about him that she could get her hands on.

She set her backpack on the floor by the chair and sat down, fidgeting constantly, as though she couldn't sit still.

"Are you on drugs?" he asked.

She stared at him. "What? No, of course not. I hate that crap."

He nodded. "Okay," he said, "just checking."

Simon hated drug addicts, drug dealers, even doctors who prescribed too many drugs to their patients. He watched her for a moment as he took out a sheet of paper from his desk drawer. "You seem to have a lot of nervous energy," he said. "That's why I asked."

I'm having nightmares!!! She screamed inside her head, but held it in, suddenly wondering if he were still as good as his reputation.

She took another deep breath to calm herself and finally said, "My dreams are scaring the crap out of me. They have to be from a past life. I'm thinking that if you can take me there and get me through whatever the hell happened, they might stop."

He had noticed the sudden look on her face and knew she had been questioning him. *With good reason*, he thought. He gazed at her a moment longer and then said, "Let's start with your name."

She relaxed a bit, her shoulders slumping, and she wanted to give him a smile but it wouldn't come. "Hannah," she said. "My name is Hannah Marie Kent."

Simon wrote down the name. The forms his clients fill out on their first visit were in the reception room. He had already decided now wasn't the time to go retrieve one. Instead, he simply asked her a few basic questions.

She continued to run her hand through her hair as she spoke. She was twenty-four, had never been married or had children, and had just started a new job as an assistant to an interior decorator.

"What led you to my door?" he asked, as he jotted down her last answer.

"I've been following you for a few years now. I even went to one of your seminars."

"Oh, which one?" he asked, looking up at her.

"It was in Memphis, January of last year."

Before my nightmares began, thought Simon.

He gazed at her as she spoke. He put her weight at 120 pounds. Her hair was light brown and hung just over her shoulders. Her eyes were a deep brown, soft and beautiful, and her skin looked smooth and unblemished. Her breasts were small and her legs were well defined. A pretty girl overall, although he thought she could use some more meat on her bones.

"Memphis, hmm." He had done so many seminars they all tended to be jumbled together in his mind. "Was I any good?"

"The group regression was interesting. I could picture the place where I once lived, but I had no sense of a time frame. I was the father of two little children, but my wife had died in childbirth. I'm thinking it was fifteenth or sixteenth century, but it's only a guess."

"Just a couple more questions," he said. "They may seem strange, but they may also be important. Please answer as honestly as possible."

She finally managed to crack a small smile. "I've also read your book," she replied. "I think I know what's coming."

He was pleased but not overly surprised. Something had obviously led her to him. "Okay then, please name three places in the United States you would like to visit."

She thought about it for a good ten seconds and then said, "New Mexico, Hawaii and Washington, D.C."

"How about three places overseas?"

This time she barely thought before replying. "Italy, Peru, Russia."

"Name three things ..." He stopped, looked at her, and finally said, "Perhaps that one can wait. Tell me about your nightmares."

Hannah sighed deeply, her breath exhaling loudly. Simon watched as the sweet smile disappeared, replaced once again by a look of abject fear.

"They're horrible," she said. She gazed into space at the wall behind him. "Horrible," she repeated.

"Which means they're probably important," Simon said. "If you've come here looking for a past-life regression I need to know what I'm looking for."

"I'm dying, always dying; trapped by dirt, stones, even fire. I can never get away. It's as if an entire mountainside is falling on me. Like an avalanche but with dirt instead of snow. Some mornings when I wake up I still have this burning taste in my mouth."

"Nothing in your current life ever happened like that? Maybe playing at the beach, being buried in the sand, and a brother or someone went a little too far?"

"No, nothing like that. I don't even know who my birth parents were. I was given up for adoption the day I was born. I don't know why; too young, wanted a boy, unwed mother." She skipped a beat, and then added, "Who cares? It is what it is."

He winced at the comment and closed his eyes. His own nightmare returned for a moment, his hands becoming instantly clammy as beads of sweat broke out on his forehead.

"Doctor Taylor? You okay?"

He looked at her and realized his own fear was showing. He ran his hand across his face and tried to regroup.

"Sorry," he said. "You do have parents that adopted you then?"

"I did," she said, "but they died when I was nine. Auto accident. My grandparents raised me and my sister after that."

"Sister?"

"Yes, I have a sister. She was adopted too."

"A twin sister?" asked Simon.

"No, not a twin, and not a blood relation either. Our parents adopted her a year before they adopted me. Her name is Jessica. We may not be related by blood, but she's my closest friend in the world."

He nodded as he jotted down the information.

"How often do you have these nightmares?" asked Simon.

"I've had them since I was little," said Hannah, "but they didn't come that often. I'd wake up sweating and screaming; scared the hell out of my mother and father. But lately they're coming on a regular basis, sometimes two or three times a week."

He watched as she looked down at her hands in her lap. It was obvious to him that these dreams were tremendously upsetting to her.

"I can't take them anymore," she mumbled, more to herself than to him.

For a moment he thought she was going to cry, but she held it in. "So you're thinking they must be remembrances of a past life of yours?"

"I do," said Hannah.

"And you want me to help you find it?"

"Please."

"Okay," he said after a short pause, "I'll try to help you out, but any future appointments you may want will have to be in the daytime." Simon cracked a smile and was rewarded with a smile back.

"Yes, doctor," said Hannah.

As upset as he had been by her intrusion a few minutes ago, Simon was now happy to have his mind taken off his own problems. "Okay, let's get started," he said. "Now you may go lie on the couch."

Hannah arose, went to the couch across the room, and lay

down. As Simon approached she said, "I'm very nervous, but I do meditate regularly, so once you start I think I'll be okay."

"That should certainly help," said Simon, as he moved a chair next to the couch. He made sure the digital voice recorder, situated on a table to the left of the couch, was ready to go. The DVR had replaced his old stereo system, which he'd left back in South Carolina along with most everything else, after his own nightmare had started.

He began the session as he always did, by having Hannah relax each part of her body from toes to head. Her breathing calmed into a gentle rhythm as she did this, and Simon could sense the tension leaving her. When he finished he asked, "Are you relaxed now, Hannah?"

"Yes," she replied, her voice soft, barely above a whisper.

"I'm going to start counting backwards from ten to one. As I do I want you to picture yourself descending a spiral staircase. You will become more peaceful with each step you take, and when I reach one you will be standing in a hallway, in front of a door, completely at ease. Do you understand?"

"Yes," she said again.

He took her through the process in just under a minute. When he finished she appeared to be almost asleep.

"Are you fully relaxed now, Hannah?"

"Yes." Her lips hardly moved.

"We're going to go back in time now, Hannah. Just a little bit to begin with. I want you to picture opening the door and walking on through. As you do, you will be going back in time."

He had recently added the door to the process, thinking that it might help some clients to actually picture going back in time.

Hannah lay still on the couch, eyes closed, barely breathing.

"Have you passed through the doorway, Hannah?"

"Yes," she said.

"I want you to go back three or four years to an event that made you happy. Can you find a time back then that stands out for you?"

She was quiet for a moment, but finally managed a weak "yes."

"Very good, Hannah. Tell me about that day. Where were you?"

"Fort Lauderdale. It was spring break, hot and sunny. I was on the beach with my friends; Carol, Susie, Max." Her face brightened at the remembrance.

"Is Max a boy?" asked Simon.

"No, her name is Maxine. We call her Max."

"Does something special happen on this day, Hannah?"

"No, nothing special. It was just a great day with friends. We swam, drank beers, checked out the guys. That night we went to a party."

"Did you make any new friends, special friends, at the party?"

"I met a guy there, very nice and well-mannered. Not what you find too often on spring break. He was cute, too. But nothing ever came of it. I never saw him again."

"Very good, Hannah. You're doing fine. Now let's go back a bit farther."

He took her back to the age of twelve and asked her to find a happy memory.

She answered far quicker than he expected. "There's one day I remember."

"Can you tell me about it?"

"It was January and we were visiting an uncle of mine," said Hannah. "He lived on a farm in New York. It had snowed the night before, a really big storm. I had never seen snow before because I had always lived in Florida. I helped to shovel it, and later I was able to go sledding down one of the hills on the farm. I had so much fun that day."

Simon again told Hannah she was doing fine and took her back once more.

"Hannah, now I want you to go back to when you were very young, maybe just a year or two old? What is the first thing you recall from this lifetime?"

She went back farther than he had planned, at least for the moment. "I knew my mother wasn't going to keep me," she said.

She had said she was given up for adoption the day she was born, so Simon guessed she had gone back to the womb. "Did you realize this before you were born?" he asked.

"Yes, I knew it. I had chosen that path."

"Why did you choose a life as an adoptee?"

"Karma," she said.

"You had given up a child in a previous life?" asked Simon.

"More than once," Hannah replied. "I needed to see the effect from the opposite point of view this time."

"Do you understand why your mother gave you up for adoption?"

"She was young, still in high school, and very smart, with plenty of opportunities to attend college. She wasn't ready for me, yet she still wanted to keep me. Her parents wouldn't hear of it."

"Her parents made her put you up for adoption."

"Yes."

She had just told him minutes earlier that she didn't know why her mother had put her up for adoption. Now her subconscious mind had given her some answers. Even if the rest of the regression went poorly, Simon thought that Hannah would appreciate what she had just told him.

It was time to move to the next step; the regression into a past life. Some clients did this part easily, some had great difficulty. Simon hoped Hannah would be a good subject, because he really did want to help her with her nightmares.

"Hannah, I want you to go back into your past now, back to past lives you've previously lived. Try to find the life or lives that are causing you to have the dreams you are having now." He wanted to avoid using the word nightmare during the regression. "Take your time, there is no rush."

Simon waited anxiously. This was the critical spot in any

regression. Most people could go back in time all right, but it was a crap shoot from there. Some people just touched on many lifetimes, barely giving any information on them, moving quickly from one to the next. Others could offer up some intriguing insights about certain lives, but still didn't stay too long in any one era. The good ones happened when a client could recall major portions of a prior lifetime in accurate detail and get to the root of a current problem.

The great ones … well, there weren't too many Jill Palmers in the world as far as Simon was concerned. Jill had been his finest regression client ever. His book, <u>Past Life Memories</u>, had been a best-seller because of her. He often wondered if he would ever find a client that good again.

He looked at Hannah and hoped she would be the one. He wanted to help her. After all, they were compadres of a sort.

The nightmare twins.

Simon wanted to free her from her awful dreams. He wished someone could deliver him from his. Images of the past swirled in his imagination and he was suddenly lost in his thoughts again. Ten seconds went by; then ten more.

Hannah's voice brought him back. "I'm there, Doctor."

The sleepy sounding voice startled Simon, and he realized he had lost his concentration once again. He shook his head as if to get the cobwebs out and tried to remember where they had been in the regression.

"Okay, Hannah," he finally said. "Know that nothing you remember from any previous life can hurt you now. They are just memories."

"Okay," she said.

"Tell me about the life you've found, Hannah. Where are you?"

Hannah lay on the couch, still and quiet. "So long ago," she said.

"Have you found a lifetime that fits your dreams?" asked Simon.

"Not sure."

"Can you tell me what year it is, or where you are?"

"No," she said. "There's really not much to go by. It's cold, and the ground is covered with snow, lots of it. Some place like Siberia, I guess."

"Are you a female in this life?" asked Simon.

"No, I'm a man. I seem to be mid-twenties, maybe thirty years old."

"Is there anyone else with you?"

"No, I'm alone." A small smile creased her face as she added, "I think I'm lost in the wilderness."

"Can you tell me how you are dressed?"

"As you would expect for the freezing cold," she said. "Heavy coat made out of fur of some kind, and a fur hat too; boots nearly up to my knees, but no gloves. I have some kind of fabric wrapped around my hands to keep them warm."

"What happens to you, Hannah? Why did you return to this lifetime?"

She paused for a while before finally answering. "I freeze to death. I'm weak, hungry, and I finally pass out. It is snowing when that happens, and eventually I'm covered with snow. I never get up."

It wasn't the dirt of her nightmares, but it was a start, and she had been buried.

"Remember, Hannah, this is only a memory. You are lying on the couch in my office and you are fine."

"Yes, only a memory," she replied.

"Can you tell me anymore about that lifetime?" he asked.

"No."

"Is this the lifetime that is the cause of your dreams?"

"No," she replied.

"Okay then, let's attempt to find another lifetime that ended in a similar manner. Remember you are safe, and it is only memories we are reliving," he said again.

"I know," she said. "I'm fine."

He hoped to find a more recent life where her recall would be better. "Let's move ahead in time to the next lifetime that is affecting your current dreams. Can you find another lifetime that applies?"

Again she paused for a while, as though she were thumbing through each of her past lives to see which one fit.

"I have one," she said.

Simon smiled, her regression temporarily taking his mind off of his own troubles. "Excellent," he said. "What can you tell me about this next life?"

"I'm a girl," said Hannah. "My name is Kali, after the goddess."

Simon knew of the goddess Kali and asked, "Are you in India?"

"India, yes."

"How old are you?"

"I think I'm about nine. I live in a small town."

"Do you live with your family?"

"Yes, of course," she said. "I have a mother and father and nine brothers and sisters."

"That's wonderful, Hannah. Do you recognize anyone from that time period that you know now?"

It was one of the wonders of regressions. People could recognize family and friends in their past life who were with them now in their current life, although the opposite never seemed to be true, at least on a conscious level.

She paused again, and Simon saw her head move slightly, as if she were checking out her family of long ago.

"I do," she said, a surprised sound to her voice. "That's my grandmother!"

"Your grandmother in this life?" asked Simon.

"Yes. She is one of my sisters. Her name is Sevaley."

Wanting to make sure he had it right, Simon asked, "So your sister Sevaley during your life in India is now your grandmother?"

"Yes. And Gupta, my brother, is now my Uncle Dan. It was his farm in New York where I was sledding."

"That's excellent," said Simon. "Can you tell me what

your life is like there?" he asked. "Do you go to school?"

"School?" She seemed to search for the answer, and then said, "No, I don't think so."

"Do you know what year it is?"

"No. It seems to be very far back."

Simon was always amazed by how far back his clients would sometimes go. Over the years he had regressed clients who had gone back to ancient Egypt or the era of Jesus, and a few who had gone back over three thousand years, as Hannah may be doing now.

"Tell me about your village," said Simon.

"It is very small, about four hundred people," said Hannah. "It is situated at the bottom of a large mountain. We grow our own food, and everyone in the family works in the field. All the children work, even the very young ones."

Simon was about to ask another question when a great smile came over Hannah's face.

"Ashoka is coming," she said, obviously pleased.

"Who is Ashoka?" he asked.

"He is the boy I love and want to marry some day."

"Do you recognize Ashoka as someone you know in this life, Hannah?"

"No, I don't know him now."

"Hannah, can you go ahead in time to the day you and Ashoka marry?"

"No," she replied. "We never marry. The rains come."

"How old are you when the rains come?"

"I'm still nine, maybe ten," said Hannah. "The monsoon hits us in the middle of the night. We are all sleeping, and when we wake up it is too late."

"Too late for what, Hannah? What happens?"

"Mudslide," she said wistfully. "Too late to escape the mudslide. The mountain comes down on top of us."

"Hannah, remember you are in my office, safe and warm. There is no reason to be fearful. Can you look down over the scene and tell me what happens?"

She shivered suddenly and her entire body moved on the

couch. "It was quick. I awoke only when I heard the others screaming. Then I was washed away in a sea of mud. I died almost instantly."

"Is this the cause of your dreams?"

"I think I do dream about this on occasion, but it is not the one that wakes me up screaming."

"Can you tell me anything more about this lifetime?"

"No," she said, "I've moved on."

Simon was disappointed she wasn't staying within the lifetimes for a longer period so that he could gather more information about them, but at least she was finding lives that might explain the nightmares she was having.

Still, he wondered if they would get much more out of the regression. They had two lifetimes where she had died a sudden death and been buried under snow or mud. However, neither lifetime could explain the burning taste in her mouth that she had talked about. He wondered if they would find another lifetime that fit.

"Okay, let's move ahead and see if there are any other past lives of yours that might be causing the dreams that you are currently having."

"Nightmares," she corrected.

"Yes," said Simon, his attempt to avoid the word apparently obvious to her. "Is there any other life in your past that fits our criteria?"

She paused for a moment, and then a sudden whimper escaped her.

"Are you okay?" asked Simon. "Should we stop?"

"No, I'm alright," she said, but her voice had an unexpected shakiness that worried Simon.

"Have you found another lifetime that fits your situation?"

"I have, but it is not pleasant." She paused again, her eyes appearing to squeeze tightly as if she were in pain. "This is definitely the cause of my nightmares. There are two major catastrophes during this lifetime. I survived the first one."

Simon assumed she was telling him she didn't survive the second one. "Are you there now?"

"Yes."

"Are you a male or female in this life?"

"I'm female," said Hannah.

"What is your name? Can you tell me?"

"My name is unimportant."

Another first; no client had ever said that before. "Why is your name unimportant?" he asked.

"I'm a slave," said Hannah.

He thought of the slave trade and asked, "Are you in Africa?

"No, not Africa," she replied. "I was born a slave. My mother is a slave."

"Are you a dark-skinned person in this lifetime?"

Hannah appeared to look herself over for a moment before answering. "My skin is a golden brown. I think I might be Spanish or Portuguese."

"Tell me about the clothes you are wearing," said Simon.

"I'm wearing a wrap of some kind made out of cloth." She paused again as if searching for the right word, and then added, "A tunic."

Although this new life seemed to have shaken her, Simon was hopeful that this remembrance would bring back more memories for Hannah than the other ones had.

"You said there were two incidents that occurred in this life. Let's go back to that first incident if you can. Tell me about that one? How old were you when it happened?"

"It was an earthquake," said Hannah. She thought for a moment and then said, "I was about twenty-five."

"Do you know the name of the town you are in?"

"Yes," said Hannah. "I know."

She gave him the name, and Simon recognized it instantly. It was a place he and his wife Nora had visited on two different occasions during their trips to Europe. He had been so enthralled by the visits that he had come home after their first trip and read all he could about what had happened there.

It was a history he knew very well.

The question was whether Hannah had lived there during the times that Simon knew about.

"Hannah, can you tell me what year the earthquake takes place?"

She told him immediately, and Simon knew they had found the cause of Hannah's nightmares.

Pompeii.

TWO

Simon hoped that Hannah's recall of her life in Pompeii would be more thorough than the other lives she had mentioned so far. "Let's go back to your name. Even though you are a slave, you must have a name."

Then an amazing thing happened. Except for an occasional question from Simon, Hannah Marie Kent spoke non-stop for forty-five minutes.

"My name is Helvia. I was shaken awake by my mother that morning. She said 'Helvia, get up. The sun has been up for five minutes now.'

"I stirred for a moment, and then my eyes popped open as I realized what my mother had said. The day of a slave started at sunrise in the household of Decimer Macer. There was much to do early in the morning.

"I stood up quickly and felt a crick in my back from sleeping on the hard kitchen floor. Then I rolled up my bedroll and stored it away. I was the only slave sleeping in the kitchen. The others all slept in the hallway. That is why I hadn't stirred when the rest of them did.

"I joined my mother and the other slave girls at the back door and we headed out to begin our shopping."

Simon remembered reading that slaves were not allowed to enter or leave through the front door. "Can you tell me what you look like, what your appearance is?" he asked.

"I'm very tall; nearly six feet. Thin yet muscular. I have a small round face, brown eyes with spots of gold in them, and short dark brown hair. I'm the tallest of all the women in the household. My height often draws the attention of men, most of whom are shorter than me.

"The day is bright and sunny as we walk towards the market. This is one of the best times of the day for us. We are free to roam the streets and be ourselves for a few hours. Of course, we must accomplish our task of purchasing the day's food supply, but we are out on our own.

"The streets are busy, but it is nearly all slaves who are out, running the same chores as we are. I know many of them, but there is little time to stop and chat.

"The market is already crowded when we arrive. Buying food for the household is always the first item of the day. My mother, who is the oldest of our group, acts as the leader. She sends us off in different directions; some to buy meat or fish, others to buy vegetables and beans.

"She tells me to 'Get the fish today', and points out a merchant with a stand on the corner of the street. He is one we trust more than others, although most of the merchants are honest. They have public scales run by slaves to keep them that way.

"I make my way to the front of the line, occasionally slipping ahead of another shopper who wasn't paying attention. There are fourteen people in our household to take care of, not counting the slaves. When I arrive at the front I purchase about fifty pounds of fish. It is put into a basket that I balance on my head. It is the easiest way to carry it through the crowd.

"I rejoin the others. We are all laden down with our purchases, but we are used to it. No one complains except for Julia. She is just fifteen and has only been with us for a few months. She has not yet built up the stamina that she needs, but she will over time.

"My mother looks at me and says, 'We'll take this home, and then you can go back out for the bread. Take Julia with you.'

"My mother knew I had an eye for a young man who worked at one of the bakeries, but she was not being overly kind to me. She showed no favoritism to me over the other girls. It was simply my turn. However, I was delighted. It meant that I would not have to go for water, which was the toughest chore of the day. Standing in line at the fountain, then filling your jug and carrying it back to the home—Ugh!—we all hated that chore.

"When we returned home I brought the fish into the kitchen and set it on the counter, and then I turned to Julia and said, 'Come with me.' Immediately she asked where we were going, whining like the little girl that she was, and my mother yelled at her to 'just do as you're told'.

"I told her we were going to get the bread, and that brought a smile to her face. She put down the meat she had been carrying and her arms hung limply to her side, all energy gone. Yet I knew in a few more weeks she would be much stronger.

"We walked back outside and turned left. We had passed half a dozen bakeries before Julia asked, 'Why don't we just go to the closest one?' There were over thirty bakeries in the area because so much bread is needed each day. Only a few homes have their own ovens.

"'Are you in such a hurry to return to the work at home?' I asked her, and when she said no I told her, 'There's someone I want to see,' and I guess the look on my face gave me away, because she answered, 'Oh, a boy.'

"'Not a boy, a man, I replied. His name is Stephanus.

"We arrived at the bakery to that wonderful smell of fresh baked bread that always made my mouth water. I saw Stephanus in the back and knew he had been there since midnight. He was turning the grinding stone that crushed the grain into flour. Some bakeries used donkeys to turn the stone, but if there wasn't enough room for a donkey, slaves would be used.

"Stephanus is two inches shorter than me, but extremely muscular. Walking in a circle for hours on end turning the stone was back-breaking work, and he had been doing it for years now. His thick black hair glistened as sweat poured off his brow.

"I recognize him! He is Ashoka from my life in India."

Simon was stunned by the sudden story she was telling. "Have you recognized anyone else yet that you know in your current lifetime?" he asked.

"My mother is now an aunt of mine. I have not recognized anyone else.

"Stephanus finally sees me and gives me a quick wave. I smile and wave back, but my purchase is ready and I have to leave. Most days that would be the only time I would see him."

Most days? Simon wondered if this day would be different.

"We returned home and I spent the next hour preparing the food for the day's meals. It must have been around ten o'clock when my mother came to me and said the matron wanted me to attend the baths with her. The matron was Livinia Macer, wife of Decimus, who was the owner of the home and all the slaves in it. Decimus was a former soldier in the Roman Army and had been given the estate as a reward for his years of service to the Emperor.

"I immediately dropped what I was doing and walked quickly to Livinia's room. The matron didn't like to be kept waiting. I gathered together all of her toiletry supplies that she would use during her bath; different olive oils, a variety of soaps, and the change of clothes she had laid out.

"The public bath was down the street about a half mile away. Livinia walked slowly, often stopping to exchange pleasantries with other ladies that she knew. When we reached the baths the waters were already filled with naked men and women. Although there were private areas just for men or women in another part of the complex, Livinia always liked to stay in the shared pool.

"She washed slowly, chatting as she did so with the men and women around her. I handed her the different oils as needed; one for her hair, another for her face, still another to soften the skin on her arms and legs.

"After an hour I was excused, and I went to wait in the slaves' quarters. The room was bare and lacked any amenities save for a bench to sit on. I saw a friend from the home next door to ours and I sat with her, keeping the matron's belongings close at hand. Thievery among the slaves was a common occurrence, and losing my lady's change of clothing would draw severe punishment. I knew the matron would probably be in the pool for another two hours. I simply had to wait.

"My wait was short-lived, however. Suddenly the floor below my feet began to rumble and then shake. I recognized the signs of an earthquake immediately, for we often had rumbles in the area, although they had never amounted to much.

"This one was different. The intensity picked up dramatically. My friend sitting next to me suddenly fell out of her seat as the building started to rock. I grabbed the belongings entrusted to me and headed for the exit to try and find the matron. A vase fell off its pedestal and nearly hit me as I passed by.

"I managed to reach the area of the public baths just as the earthquake hit full blast. The scene was utter chaos. The floor cracked open and water was rushing everywhere. The roof to the area on my right suddenly caved in, and I looked that way just in time to see one of the city's leading senators crushed by the debris.

"I rapidly gazed left and right to try and find Livinia, but naked bodies were running helter skelter and I couldn't see her anywhere. It was only when I heard a doleful cry of 'Help me' that I recognized the matron's voice and finally saw her. She apparently had just removed herself from the bath when a nearby statue split in two and fell on top of her.

"I rushed up to Livinia as quick as I could, trying to avoid falling bodies, sliding debris and rushing water. The shaking became worse, and twice I was knocked down by others who were attempting to exit the bathhouse. By the time I finally arrived at the matron's side it was too late. Her cry for help had apparently been the final words she had uttered.

"The shaking stopped a moment later. In all it had probably lasted about forty-five or fifty seconds. I think I went into a state of shock for a while. Seeing my matron's body crushed and bleeding was horrifying to me, and there were more bodies scattered around the room. Even most of the people who survived suffered injuries of some manner or other."

"Were you injured at all?" asked Simon.

Hannah's head moved from side to side as if examining her body. "I have a cut on my leg. I don't even know how I received it, but that is all. How is that possible? I wander outside and see devastation everywhere. Many homes are completely destroyed, the roofs caving in and crushing them."

Simon was aware from all the reading he had done that homes at that time had heavy wooden beams and terra cotta tiles that made up their roofs. Their weight was tremendous, and deadly during an earthquake.

"I begin to make my way back to my matron's home, but it is difficult. The streets are filled with people, both slaves and free. Many are in shock as I am, seeing but not believing, and homes and businesses everywhere are in ruin. I eventually manage to make it home, but I wish I hadn't. The sight brings tears to my eyes. At least eighty percent of the home is in rubble.

"Julia is the first one I find. She had almost made it outside before a chunk of stone fell on her, crushing her legs. She is alive but unconscious, pinned by the heavy weight, and she will die shortly.

"I need to find my mother, but when I do she, too, is dead. One of the slave girls who survived tells me my mother tried to move everyone else to safety but then ran out of time for herself. She was a hero, but now my mother is gone."

Simon realized that Hannah was extremely agitated at this point, and decided it was time to move on.

"Hannah, let's jump ahead in time a few years. Try to find a time when you are happy again. Tell me about it."

Instead of a few years, Hannah jumped ahead just an hour or so.

"Stephanus is alive!" she proclaimed.

"Amazingly, the bakery where he works suffered very little damage, although all around it there is destruction. The baker and Stephanus are standing outside the shop, looking stunned, when he suddenly sees me. I rush into his arms and he holds me tight. The baker doesn't complain. He is in as much shock as everyone else."

"Did Livinia's husband survive the earthquake?" asked Simon, momentarily forgetting his name.

"No. It was said the ground opened up and swallowed him whole."

"How do you survive in the coming days?" asked Simon.

A look of agony comes over Hannah's face. "It is so sad," she says. "We thought that help from Rome would arrive quickly, but it does not. Chaos is everywhere. Slaves have no masters; masters have no slaves.

"Later that day the baker would find that his wife is among the dead and his home destroyed. I am fortunate. The baker takes me in because he sees I am so close to Stephanus. We sleep at the bakery, but there is little work to do there for the baker has few supplies. It turns out the ships carrying the grain were in the harbor at the time of the quake. Some sailed away, but a great many sank because of the waves the quake caused."

Simon knows that reconstruction in the area was very slow and tries once again to move Hannah ahead in time.

"Let's go to the time leading up to the next disaster. Are you still with Stephanus? Do you still live in the same town?"

Hannah paused, as if building up the strength to relive yet

another major disaster.

"Yes, I am with Stephanus. We have two children now, both boys."

"Do you recognize the boys as people you know in your current life?"

"I do," said Hannah. "One was my adopted father, and the other boy is now my sister Jessica. We are still together."

"But you don't recognize Stephanus yet as anyone you know now?"

"No," said Hannah, who then continued her story. "We have moved to the next town over."

Simon remembered his Pompeii history and asked, "Would that be Herculaneum?"

"Yes," said Hannah. "It too suffered damage from the earthquake, but not nearly as much. Their recovery is quicker."

"Are you still with the baker?"

"No, he has died. But he did a wonderful thing for us before his passing. He gave us our *freedom*!"

She nearly yelled the word. Simon was thrilled that her recollection of the event caused her so much joy.

"When he found out how much Stephanus loved me, he invited me to move with them to Herculaneum. There had been a baker who had passed away, and Stephanus' owner took over his shop. I was still a slave at that time, of course. The baker put me to work in the bakery. I helped make the loaves and put them into the ovens. It was not really hard work, and he treated me well.

"I guess about six years went by and then the baker became quite ill. He realized that he was dying, and since Stephanus had been so loyal and hard-working over the years, the baker decided to give him his freedom. We were thrilled, but then when he told us he would give me my freedom also, well, it was a joyous day.

"But that wasn't all. He had no family left at that point, so he gave Stephanus the bakery as well. Words cannot describe how happy we were."

Simon glanced at the clock and noticed how late it was becoming. He was surprised, and realized that for the first time in a long while he was happily engaged in what he was doing. Still, he felt the need to move ahead. "How many years before the second disaster were you given your freedom?"

"About ten."

"And your life was …"

"Wonderful!" cried Hannah. "We had two more children, a girl and a boy. They were a joy to our hearts, although I do not recognize them in my current life. The bakery was busy every day, and Herculaneum was a more prosperous town than Pompeii had been. After a while we became quite wealthy."

"Let's go to your final days," said Simon. "Remember, this is only a reviewing of that lifetime. Nothing can hurt you now."

"I know," replied Hannah. "It is simply a past life that I once lived."

"That's right," said Simon. "Can you tell me how it starts?"

"The wells dried up."

"The wells?"

"That was our first clue. Of course we didn't know what was about to happen. We had no idea the mountain could do such a thing."

"You didn't know it was a volcano?" asked Simon.

"No," Hannah replied. "I don't think anyone knew. We used to pray to the mountain to keep us safe and bring abundance. When the wells suddenly started to dry up we knew something must be wrong, but we had no reason to believe it involved the mountain.

"Then when August began the earth cracked open, as if someone had used a giant ax to break it in half. It was similar to the way the ground broke open in the Pompeii earthquake. I remember Stephanus mentioning to me how rough the seas were becoming. Waves like we had rarely seen in the harbor, and we began getting small earthquakes on a regular basis.

"I guess the last precursor was the animals."

"The animals started acting up?" asked Simon, knowing that they often knew of impending danger before humans did.

"Yes. The dogs and horses were going crazy and the birds flew away. By then the quakes were coming every day."

"And then?" asked Simon, leaving the question open.

Hannah was pensive for a moment as she recalled the event.

Simon thought she was becoming frightened and told her that she could just float above her body and watch the scene below. "You can't be harmed by this. It's just a memory."

"And then the world blew up," she said.

Simon waited, knowing the story would come.

"It must have been around noon time," said Hannah. "Stephanus and I were at the bakery, although there were few customers. Everyone was talking about the constant quakes and strange happenings. I remember one man saying his three dogs had run off. They just disappeared.

"Suddenly there was a tremendous explosion, like nothing I had ever heard. We all ran out into the street, wondering what had happened. The top half of the mountain was gone! We couldn't believe our eyes. Stones and hot ash were flying up into the air. Madness erupted in Herculaneum and reminded me of those days in Pompeii.

"We were fortunate at first, for the winds were blowing south and kept much of the debris away from us. Poor Pompeii was getting rained upon by all of it, again taking the brunt of the disaster.

"The rest of the day was just chaos and confusion. People from Pompeii were fleeing the town, many of them coming through Herculaneum as they made their way north. Others tried to sail out of the area, but the waters were incredibly rough and many boats sank.

"As the day turned into night there were black clouds throughout the sky and it looked as though the wind were on fire. And the quakes just kept coming, over and over again. I'd never been so frightened in all my life, not even in Pompeii.

"Around midnight we received word that many of the people were heading to the boat houses on the shore, thinking that it would be safer there from the falling debris. Stephanus thought it was a good idea, and by that time I would have agreed to anything that took me farther away from that mountain, so that's where we headed."

Hannah paused, and when she resumed her voice had a mournful, haunting sound.

"It was too late. Rivers of lava were flowing down the side of the mountain heading straight for us. If I live a thousand lifetimes I'll never be that scared again.

"And then I died."

Simon did not ask for details. He had read numerous accounts of the event and knew the horror of it. It was time to bring Hannah back.

"Hannah, in a moment I'm going to count from one to three, and when I say three you will return to the present time. We have discovered why you are having such terrible nightmares. Now there is no need for them to bother you ever again. You will sleep peacefully from now on. Do you understand?"

"I do," said Hannah.

"Okay, then … one, two, three."

Hannah's eyes popped open and she turned her gaze to Simon Taylor; then she burst into tears. Hannah's tears rained down for nearly a minute before she finally regained some semblance of composure.

"Oh my God," she eventually said, "what a horrible way to die."

"I gather that we have found the cause of your nightmares," said Simon.

Hannah slowly looked up at the doctor, sniffled one more time, and then nodded her agreement. "Yes," she finally said, "many of my nightmares have been similar to that."

Simon told her about his two visits to Pompeii. He assured her that the details of her recall were accurate from the history he knew and that she was not making them up.

Not that she doubted it for a second. "The last scene in Herculaneum," she said, "was just like my worst nightmare; a wall of burning fire slamming into my body. That's the one that always had me screaming the loudest."

"Yet you did leave your body before the flow hit you, did you not?"

"Yes, I did," said Hannah. "I was floating about twenty yards above myself—that sounds funny to say—when I died. And I can assure you, death was instantaneous. It was just devastating."

"Yet since you had left your body already, you didn't actually feel pain, did you?"

"I … didn't. You're right."

She had a mystified look on her face that Simon had seen many times before.

"When our spirit leaves the body it no longer feels the pain and suffering that the body goes through in its final moments," said Simon. "I've had clients who died in plane crashes who felt no pain, because they left the body before the plane hit the ground."

"Yet the memory of what happened to me stayed with me and caused my nightmares," said Hannah.

"Yes, it certainly seems that way."

"But why would I be having dreams now about a life that ended nearly two thousand years ago?"

"I don't know," said Simon. "Perhaps the memories are important information you need for what's ahead of you."

"Ahead of me? What do you mean, like more earthquakes?"

"I honestly don't know why you would be dreaming about a life so long ago." He talked with her a while longer until her fear seemed to be gone. He hoped the scenes she had just witnessed would not bring her more nightmares but would instead cause them to cease.

"You also learned something about your birth mother," said Simon. "Do you remember what you said when you were in the womb state?"

"She wanted to keep me," said Hannah, as another tear started to form on her cheek. "Her parents made her give me up."

"I hope that also brings you some comfort," said Simon.

"It does," said Hannah. "More than you know."

Simon noted the time and said, "Well, I hadn't expected to be in my office this late. It's after ten thirty."

"I'm sorry to have barged in on you like I did," said Hannah, "but I ..."

He cut her off with a wave of his hand. "All things considered, I'm glad you did."

"Thank you," she said, and she arose to go.

Before she left, Simon asked if she wanted to return for more regressions. While she had started off slowly, the regression to Pompeii and Herculaneum had been extraordinary. He was hoping that maybe she could do it again. However, Hannah was non-committal.

"I'm going to have to think about it," she said.

"You did meet Stephanus again after seeing him in India. It certainly appears that he could be a soul mate of yours, or at least someone you always reincarnate with. Maybe he will continue to show up in more regressions."

"Perhaps," Hannah said, "and I will think about coming back; honest. But for now, I just want to go home and see how well I sleep."

"I understand," said Simon, "and I certainly hope this will be the end of your nightmares." He handed her one of his business cards and told her to feel free to call anytime.

As Hannah neared the door she tried to hand him a fifty dollar bill. "I know your sessions aren't free," she said. "I hope this is enough."

"Under the circumstances, I think we'll let this one slide," he said. "To be honest, I think I should pay you for such an amazing story."

Hannah left a moment later, and Simon sat back down at his desk, intending to tidy up for just a minute before leaving.

As he did, his gaze caught the picture of Nora that sat on the corner of the desk. He slumped back in his chair as his mind wandered yet again.

THREE

Fourteen months ago Simon Taylor had been riding high. His psychology practice in Willis, South Carolina was thriving; his book was still hanging around the best-seller lists; he had speaking engagements around the country explaining past-life regressions; and his marriage to Nora, the woman he believed to be his soul mate, was as strong as ever.

He and Nora had met at a gathering of local medical practitioners. She had come with her boyfriend, a doctor who had just finished his residency at Boston General and had moved back to South Carolina to open a family practice.

Simon had come to the party alone. He had never dated very much and was too busy to worry about it. One look at Nora had changed his mind. She was smart, funny, and loved her work as an emergency room nurse. Standing five foot eight, she was slim yet strong, with short black hair, grayish eyes, and long eyelashes that most runway models would kill for.

Simon moved in to talk with her as soon as her boyfriend wandered off, and by the end of the night he was asking her out. She declined at first, telling him she was in a relationship, but his persistence finally earned him a lunch date.

It had taken off from there. They were both dedicated to their jobs but thoroughly enjoyed the time they spent together.

Neither one wanted children. Nora moved in with him three months after their first date, and a year later they married. They never regretted it.

The one thing they made sure to do every year was plan their vacations together. They had gone on an African Safari, relaxed on the beaches of Maui, and toured Europe by car, train and boat.

When Simon's book had been released and become a best-seller, Nora was thrilled for him. Their combined income made them one of the richer families in the small town of Willis, yet they had no desire to move to bigger, more exciting cities. Willis was their home. They loved their jobs and they loved each other. Life was perfect.

In February they had celebrated his forty-first birthday. Nora threw him a surprise party the day before his actual birthday. Twenty-two of their closest friends were there, and Simon had been thrilled. Although both drove top of the line BMW's, she gave him a Jaguar XKR-S Convertible as a present, knowing he had always wanted one.

Three weeks later they were making plans for their 13th anniversary and trying to decide where to go on their summer vacation.

It was a Tuesday evening, cool and rainy. Simon had stayed around the office until nearly nine, making notes about two new regression clients he had seen that morning, and talking for almost a half hour with one of his hypochondriac patients who was sure she was dying of some flesh eating disease.

He had to pick Nora up from work at ten because her car was in the shop and she refused to drive his stick shift. He had planned on taking his BMW home and using the Jaguar, but the rain caused him to change his mind.

He showed up at the emergency room fifteen minutes before her ten o'clock shift ended. The receptionist recognized him immediately and buzzed him in. He walked back to the main desk and said hello to the two nurses who were sitting behind the counter. Nora spied him from down the hallway and gave him a quick wave. Simon settled into a nearby chair and began thumbing through a copy of Archeology Magazine.

Nora was just getting ready to leave when a police car drove up to the ambulance entrance of the emergency room. Two officers emerged from the front seat, opened the back door and pulled out a twenty year old male named Miguel Diaz, who was obviously high on something. He also had a heavy bandage over one arm.

"Definitely going to need stitches," Simon heard one of the officers say.

The two cops struggled mightily to get their prisoner into the ER. The man was kicking and screaming, though much of what he said was unintelligible.

Nurse Doris Wegman said, "Bring him in here," pointing to an empty room near the area where Simon was sitting.

Patrolman Thomas Jones, just four months on the force, had been riding with his Sergeant, a fourteen year veteran named Angel Marino, when they had received the call. The two men managed to get Diaz to sit on the bed, and then Jones undid one of the handcuffs, which belonged to the Sergeant, and quickly reattached it to the rail on his side of the bed. The crazed kid was still struggling to free himself, his freed arm now flapping around as he tried to avoid the grasp of Marino. Jones, fearing there might still be trouble, undid the clasp holding his billy club in place.

Nurse Wegman tried to calm the man, but Diaz paid her no attention as his screams echoed throughout the hospital's hallways. Nora had been heading towards Simon when she saw that Doris might need assistance. She held up a finger to Simon, said "I'll be with you in a minute," and then entered the room to help Doris.

Patrolman Jones was attempting to remove his cuffs from his belt in order to hand them to the Sergeant so they could cuff Diaz's other hand to the railing on Marino's side of the bed. However, Diaz managed to yank his right arm free of the Sergeant's hold just as Nora was arriving at the bedside.

Fate took over from there.

Miguel Diaz reached across the bed and grabbed Officer Jones's billy club. He pulled it free and swung it wildly.

Nora had no time to react. The club caught her flush on the nose, slamming it backwards into her head. It was a lethal blow that killed her instantly.

"Nora!" screamed Doris.

Simon heard someone yell his wife's name and was off his chair in an instant. He rushed into the room, saw Nora on the floor, and ran to her. He knew as soon as he reached her that she was gone.

One second a smile and a wave; the next, tragedy.

He was devastated beyond belief. He sat on the floor next to his wife, cradling her head in his hands as he sobbed uncontrollably.

The next few days were blurs in his memory bank. He went through the wake and the funeral in an almost catatonic state, hoping beyond all reason that this was just a dream that he would soon wake up from. Both Nora's parents and his own attempted to comfort him as best they could, although they too were grieving. Nora had been her parents' pride and joy. She was also their only child.

Simon was lost for weeks, as though adrift on a rowboat in the ocean with no land in sight. The thought of resuming his life without his beloved Nora was almost unbearable for him. He closed his office, first for two weeks and then for two more. He cancelled all of his speaking engagements and seminars that he had been scheduled to attend.

Melinda, his secretary and jack-of-all-trades, called nearly every day to check up on him. Friends stopped by on a regular basis, bringing him casseroles, cookies, and homemade soup.

Nothing helped.

He was in as big a depression as any of his patients had ever been. His parents and a sister stayed for a few days after the funeral, but he wouldn't let them touch any of Nora's belongings. Eventually they had to return to their own lives and he was left alone. He stayed inside the house most of the day, wandering around and wondering, *What would Nora do?*

In time he went to counseling, joined a survivor's group and tried to move on, but the process was arduous and had little effect.

When the million dollar check arrived from the insurance company that held Nora's policy, he cried for nearly an hour and almost tore it up. He didn't need the money.

He just wanted his Nora back.

It was Melinda who finally helped him get out of his funk and back to work. She came over one day, sat him down on the couch, and told him to listen. Melinda didn't hold back.

"Nora wouldn't want to see you like this," she said. "Both of you were in the business of helping people. What happened to her was tragic, but if there is one thing you've learned from all the regressions you have taken people through, it's that we never know how much time we have, and life can end suddenly. You also know that her spirit left her body before she died. She was watching from above, and I'm sure she's been watching you ever since. Do you think she's happy with what she sees?"

He looked up at Melinda at that point, angry for a moment and about to respond, and then … he knew she was right. The tears soon followed. "I miss her so much," he cried.

"I know," said Melinda, "but it's time to move on. People need you, and you need to get back to work."

He reopened his practice five weeks after Nora's death, only to find that many of his patients had switched to other doctors. Work was slower than it had ever been. However, his Tuesday morning regression clients had been waiting for his return, and within a month the entire day was strictly for regressions.

The first nightmare hit two months after Nora's passing. He could never recall exactly what it was because he woke up screaming. After that they came on an irregular basis but at least once a month. Oftentimes it was a billy club flying through the air about to hit the woman he loved. On other occasions they had nothing to do with Nora's actual death but were just as horrid.

Four months later Simon decided he needed to move away. Willis no longer held pleasant memories for him. He gave his patients a one month notice that they needed to find another psychologist. Most were unhappy to see him go but understood the circumstances surrounding his decision. In the end his final week consisted solely of regression clients.

Oddly enough, determining where to move was decided by his Jaguar. At first he thought he would sell the car, since it reminded him of Nora whenever he saw it. Then he remembered it was the last gift she had given him, and he sold the two BMW's instead. Since the Jaguar was a convertible, he determined he needed to find a warm weather spot. A friend suggested Sarasota, an artsy community on the Gulf coast of Florida, and Simon figured it was as good a place as any.

He sold his home, including most of the furnishings, and moved to Sarasota seven months after Nora's death. He purchased a condo on the waterfront and bought all new furniture. Other than the car, photo albums and some personal items of Nora, he left nearly everything else behind in South Carolina.

He decided not to open a psychology practice at first. He simply didn't want to deal with other people's problems. Instead, he began accepting speaking engagements at body and soul seminars around the country, continually running into the same speakers—Dyer, Chopra, Choquette. He was still awed by the idea of past-life regressions, and eventually he came to the conclusion that he should simply go back to doing those full time.

Besides being one of the leading arts communities in the country, Sarasota was also a hotbed of new age activities. It seemed like the perfect area to continue his work, so two weeks into the new year Simon opened an office on the fourth floor of a twenty-four story complex in downtown Sarasota and went back to work.

Word that the famous author had opened up shop spread quickly. It seemed everyone wanted to give regressions a try, and Simon was soon working four full days a week. Many came just once, apparently so they could tell their friends they did it. A few came two or three times, but no one had come more than that. Some were extremely interesting; most were run of the mill.

He was helping people, however, and that made him feel better for short periods of time. One woman overcame her fear of flying after learning she had been a pilot back in the 1930's and had died in a plane crash. Once she released that fear from her past life she no longer had a problem.

His best success of late had been a man in his fifties who had an abject fear of guns. Just seeing someone wearing a gun—a cop, a security guard, or anyone else—made his stomach turn. This had caused him to be ridiculed by the rest of his family, who were all hunters and members of the local gun club.

Simon regressed the man back to Kansas in the 1840's. It turned out he was the town drunk, and cowboys used to love to make him dance by shooting bullets at his feet. This had gone on for years. One day, however, an errant shot had struck him in the leg, nearly killing him.

Simon explained to him that that life was over now and he no longer had to carry the fear of guns with him.

Simon hired a new secretary when he opened up shop, a plump woman nearing fifty named Grace Baxter. She was straight-laced, rarely smiled, and was just the type of person he wanted to be around. She was also close-minded when it came to regressions and thought all this reincarnation nonsense was just malarkey, but times were tight and she needed the job.

Unfortunately for Simon he still had to go home at night. The condo was empty and quiet, and constantly reminded him of the woman he was missing.

And the nightmares followed him from Willis to Sarasota.

They had resumed one night a week after he had moved in. He dreamed of Nora running towards him, happy and carefree. Then her face would contort into a gush of agony and she would fall at his feet. Sometimes it was a shotgun blast, other times a knife in the back, and still others a billy club to the head.

The nightmares came regularly. Talking about them to the counselors in Willis hadn't helped, and they hadn't let up since he'd moved to Florida. He had hoped delving back into regressions would change things, but they hadn't. He still had to go home at night and face his demons.

He wasn't sure how much longer he could hold on.

It was after eleven before Simon finally headed home after Hannah's regression. His condo was less than two miles from his office. He steered the Jaguar into his underground parking space and took the elevator to the fourteenth floor. There were only two condos on each floor that faced west, two more on the other side that faced east. He turned right off the elevator and unlocked his front door.

The door opened into his kitchen, a large square shaped room with a work island in the middle. There were eight cabinets on the walls and four more on the floor under the counters. More than half were empty. Simon had purchased the basic accoutrements that one person would need and not much else.

The kitchen led into the living room and the dining area. The living room was also sparsely decorated. Simon had bought a sofa, love seat and chair, and had a large screen television sitting on top of a stand, but the walls lacked pictures of any kind. An end table by the love seat had a framed picture of him and Nora that, oddly enough, had been taken in Pompeii. The other end table had a light; nothing more. Only the coffee table in front of the sofa showed outward signs that someone actually lived here. It was filled with magazines and old mail, much of it unopened. Sliding glass doors at the back of the living room led to a balcony that overlooked Sarasota Bay.

The dining area contained a table and four chairs, which Simon rarely used, as he generally ate on the couch while watching television.

The condo also contained two bedrooms. The master bedroom that Simon slept in was actually well furnished. A queen-sized bed sat in the middle. He had purchased the queen size out of habit, because that is what he and Nora always had. A large dresser stood to the left of the bed, and a walk-in closet provided more than enough room for his wardrobe. A nightstand by his bed was furnished with a light, a digital alarm clock, and another framed picture, this one of a smiling Nora in a bikini, taken a few years ago on Maui.

The master bathroom was spacious and included a Jacuzzi, but the two washbasins always reminded Simon that someone was missing.

The other bedroom was currently being used as a storage area, filled with boxes of assorted items that Simon had yet to get around to unpacking. The second bathroom, which he rarely used, had a towel by the sink and a roll of toilet paper; nothing else, not even a shower curtain.

Simon made a martini and took it out to the balcony. The recent humidity that April's heat brought had finally abated so that he could sit outside without perspiring, and tonight there was a cool breeze blowing off the waters. He loved the view from here that looked out over the bay. The sunsets were spectacular from this vantage point, and Simon enjoyed watching them whenever possible. He didn't understand why anyone would purchase a condo on the eastern side of the building, which gave them a view of downtown Sarasota and a sunrise mostly blocked by skyscrapers.

The balcony had plenty of room for a small table and two chairs, but only one chair was currently situated there. The second chair that had come with the set was in the second bedroom. The only other item on the balcony was a wind chime that Simon had found in a second-hand shop. It had sand dollars hanging on it and it made him think of Nora. She had loved sand dollars, and after her passing he had found a large box of them in her closet.

He often talked to Nora while standing on the balcony, telling her about his day and letting her know how much he missed her. When he was finished talking he would look at the wind chime and ask, *Did you hear me, Nora?*

Although the chimes often made a song in the breeze, they had never moved when he asked that question.

Simon sat at the table and sipped his martini as he thought back over Hannah's story. The fact that he knew so much about Pompeii and Herculaneum had made it extremely enjoyable for him. Now his thoughts turned to his visits there with Nora. She had been enthralled by the place and fascinated by the discoveries the archeologists had made. Oddly enough, the one she talked about the most to her friends concerned the bread they had found in the oven of one of the bakeries, still intact after nearly two thousand years.

Simon smiled at the memory as he looked out over the waters of the bay. They were calm tonight. *Peaceful*, he thought. He wondered if his life would ever feel peaceful again. There had been an ache in his stomach since the day Nora died that wouldn't go away; sometimes he thought it never would. *Time heals all wounds*, his friends would tell him, but he doubted if that were true. The move away from Willis had not stopped him from thinking about her every moment of every day, and he certainly didn't think that wound would be healed for a very long time.

He hadn't dated since the funeral, hadn't even thought of dating. His 42nd birthday had passed with no celebration at all. Who could ever replace the love of his life? He had never had a regression himself, yet he was sure Nora was his soul mate. He was certain that they had spent countless lifetimes together and would again, as soon as he was finished with this life.

Thoughts of suicide had rattled around in his brain like the Sirens calling the sailors to their watery grave. He had come close on the anniversary of Nora's death, taking a carving knife out of a drawer and holding it to his chest. One good shove into his heart and it would all be over. He and Nora could be together again.

He had held the knife there for nearly two minutes, and then he slowly put it back where it belonged. Someone had told him once that those who end their life early, before they have learned all the lessons they have come here to learn, are forced to go back and do it all again.

So he carried on. Lonely and depressed that he was without his true love, yet unable or unwilling to end it all and risk the chance of having to do it all over again.

What am I going to do? he sighed.

Then he went to bed.

The next morning as he drove to work, Simon again replayed Hannah's regression in his mind and his mood lightened just a bit.

Grace noticed as soon as he came in. "You seem to be in good spirits today," she said.

Simon told her about his late night client and how she had regressed to Pompeii.

"Pompeii, huh? Like she couldn't have gotten that out of any history book."

Simon looked at her, shook his head, and smiled. "Oh, Grace," he said, "when are you going to believe that the work I do here isn't poppycock?"

"I work here because I need the job," said Grace. "Doesn't mean I have to believe I've lived a hundred lives or more."

"I think we need to regress you someday, Grace, and find out why you're so cantankerous."

Grace Baxter gave him an evil eye and said, "That ain't never gonna happen."

Just then the door opened and the first client of the day entered the room.

"Hi," said Grace, amazingly transforming into the efficient secretary she was, "Are you here to go back in time?"

At that same moment, Hannah Marie Kent was making breakfast in the tiny kitchen of her three room apartment. She was singing an old Moody Blues song from the '70s that had been the last thing she'd heard as she fell asleep.

Hannah had slept soundly. She had awoken feeling refreshed and alive, something she hadn't felt in a long time. No nightmares, no screaming; in fact, no dreams at all as far as she could recall. She felt fantastic, and she believed there was a solid chance that the days of horrid nightmares might be over.

She had enjoyed her time with Doctor Taylor. It was obvious that he wanted to help her as best he could, and she thought the regression had gone well, although she had rushed through the first two lifetimes. The time in Pompeii and Herculaneum, however, had been vivid to her. It was as though she had just been there last week, not two thousand years ago. She had smelled the bread in the bakery, felt the uneven roads under her feet, and relived the shaking of the earth during the quakes. It had all seemed real to her as she went through it.

It was also obvious to her that the doctor was carrying a great weight on his shoulders, a pain that he could barely withstand. She knew about the tragic death of his wife; had read countless stories about it when it first happened. Overall he had seemed like a decent fellow, and Hannah prayed that he could overcome his own demons.

She hoped he had healed her of her terrible nightmares. Sure it had only been one night, but Hannah was confident that her peaceful nights would continue. Her conscious mind now knew that her horrible dreams were just carryovers from the past and could be let go.

Hannah took the eggs she had scrambled and the two slices of microwaved turkey bacon over to her table and sat down. As she ate, Hannah debated whether or not she should return to see the doctor again. If her problem was solved, then there was only one reason for her to go back.

Stephanus.

She was a firm believer in soul mates. She oftentimes felt a connection to a person she had just met that made it seem like they had known each other forever. She was certain that was a sign that the two of them had known each other in a previous life. How else to explain it? Once she had even stated the fact out loud, saying "I'm sure I knew you in a prior life" to the startled recipient.

She thought it might be fun to see what other lifetimes she had lived. Hopefully they would be happy ones to offset last night's remembrances, and maybe Stephanus would show up in more of them. In the end she decided to wait before making a decision.

Just to make sure those nightmares were really over.

Hannah glanced at the clock as she ate, not wanting to be late for work. She loved her job at Designs By Florence. Her boss, Florence Davidson, was a dream to work for, and she had taught Hannah so much in the three months that Hannah had been employed there.

Hannah had loved interior design for as long as she could remember. Her adoptive mother had always encouraged her to give her opinion on things, and how the house should look was always a topic that Hannah was commenting on, even at such a young age.

Things had changed after her parents died in the car accident. Her grandparents were wonderful people, but they were set in their ways and had little interest in changing their home around to suit the girls. The best Hannah could do was decorating her own room to her liking.

By the time high school rolled around it was obvious to Hannah that decorating was the field she wanted to pursue, and fortunately she had a guidance counselor who thought it was a great idea. She was never an A student, but she was intelligent and could have gone to college to study math or science had she desired. Instead, she had attended Southwest Florida College in Bonita Springs. Four years later, she had a Bachelor's Degree in Interior Design.

The career had a rocky beginning. She had been hired

right out of college by a company in Tampa. However, she always seemed to be at odds with the owners, a husband and wife team, and their ideas never seemed to mesh with Hannah's. After a year and a half on the job she was miserable. Exacerbating the situation was an off-and-on again relationship with her boyfriend, who was two years younger than she was and often acted even younger than that.

It had all come to a head on a rainy day a week before Christmas. Hannah just wanted to get away from it all, and so she did, breaking up with the boyfriend and quitting the job all in the same day. She moved back in with her grandparents in Sarasota for three weeks until she found employment with Florence. A week after finding her job she moved into her current apartment.

Florence Davidson was the exact opposite of her former bosses. She loved to hear Hannah's ideas, and she taught her tricks of the trade that Hannah had never learned in school. Now Hannah loved going to work.

She had not replaced the boyfriend, however, and was in no rush to do so. She had plenty of girlfriends and enjoyed her time with them, and she loved the freedom of not being tied down. As she swallowed the last bite of her breakfast, Hannah found her mind wandering back to a bakery in Pompeii and a man named Stephanus. She smiled every time she did so.

One of her girlfriends was an outgoing spiritualist named Madison Perry. Madison read tarot cards, and Hannah decided it was time for a reading. She took out her cell phone and gave Madison a call.

"Hey, girlfriend," she said after Madison answered.

"Hannah, is that really you? It's been two weeks since I've heard from you. What have you been up to?"

Hannah decided to wait until she saw Madison to tell her about the regression. "Just the usual stuff," she said. "I think I need a reading. Do you have any time open?"

"For you, of course I do. Let me check my book." Madison was back on the line ten seconds later. "Today's actually kind of busy for me," she said, "and tomorrow I'm doing a fair."

"A fair? Where?" asked Hannah.

"The Sarasota Metaphysical Society is putting on a fair at the Davit Convention Center. I'll be doing readings there all day from ten to six."

"Why don't I come there then?"

"Because I'd only get to talk to you for twenty minutes, and that won't do," said Madison. "How about you come by my place Sunday morning for breakfast, and I'll do your reading afterwards?"

"Sounds good," said Hannah. "It will be great to see you again."

"Been too long," said Madison, and then she hung up. Madison hated to say goodbye.

Barry Homan

FOUR

Hannah arrived at Madison's home just after nine Sunday morning.

Madison lived alone in a double-wide mobile home just over the Bradenton line in Palmetto. She was dressed in a light blue satin robe that flowed as she walked. The garment reflected the décor of her home, which had muted pastel colors in every room and was tastefully decorated.

"Come on in," said Madison, as she opened the door following Hannah's knock. "You want one of my green smoothies?"

"Thanks anyway," said Hannah, "but I'll pass." She knew her friend started every day with a drink consisting of spinach, kale, honey and numerous other ingredients that were supposedly healthy for you. Hannah had tried it once but wasn't impressed.

Madison poured Hannah a cup of coffee instead and then picked up a plate of scones and brought them over to the kitchen table. "Made them this morning," she said.

Hannah chose one and took a bite. "Wow, these are delicious."

"And they're good for you," said Madison. "None of that crap that the store bought ones put in them."

Madison had been on a health kick ever since Hannah

had known her. She was five foot four and 130 pounds, with red hair she always kept short, hazel eyes, and freckles all over her body. They had met by chance one day at the beach while waiting in line at the food stand. Five minutes into their conversation you would have thought they were old friends. They'd been close ever since.

"So how was the fair?" asked Hannah.

"Terrific," Madison replied. "Unbelievably busy. I barely had time to eat. I did thirteen readings, twelve of which were great. The other one, I don't even know why she sat down. Had a frown on her face from the get-go, said the reading meant nothing to her and was a waste of her twenty dollars. I think some people just want to be able to say that the cards have no validation. Why they even come to a spiritual fair is beyond me."

"Were there many readers there?"

"About ten of us, I'd say, plus two dozen vendors. That cute guy who sells the salt lamps was there, but I barely had time to say hi to him."

"Anyone else who read tarot cards, or just you?" asked Hannah.

"Madge Watson was there. You remember her? She's the elderly lady with the purple hair."

Hannah let out a giggle. "Oh yes, I remember her. No one who'd ever seen her could possibly forget that one." She took another sip of her coffee and then said, "You'll never guess what I did last Thursday."

"What was that?"

"I had a past life regression."

"Do tell," said Madison, a look of excitement coming over her. "Who did you go see for that?"

Hannah took another bite of her scone and washed it down with some more coffee, and then she said, "Well, you've heard of Doctor Simon Taylor, haven't you?"

"I remember you talking about his book once or twice, but I don't know that much about him."

"You should," said Hannah. "He's one of the leaders in the past life regression field. He wrote that book a few years ago and it became a best seller. It talked about some of the regressions that he had done, how interesting they were, and how many of them seemed to prove that our spirit doesn't die when our bodies do. Instead, it reincarnates over and over again."

"I certainly believe that," said Madison.

"His major story was about a lady who had a unique ability to return to a previous lifetime from one session to the next and pick up the story where she had left off. He'd never had a patient do that before and probably hasn't since. She went back to three different lifetimes in all, and it was just fascinating reading.

"A while back, must be more than a year ago now, his wife was killed by some kid high on crack or something."

"Oh my god," said Madison.

"I read about it at the time. He was waiting to pick her up from work when it happened. I think it messed him up for awhile. Anyway, I knew that he had moved to Sarasota and had opened an office here, so I checked him out and discovered that he was doing regressions again. I'd been having these awful dreams about dying horrific deaths and I just couldn't take them anymore."

"I remember you talking about them," said Madison.

"So I went and knocked on his office door Thursday night. He was closed, and none too happy about it, but he finally let me in, and he ended up doing a regression on me."

"And what happened? Did it work?"

"Believe it or not it did, although it started out kind of shaky. First I went back to some winter wonderland. I have no idea where it was. I was a man. I didn't see anyone else around me. I was thin and frail and I died in a snow bank."

She then told Madison about her time as a young girl in India.

"It was weird. I couldn't seem to get out of those lives fast enough. I wanted to know more, but my mind just sort of jumped right out of them to the next one. But I guess I know why."

"Why is that?" asked Madison.

"I think my spirit was in a hurry to get to the third lifetime, and this one is going to blow your mind."

"What happened?" cried Madison.

"I used to live in Pompeii," said Hannah, and she saw Madison's eyes pop open wide. She spent the next twenty minutes recounting the story, trying to remember as many details as she could. When she finished she could see the stunned look in her girlfriend's eyes.

"So you did leave your body before you died," said Madison. "I've always believed that was the case."

"I did, thank God."

"I've been to lots of channeling sessions," said Madison, "and the spirit world always tells us that's what happens. It's nice to hear it from you to sort of confirm what they say."

"I can't believe I was a slave," said Hannah. "Can you imagine?"

"Well, if we have lived countless lives, I guess at one time or another we must have been just about everything."

"So," said Hannah, "now I need a reading to find out when I'm going to find Stephanus in this lifetime."

"If only it were that easy," said Madison. She arose, took a minute to clear the table, and then said, "Follow me, and we'll see what the guides have to tell you."

Madison led Hannah to a room at the back of the mobile home. This was her reading room. A card table sat in the middle of the floor with two chairs on opposite sides. The table was covered with a cloth of dark blue and purple that had a Celtic cross design. Light brown curtains hung in front of the window. Two walls were painted a light green; the other two walls were a soft red. Hung on the walls were framed pictures of Madison's favorite tarot cards; the Hermit, the Lovers, and the High Priestess.

Madison took the chair on the left and said, "Have a

seat."

"I love this room," said Hannah, drawing a smile from her friend.

The tarot cards were inside a brown pine box that was on the table. Madison took them out and removed the satin cloth that surrounded them. Hannah had received two previous readings from Madison and had noticed the box both times. "Do you always keep them in that box?" she asked.

"I do. I take good care of my cards and they take good care of me. Now let's see what they have to say about you. First off, we need to formulate our question."

"I want to know about my love life and whether or not my soul mate is coming," said Hannah.

"All right," said Madison. She held the cards to her forehead for a moment as she said a small prayer. When she finished, she said, "I think we should do a reading for the next three months. How's that sound to you?"

"Okay," said Hannah. "I trust your judgment."

"Good. First we're going to mix the cards."

Hannah knew that some tarot card readers only read the cards in the upright, but the really good ones read them both upright and reversed. The cards had all been going in the same direction when Madison took them out of the box. Now she was going to change all that.

Madison cut the deck in half, faced the two halves head to head, and shuffled. "Now they're mixed," she said, and showed Hannah that some were upright while others were upside down. "Now I'm going to shuffle the deck three times, and then cut the cards with my left hand into three piles." She did all that, and then put the deck back together. "Are you ready?"

Hannah just nodded yes.

Although she was only twenty-six years old, Madison had been doing tarot card readings for nearly ten years. She had developed her own routine, which she followed to the letter every time. The client never touched her cards. She wanted her vibrations on the cards; no one else's. She always laid out all ten cards of the spread before commenting on any of them.

The overview was just as important as each individual card. Occasionally, however, it was hard for her to hold it in, and when she turned over the sixth card in Hannah's layout, a grin came across her face.

"You're smiling," said Hannah. "I hope that's good."

"It's an interesting reading," said Madison, as she laid down the last card. "As you probably remember, the first thing I look for are the major arcana cards. You have three." She pointed them out to Hannah. "You have Strength, the Hanged Man, and the Moon reversed. Having three major cards out of ten means that some of what is going on in your life is out of your hands. It's just karma working itself out. All three are great cards. The moon is actually better in reverse than in the upright.

"Next I look for court cards, and you have one—the Queen of Swords reversed. Something has been going on in your life that has been draining your energy. It's in the third position," said Madison, pointing it out to Hannah.

"Isn't that my base, my foundation?"

Madison smiled at her. "Hey, you remember. Yes, that's the basis of the current situation. The queen very often is an actual person in your life. However, your nightmares could very well be the cause of your energy drain."

"Probably," said Hannah.

"Next I look to see if you have three or more of any suit. The queen is your only sword; that's good. Swords are a difficult suit. You also have one pentacle, which is the suit of the physical and material. You only have two wands. However …," Madison looked at Hannah and smiled broadly, "you have three cups, the suit of love and emotions."

"So am I going to meet Stephanus soon or just some schmuck in a bar?"

"I may have that answer for you," said Madison, "but let me start at the beginning." She scanned the entire layout for a moment before starting.

"Your first card is the Ace of Cups. As I said, cups are the suit of love and emotions, and aces, in any suit, always show beginnings. In the upright, this card promises good things to come in any area of question, and based upon your question and the other cards in the layout, I would have to say that a new relationship of some kind is certainly possible for you. This is also a card of emotional renewal, a return to wholeness, so I'm guessing that those bad dreams of yours may be gone—for good."

"That would be fantastic," said Hannah, "and if last night's sleep was any indication, I think you may be right."

"The ace is covered by the Hanged Man. This covering card is always read in the upright, even if it comes out of the deck reversed. It can reveal the forces in opposition to you that are affecting you. It can be good or evil, positive or negative.

"In this case you have a great card here. The Hanged Man is a card of spiritual growth and wisdom. It shows your life is in transition, but it always involves a period of suspension. Nothing is going to happen quickly, but your intuition is going to be heightened and you should listen to it."

"That little voice in my head that keeps trying to tell me things, huh?" said Hannah.

Madison smiled. "Yeah, that one. Pay attention to it, okay?"

"Okay," said Hannah.

"As we've already discussed, the Queen of Swords reversed is in the third position, the base of your problem. Your energy level has been low lately. About three quarters of the time when a queen or king shows up in a reading, it refers to an actual person. Hopefully that's not the case here. You haven't been having any trouble with another woman in your life, have you?"

"No," said Hannah. "Outside of friends and family, the only woman in my life is my boss, and she and I get along great."

"That's good," said Madison. "A Queen of Swords reversed is a dangerous enemy to have."

"The Five of Wands reversed is in the fourth position.

This is what is behind you in your recent past and is slowly moving away. The things that have been bothering you are dissipating and new opportunities will begin opening up for you. Like the Ace of Cups, it promises new beginnings. However, like many of the wands in reverse, it also signifies that things may be delayed, so you may not get your answer within this three month period.

"The fifth card, the card that crowns you, is the Moon reversed. This reveals your hopes and aspirations for the future and represents the best that can be hoped for under the circumstances. This is one of my favorite cards in the deck, even though it is not necessarily a good card. I like to think of it as a card of mystery. In the upright it can show a dark, perilous period in one's life; secrets that are held within the recesses of the soul. It's another card that tells you to listen to your gut feelings."

"Seems like my guides are trying to tell me something," said Hannah wistfully.

"Ah, but you have the card in reverse, which is much better. Changes are coming for you, but they will not be as disruptive as they would have been if this card had been in the upright. You will have peace and clarity, but be careful. This is not the time to be taking any risks.

"Now," said Madison, "here comes the good part; card six, your future, which is heavily connected with card ten, the outcome. Here you have the Six of Cups, which gave me a tingle through my body when I saw it, considering your question and what you just went through with your regression."

Hannah sat listening, eyes wide, wondering what was coming next.

"Again, cups are the suit of love and emotions, and the six of cups upright is a very karmic card. It tells me that someone will be coming into your life that you have known before. It could be someone from earlier in this lifetime, back when you were a child, who will be reentering your life."

Madison paused and looked up at Hannah, a big smile coming over her face. "Or it could be someone from a past life whom you have a karmic connection to."

"You're kidding," said Hannah, a look of bewilderment coming over her.

"It has other meanings, of course, but considering your question, I'd say this is the one that fits."

"That's kind of freaky," said Hannah.

"I'd rather look at it as incredibly interesting," said Madison.

"The next card doesn't look good though," said Hannah, pointing to the card in the seventh position.

The Five of Cups reversed showed a man in a long black coat with three spilled cups in front of him and two behind him still upright. It was obviously a card of sorrow.

"A very difficult card in the upright," said Madison, "but you have it in the reverse, and again this is a card that is better reversed. It shows that your current difficulties will be overcome. You understand the problems that you've had and now you are prepared to start again. You've gotten over the break-up with what's his name and you're ready for a new relationship."

"You didn't like him much, did you?" asked Hannah.

Madison had only met the man once, when Hannah had come home for the holidays and brought him along. "Not much," Madison replied. "But everything in life is a lesson, and I guess you had to go through that to arrive at where you are now. Anyway, in the seventh position, this card shows your fears, so the question is, are you ready to move on?"

"I think I am," said Hannah, "although dating hasn't been at the top of my list lately. I've been so involved with my new job, wanting to get off on the right foot."

"And you have, haven't you?"

"I have. I love the job, and Florence is wonderful to work for."

"So you can release whatever fear of dating you may have been holding on to and move forward, right?"

"Right," said Hannah, offering up a small fist pump.

"Good. Next we have the Two of Pentacles in the eighth spot. This is the card of the environment, of the people around you who are close to you. It shows how they view you at the moment. Pentacles are the suit of money and deal with the physical and material. The two is a card of harmony and balance. It shows that you can handle more than one situation at a time. It also shows pleasure and happiness to come, which seems to be in so many of your cards today.

"Then we have the Two of Wands in the ninth position. It's in the upright and shows your hopes for the future. The card shows a man waiting for his ship to come in. Everything is going along fine, but there is a time element involved. You have to wait for the time to be right. If you had the next card, the Three of Wands, you would see the ships in the harbor; the wait would be over. This tells us that you will have ultimate success, but it's going to take a while longer."

"Another card telling me it won't happen in the next three months?" asked Hannah.

"Probably not," said Madison.

"Well, I'm not really in a rush," said Hannah, "although having sex again sure would be nice."

"Finally," said Madison, "you have this great finishing card; Strength. Strength shows the application of emotions, love, and patience to conquer all the situations you are facing in the physical world. You can recognize your fears and overcome them, and your guides are assuring you that you can do this. You're a strong woman, Hannah."

"Wow, that was a great reading, Madison. Thank you so much!"

"You're welcome," said Madison. "He may not be here in the next three months, but it seems like your karmic lover is on his way."

FIVE

It was a Tuesday morning three weeks after Hannah's late night visit when Simon took another step forward in overcoming the loss of his wife. It happened in a most unusual way.

He read his book.

He had an entire day free. No appointments on his calendar, nowhere to be, nothing to do. He had just finished his breakfast, a bowl of oatmeal, toast and coffee, and was wandering around his condo wondering what to do when he saw the book lying on the bottom shelf of his coffee table. It was one of the complimentary copies he had received from his publisher during the original printing.

Simon picked up the book and sat on the couch. He thumbed through it for a few minutes, reading a snippet here and there. He'd been proud the first time he saw his name on the cover, and it still gave him a sense of satisfaction; not because the book had made him a great deal of money, but simply that he had accomplished such a task. He would have been just as happy if the book had never sold a copy; simply seeing his name on it was enough.

He thought of Jill Palmer, whose story had really given the work its sizzle, and he opened to that part of the book.

"Page 74", he said out loud, well aware of where her tale

began.

Her story had been compelling. She was a non-believer, coming to see him only to please her friend. Even after her first few visits, where she told a tale so complete that it had to be true, she still didn't want to admit that it had anything to do with reality.

Over the course of eight regressions, she had returned to lives in Ireland, London, and Boston, and each time she had met up with a man who, by journey's end, she was sure was her soul mate.

A few years later Jill had married, undoubtedly thinking she had met her soul mate again, yet she had never tried to confirm that with another visit, and he had never come in either. Simon had been somewhat perplexed by that at first, but after a while he thought he understood. What if a regression had shown that her new husband was not the same soul from those previous lives? What then?

Besides, Simon knew from his extensive research that soul mates did not always come back as husband and wife. Your soul mate could be your brother, your mother, or your best friend. The only thing that appeared certain was that they always reincarnated to be with you in some capacity.

Simon read Jill's story slowly, letting it wash over him like a gentle wave. He stopped often, and tried to imagine how she had been feeling as she went through the regressions. When had she suddenly started believing? What had it been like to see this soul mate over and over again in the regressions and yet not know who he was in her current life? She had recognized countless people in her regressions, but didn't know him.

Had she married him in this life?

Simon still heard from Jill, now Jill Harmon, on occasion, and she had contacted him several times after Nora had passed. He knew she was happily married. In fact, her last call some four months ago had informed him that she was pregnant. Both Jill and her husband Michael had been shocked by the news at first. Michael's only daughter had just graduated college, and Jill had one son in college and one in high school. Jill herself was nearly forty-five, if Simon recalled correctly. However, Simon could easily hear the joy and excitement in her voice when she gave him the news.

"One of my Irish boys wanting me to be their mom again, no doubt," she had said, "although it appears they're coming back as a girl this time."

"And you who used to be a non-believer," Simon had replied. "Look at you now."

Jill had laughed, and Simon had smiled for one of the few times back then.

He finished reading her tale and put the book down. "What's our story, Nora?" he said, looking up at the ceiling. "How many times have we been together?"

He thought the answer was dozens, or maybe even hundreds. How many lifetimes had they lived on this planet? Perhaps they had lived on other planets too. Who knew?

We come here for a reason, the spiritualists say; to learn lessons, to grow closer to God, eventually to return to God. What lesson was he learning now? Why had they agreed to come back again only to have his beloved leave so early in life? If it was a karmic lesson, it was one he couldn't wrap his head around.

He lingered on the subject for an hour more, and somewhere in that hour his black cloud burst and the sun finally began to shine through. He would see his Nora again in the next lifetime, and for many lifetimes after that, and while he was still greatly saddened by the loss of his love in this time period, he knew it was his job to move on.

He placed the book back on the table as he thought of Jill one more time. Her lives with her soul mate had ended abruptly each time, and yet he or she had carried on, because that was all you could do.

He felt a weight lift from his shoulders, and he said, "Thank you, Jill." Then he walked out onto his balcony and looked at the heavens. *I think I'm going to be okay now, Nora*, he thought. The wind chimes didn't move, but Simon was pretty certain that Nora had received the message.

Two days later, Simon flew to Denver, Colorado, where a three-day body and soul conference was taking place. On Friday he did a workshop from nine to five with Thomas Mann, a well known spiritualist who gave messages from the other side. It was the third time that they had shared the stage together, and the two men had developed a friendship and a healthy respect for one another.

Three hundred people packed the crowded auditorium to see in person these two men whom they had heard and read so much about. In the morning each man spoke about his specialty for about an hour, and then they took questions, sitting side by side on the stage. After the lunch break, Simon had the floor from one to three. He did a group regression for the entire audience and then asked them what they had seen. Some of the responses were quite amazing, as was usually the case.

"I saw my mother in a past life," cried one of the attendees, a young woman from Omaha. "I was a man back then and she was my brother. I think we lived in Scandinavia. There was snow on the ground and we were stalking wild animals. I was wearing animal skins and carrying a bow and arrows."

It was obvious to everyone that the young lady was excited, and she confirmed as much when she finished by saying, "That was awesome! Thank you so much."

Simon asked if anyone else would like to share what they had experienced and hands flew up around the room. A man in his fifties said that he had gone back to a life in Germany where he had been a college teacher. A woman from New Jersey claimed she had been a housekeeper for a famous painter; she thought it was Monet, because of the wonderful garden he had, but she wasn't sure. Another woman claimed she had been a matchmaker in Italy.

They could have continued for another hour, but three

o'clock came quickly, and it was Thomas Mann's turn to take the stage. He had arrived back at the auditorium just ten minutes before he was due on stage and had not heard the reincarnation stories.

For two hours he brought through messages from loved ones for the people in the audience. At one point he was in the middle of a message for a husband and wife from Idaho when he suddenly stopped and said, "Excuse me one moment. I'm being interrupted by a rather loud spirit on the other side who insists on saying something." He paused a moment and then said, "Is there someone here from New Jersey who spoke earlier?"

The lady who had given her story to Simon raised her hand and hollered, "Over here."

Thomas Mann looked at her and said, "Monet says hi."

The audience gasped in unison, a chill running down the spines of many, and then they broke into applause.

Mann looked skyward and said, "Now may I return to my other message?" and shortly thereafter said, "Thank you."

The weekend conference was a huge success. Simon had a 90 minute workshop on both Saturday and Sunday with space being limited to thirty people. Both had sold out, and more tales from previous lives had been brought forth. Not only that, but the bookstore had sold over eighty copies of his book during the event.

The flight home found him satisfied and relaxed, and Simon realized he hadn't felt that way in a very long time.

He entered his office on Monday morning raring to go, and Grace noticed.

"You're smiling," she said. "Must have been a good weekend."

"It went very well," said Simon, "and I'm feeling a great deal better overall, thank you very much." He knew Grace had been worried about him ever since she took the job, although her hard-crusted exterior rarely let that show.

"That's nice," she grumbled, as if to prove the point. "You have a full day ahead of you; six appointments in all.

The first one should be here any minute." She paused a moment and shook her head, then said, "Amazing how many people believe this stuff."

Simon actually laughed. "Oh Grace," he said, "what am I going to do with you?"

His first client after the lunch hour was waiting for him when Simon arrived back at the office.

"He's been here twenty minutes," said Grace. "Can't wait to meet you." She rolled her eyes as she said this last part.

"Grace, be nice," said Simon. He took the questionnaire from her that the client had filled out and said, "Give me two minutes, then send him in."

He sat at his desk and gave the form a quick glance. He was always curious whether or not the places a client listed as spots they would like to visit were actually destinations of past lives. The form he held in his hand listed Hawaii, Barbados and France. They sounded more like vacation spots the gentleman hoped to visit in this lifetime, mused Simon. Still, one never knew.

Another question on the form asked for three things you are afraid of. It was the question he had stopped himself from asking Hannah Kent. This form listed fire, snakes and marriage, and Simon let out a laugh. *A man with a sense of humor,* he thought.

The door opened a moment later and Grace led the man into the room. She always introduced his new clients, and this time she said, "Simon Taylor, this is Hollis Brown."

The two men shook hands, and then both took a seat as Grace left the room. Hollis was about five-eleven, and Simon put his weight around 175. He was prematurely balding, and Simon guessed that in five years any semblance of hair would be completely gone. The form he had filled out put his age at thirty-four. He wore glasses with thick black frames and could have passed for a college professor.

"Interesting name," said Simon. "I seem to remember

that name in a song back in the '60's."

"My dad was a big Dylan fan," said Hollis. "Still is, actually."

"As I recall," said Simon, "that song …"

Hollis interrupted him and finished the sentence. "… had a rather tragic ending, yes. My dad always told me he liked the name and didn't care what the song was about."

"So do you go by a nickname?"

"Some of my friends call me Hal, but to be honest I like the name Hollis. Unique, you know."

"Well then, Hollis it is. What brings you here to see me today, Hollis?"

"This," said Hollis. He stood up, turned a bit to his left, and lifted the bottom of his shorts about three inches.

Simon saw a deep reddish-brown spot about the size of a quarter on the man's outer thigh.

"I was born with this," said Hollis. "No one could ever explain why. It wasn't something that happened because of the birth. You know, it's not a forceps mark or anything like that. I don't even think about it most of the time, but every once in a while I'll get a throbbing pain there that lasts for some time before it dissipates. I'm hoping you can tell me what caused it."

"And what led you to me?" asked Simon. "Did you read my book?"

"Your book?" said Hollis, a quizzical look on his face. "No, I didn't know you had a book out. I met a lady in a bar. We talked about all sorts of interesting subjects and eventually the conversation turned to soul mates. You see, I was married when I was nineteen. It didn't go well. Both of us were too young and too stupid, and by the time I was twenty-two we were divorced. I thought I'd be married again in no time, but I just can't seem to find the right person. Anyway, this lady had been to see you, and she suggested I go."

"If you don't mind my asking, what was her name?"

"I don't mind, and neither does she. Her name was Maria Vasquez, and she said to say hello."

Simon had a vague recollection of the woman. She had

come in shortly after he had opened the Sarasota office, and she had been a stunning woman to look at. As he recalled, the regression hadn't gone all that well. Then again, he may have her totally confused with another woman. Back then his mind had still been in a fog.

"Sounds like you had a connection with her. Have you seen her since then?"

"Oh no," said Hollis. "She's married. That night she was just out with her girlfriends. We talked for a couple of hours, but I haven't seen or heard from her since."

"So you're thinking this mark on your leg is a carryover from a past life. I'm afraid there's no guarantee about that."

"I realize that. I never even considered such a thing until talking with Maria. She seemed to think it was a possibility, so I decided to check it out. And I suppose learning about a past life might be pretty interesting also."

"Well then, let's get started, shall we, and see what we can come up with."

"A few questions, if I may?" said Hollis.

"Certainly," replied Simon. "What would you like to know?"

"How long have you been doing this?"

"Oh, it's been about six years now, I guess."

"Did you always believe in past lives?"

"I've always felt there was more to life than just one chance. I believe God to be a loving God, and therefore I couldn't understand how a baby might live for just a few hours and then pass away. I couldn't explain the starving children in Africa, or even in our own country, if that was all there was to life. Instead, because I do believe in a loving God, I had the idea that these people were living the lives they were living to teach us something. In doing so, I believe that in their next life their story will be quite different; perhaps one of luxury, or at least comfort, in payment for their sacrifice."

"Interesting theory," said Hollis.

"Over time I've come to believe that every person who

comes into our lives is there to either teach us something or learn something from us."

"So I'm here today to learn from you?"

"Perhaps," said Simon, "but one thing I've discovered is that oftentimes nothing is as it appears."

"What's your book about?"

"You're beginning to sound like a reporter," laughed Simon.

"I'm sorry," said Hollis. "I've always had a very inquisitive nature."

"My book is about my experiences with past life regressions and some of the interesting stories that have come from them. Now I suggest we get started before your time is up."

Hollis gave him a smile and said, "Okay, you win."

Simon led Hollis over to the couch and asked him to lie down. He then explained the whole procedure to Hollis.

"I'm going to have you relax your body, starting with the toes and feet and moving on up to your head. Then I'm going to count backwards from ten to one while you picture yourself descending a spiral staircase. At the bottom of the staircase will be a door. When we finish descending the staircase you should be fully relaxed. The door in front of you is your entryway into your past lives. I will ask you to step on through, and then we will have you go back in time; first just a few years, then to your childhood, then to the womb. Some amazing things have come up when my clients are in the womb stage. Finally we will attempt to have you return to a prior lifetime and see what we get. Okay?"

"Sounds good," said Hollis, and they began.

He seemed to be a good subject and his answers to Simon's questions came quickly. When asked to go back a few years to a happy moment, Hollis immediately brought up his parents' thirtieth anniversary party.

"A wonderful surprise," said Hollis. "They knew the party was coming, of course, but they didn't know that all the kids had chipped in to send them on a cruise to the Mediterranean.

They were thrilled, and my mom cried."

Simon took him back further to the age of eight, and again Hollis spoke up without hesitation.

"We went to Times Square and watched the ball drop," said Hollis. "None of us, not even my mom or dad, had ever been to New York. It was a fascinating trip. My folks might have loved it even more than us kids did. Best vacation I had as a kid."

"You're doing very well," said Simon. "Now I want you to go back further. Back past the age of two, past the age of one, and back into the womb. You can do it, Hollis. It's not difficult."

"It's squishy," said Hollis, and Simon nearly let out a laugh. He had never heard that response before.

"Do you understand what's happening while you're in the womb?"

"Yes, I'm about to be reborn again."

"Are your parents excited?" asked Simon.

"Well, yes and no. They've been through this before. I will be their second child, and another will be coming after me."

"You know this while you're in the womb?"

"Yes, I have chosen this family, and my guides have told me everything I need to know before I incarnate. They already have a girl, and another girl will come after me; three children in all."

"You said yes and no about your parents being excited. What is the no part?"

"Well, Dad is worried about the financial part of it. He keeps talking about 'another mouth to feed', but mostly he is excited and happy, just like Mom."

"That's excellent," said Simon. "You're doing very well. Now it's time to go back even further. You've lived other lives. I want you to go back to your last life and tell me about it, okay? Tell me everything you can remember. Let's see if we can find the reason for that spot on your leg."

Hollis appeared very comfortable as he lay on the couch. He hadn't had any trouble with the regression up to this point, and Simon was confident that Hollis could do as he asked.

"You can choose any moment in your prior lifetime that you wish," said Simon. "Begin anywhere you want and tell me what you see."

Hollis lay still for a moment, and then his face suddenly contorted, and he cried, "Oh my God!"

"What is it?" asked Simon. "What's the matter?"

"I'm a woman," said Hollis.

Simon again had to keep from laughing. "Very common," he said. "We oftentimes change our sex from one life to the next."

"It just seems a bit strange," said Hollis.

"Tell me about yourself. What do you look like?"

"Well, I think I'm about seventeen or eighteen years old. I live on a farm, a very big farm, so big I can't see any neighbor's homes."

"Do you know where you are, what country you are in?"

"Not the United States; Canada, maybe."

"What kind of farm is it?" asked Simon.

"Um …, I'm not sure." Hollis hesitated, trying to understand the scene in his mind. "There is a large pasture, lots of land, but nothing is growing right now. Whatever it is we grow, I think the season has ended. The fields have all been plowed over. It's cold out; freezing, like its winter."

"Can you tell me your name?"

"Yes, my mother is calling to me from the house. My name is Anne."

"That's very good. You're doing very well. Now can you tell if your leg has been injured in some way?"

"No, my leg is fine," said Hollis.

"Do you recognize your mother as someone you know in your current life?"

"Oh my, yes! That's my Aunt Doris."

"Your aunt in this life was your mother in your last life?"

"I guess so."

"How many of you live on the farm?" asked Simon.

"There are six of us in all; my father, my mother, two brothers and a sister, and me."

"That's good, Hollis. You're doing fine. Now let's move forward in time a bit to see if we can find out if your leg was hurt during this lifetime. Try and picture when the injury occurred to you."

Hollis was quiet for some time, and Simon pictured him fast-forwarding through his past life.

"I have it," Hollis finally said. "I'm much older now; an old woman."

"Are you still on the farm?"

"Oh no, I'm not even in the same area. I'm riding in a car. In fact, it appears I'm moving. The back seat is filled with my belongings."

"Are you alone in the car?"

"No, not alone. A man is driving." After a moment Hollis added, "I think he is my son."

"What happens to you on this journey that causes the mark on your leg?"

Hollis paused again, as if he wanted to see the entire scene play out before describing it.

"We have stopped by the side of the road. My son needed a break from driving and we are both hungry. We put a blanket on the ground and sat down to eat. It is actually a lovely moment. We obviously have a great deal of love for each other. When we finish, I tell him that I need to go to the bathroom before we leave. There is a copse of trees nearby and I walk over to them. It is when I am walking back that the injury occurs. I trip over a root in the ground and fall awkwardly. There is a decayed tree limb lying nearby with a broken branch sticking up. It is about two inches in length, and my leg falls on it just right. In my younger days it probably would have just given me a bruise, but now my skin is very brittle and the stick pierces my leg.

"I screamed as though I was being murdered and my son

came running. By the time he arrived I was bleeding quite a bit. He carried me back to the blanket and laid me down, and then he picked up a cloth napkin that we had been using and told me to hold it as tight as I could on the wound. He quickly collected the remnants of our meal, and then he picked me up again and carried me to the car.

"There was a town not too far away, and he drove there as fast as he dared. The local doctor fixed me up, but I walked with a limp for a while, and the pain in my leg would come and go for the rest of my life. The skin healed over time, of course, but there was always a deep red mark on my leg. It never went away."

"And the mark on your leg that you have now is in the exact same spot?"

"Yes, that is where I fell on the broken branch."

"It appears we have found the answer to your question," said Simon. "Is there anything else about that lifetime that you can recall and would like to share?"

"No, we found what I wanted to know," said Hollis.

Simon could only smile at the matter-of-factness in his voice. "I'm going to bring you back to the present now. The pain you have felt in your leg off and on is not from this lifetime. Leave it in the past. There is no need for you to feel pain there any longer." A moment later he brought Hollis out of the regression.

"That was interesting," said Hollis.

"One of the shortest regressions I've ever done," laughed Simon. "It appears you have your answer as to how you received the mark on your leg."

"Do you think that really happened?" asked Hollis.

"What do you think?" said Simon.

"I'm not sure. I guess the story is plausible, but maybe I just thought it up."

"I've had others come to see me about similar marks on their body. Once they have their answer, the scars tend to fade. Maybe yours will, too."

"That would be interesting," said Hollis. "Imagine, I fell

on a stupid stick after going to the bathroom in the woods. I was really hoping it was something much more interesting."

"So how did it feel to be a woman?" asked Simon.

"It was different. I hadn't even thought that that might happen."

"Well, you may have lived hundreds of lives, and if so I'm sure many of them were as a woman."

"It sort of gives me a new perspective. I'm going to have to do some thinking about it."

"Was your aunt the only person you recognized? How about your son?"

"No, I didn't recognize him," said Hollis. "Is it possible we haven't met yet in this life?"

"Quite possible," said Simon. "It seems you were very close, so I would be surprised if you didn't meet up with him again."

"Well, I don't know how all that works," said Hollis. "Do people normally recognize everyone from their previous lives?"

"No, not at all," said Simon, "although core family members from the past usually end up in our current lifetime as well."

"Have you ever had a regression of your own?" Hollis asked.

"No, I haven't."

"Why not? Aren't you interested in your past lives?"

"The past lives of my clients are a great fascination to me and keep me quite busy," said Simon. "I've never felt the need to inquire about my own past."

"A lot of people talk about soul mates," said Hollis. "Haven't you ever been tempted to find your soul mate?"

Simon put down his pen and stared at Hollis for a long moment. "I'm afraid your time is up," he finally said. "I hope I've helped." Then he stood up and led Hollis to the door.

SIX

The following Saturday, Hollis saw an ad in his morning paper for a psychic fair. His conversation in the bar with Maria Vasquez had covered many subjects dealing with the metaphysical, of which Hollis knew very little. He had always been an in-the-moment kind of guy and had never thought much about psychics, past lives, ghosts, or any of the other countless subjects covered by the spiritual world.

Maria had been just the opposite. She had spent two hours talking with him about her spiritual interests, including channelers, mediums and astrologers. It had certainly seemed to him that she believed in all of them, and it had piqued his interest.

His visit to Simon had been his first step. Now as he read the ad he noticed that among the listings was one for a Reverend Wil Stevens, who was referred to as a shaman. Hollis remembered reading a story about a year ago concerning a shaman down in South America. As he recalled, the man seemed to have miraculous healing abilities and was able to heal people over long distances simply by knowing their name and whereabouts. Whether all shamans could do that Hollis did not know, but he thought it might be interesting to check it out.

The fair was being held at the Widmore Center on

Greenfield Street. It was the first of May, but the temperature hovered near ninety. Hollis arrived fifteen minutes after the doors opened. He entered a foyer and was greeted by a perky young lady named Molly who handed him a paper listing all the readers and vendors.

"The vendors are all in front, sort of in a semi-circle design," said Molly, "and the readers are mostly against the back and side walls. Over here," she said, pointing to a section on the paper, "are our authors who have their books for sale."

Hollis took the paper and quickly perused it.

"Is there anyone in particular you came to see?" Molly asked.

Hollis decided not to bring up the shaman just yet. "No," he said, "I just came to see what it was like."

"Well then, enjoy," said Molly. "There's plenty to see. We have some terrific readers, and the vendors sell all sorts of interesting items."

Hollis thanked her and entered the large auditorium. He came upon the vendors first and immediately gathered that what Molly said was true. He saw a table selling crystals and jewelry, another one with incense and handbags from Peru, others selling musical bowls and salt lamps and Buddha statues. He had never realized how popular these fairs were, and as he scanned the room he noticed that the place was already swarming with visitors. He realized they must have been lining up at the door before the fair opened.

He ambled over to the author's tables. There were five in all, three men and two women. He spent a few minutes talking with a cute young girl whose book was called <u>How To Raise Psychic Children</u>. She rambled off three unbelievable stories to him before he managed to extricate himself and move on.

Finally finding a fairly empty spot, Hollis took a look at his floor plan. Reverend Wil Stevens had a table at the back of the building, and Hollis headed that way. He arrived just as the shaman was saying goodbye to an aging lady in a multi-colored mumu.

Hollis hesitated for a moment, as though deciding where he was going to go next. When he finally looked up, he saw Wil Stevens looking directly into his eyes.

"Coming to see me?" asked Wil, as if he already knew the answer.

"I believe so," said Hollis.

The shaman just smiled at him.

"Sorry," said Hollis, "I've never been to anything like this before."

"And what brings you here today?" asked Wil.

"Well, I saw the ad in the morning paper and it mentioned a shaman. I'd read about a shaman once. He was some sort of mystical healer, and I wondered …"

"You wondered what a real life shaman must look like, eh?" Wil laughed heartily, but Hollis didn't feel as though he were being laughed at. The man had a presence about him that Hollis would later describe as powerful.

"Come," said Wil, and pointing to a massage table situated near the back wall he said, "Have a seat."

Hollis sat on the table. "Should I pay you first?" he asked.

"I work by donations only. Pay what you feel I deserve when we are finished, or don't pay anything. Whatever is in your heart to do, that is what you should do."

Hollis really took note of Wil Stevens for the first time. The man was tall, maybe six foot four, and well built. Probably around 45 years old, he guessed. Blond hair somewhat unkempt, golden eyes, soft jaw line.

"Take my hand," said Wil, and suddenly it were as though they were the only two people in the room. The hand was large, warm, almost clammy, and as soon as Hollis took it Wil's other hand surrounded his.

"Relax," said Wil.

Hollis took a deep breath.

At first Wil only made a few sounds, a "hmm" and an "ah". Then he looked at Hollis and said, "You have a blockage in your heart, not physical but emotional. You've been hurt in the past and you haven't let it go yet. Ah, that's recent, from this life. You know about that one, I guess."

Hollis didn't think he had any blockages from his long-ago marriage, but he mumbled a "yes," anyways.

"You don't believe me, I know," said Wil. "That's okay. I'll take care of it later." He continued to hold Hollis' hand as he moved on.

"You have the ancient culture in you; not Druidic, but something similar. Do you know that?"

Hollis had no idea what Wil meant. "No," he said.

"I'm not surprised. It's from long ago." Wil paused a moment and then smiled broadly. "Ah, here's an interesting life. You were a monk. God, you loved that work. You'll find out about it soon enough. There's much going on with you right now; you're entering a cycle of karmic payback and rewards. It will be good for you. You've had tragedy in the past but also great joy, like all of us."

Hollis could only sit and listen, not really understanding what Wil was telling him.

"You fought against the Crusaders," said Wil. "Bravely, I might add. You were Muslim in that life. Religion has played an important part in many of your past lives. I think you came here this time to try something new, something different. That's why even this event today is strange to you, because you've subconsciously stayed away from the metaphysical. But you won't stay away any longer. Today is just the first step for you."

Wil let go of Hollis' hand. "Confused?" he asked.

"You could say that," said Hollis. "How did you see all that?"

"Just a gift I've had since childhood," said Wil. "Take off your shoes and lie on the table, if you would."

Hollis did as asked, gently dropping his loafers to the floor, and then he swung his legs up and lay down.

"Just relax," said Wil. "I'm going to get rid of that blockage for you, and then we'll see what else I can find."

Wil put a hand on the crown of Hollis' head and another

on his shoulder. Every so often the position of his hands would change as Wil made his way slowly down Hollis' body. The hands felt warm to Hollis, and seemed downright hot when placed against his bare arm.

As he moved a hand over Hollis' heart Wil said, "You've had this blockage for a long time. I'm guessing your dating life hasn't been very good lately."

"I haven't tried much," said Hollis.

"You haven't been able to," said Wil, "but that will change now."

Wil eventually arrived at the end of the table and put his hands on Hollis' feet. "You're going to feel the energy flowing from head to foot now as negative energy leaves your body." A moment later Wil asked, "Do you feel it?"

And Hollis did.

He couldn't explain it, but there was a tingle running through his ankles to his toes, like a soft electrical impulse gently buzzing in his feet.

"Ah yes, you feel it," said Wil. "I can see it in your smile."

A moment later Wil was finished. "Sit up, but be careful. You may be a little light-headed."

"Thank you," said Hollis, as he put his shoes back on and prepared to leave.

"Now you can meet the woman of your dreams," said Wil.

Hollis shook the shaman's hand once more and placed a twenty dollar bill in Wil's jar. He spent another ten minutes in the hall and purchased some cinnamon and spice incense from an attractive little brunette before he left.

After returning to his car, Hollis sat behind the steering wheel for a few minutes pondering what had happened. He had never thought that his divorce so many years ago still had any effect on him. Had he been wrong? It was true his dating life since then had been uneven and less than satisfactory, but he had always told himself that he was simply waiting for the right woman to come along. Was he really afraid to date, afraid to make the same mistake again? And what to make of the past-life information? Wil told him he had been a monk, a Muslim fighting the Crusaders, a religious person many times. Was there any truth to that, or was Wil Stevens just some guy making stuff up that he knew could never be proven?

Hollis had never been particularly religious. Every religion thought they were the right one, but there were so many. How could any of them be sure that what they taught was true? So he had avoided them all and made up his own mind about what God wanted from humans.

Had he been so religious in the past that he had decided to avoid all religions in this life? If so, how do you decide that before you are born?

He was going to have to take some time to debate these questions, he knew. Of one thing he was sure, however. He felt lighter, as if Wil Stevens had removed a weight from his shoulders. Maybe it was all that negative energy, he thought, as he started the car and drove away.

Hollis Brown had lived in Florida his entire life. His parents had been hard working people. His dad had been a full-time bookkeeper for a small appliance store in Land O' Lakes, and even now at the age of seventy Harold Brown still put in about twenty hours a week.

His mother, Louise, had been a stay at home mom until Hollis turned twelve, and then she started up her own cleaning business. She went after upper-end clients, mostly targeting lawyers' homes and doctors' offices, and within a year was making almost as much as her husband. The money helped put Hollis and his older sister, Vivian, through college. Terry, his other sister and the youngest of the family, was a tomboy who had no interest in furthering her education once she graduated high school. Instead, she had taken trade courses in school that she turned into a job as an electrician.

Hollis had no idea what he wanted to do in life while he was in high school. His father urged him to get into accounting, wanting his son to go farther than he had. Hollis complied and enrolled at Tampa University, but by his sophomore year he knew that accounting wasn't for him. Teaching was what he was suddenly compelled to do, and Hollis switched his major to Ancient History.

He bounced around between a number of high schools in the first few years after getting his degree, budget cuts and layoffs seemingly following him from school to school. Finally, after five years and three schools, he had found a home at Bay Crest High School in Sarasota.

He loved teaching. He had vowed early on to make classes exciting for the kids, knowing from his own time in high school how boring Ancient History could be. The students acted out scenes in class which helped them remember better on tests. They also took more field trips than any other class in the school, mostly visiting museums to see ancient artifacts, and they watched in-class movies on Pericles and Alexander the Great.

As a reward, the students had voted him Teacher of the Year two years running, and now he was up for the Florida Teacher of the Year Award, which was due to be announced in September.

As well as his career was going, his love life had been heading in the opposite direction. His mother had tried to set him up with numerous women over the years, but they rarely lasted more than one date.

Fellow teachers had also tried to no avail. He simply didn't seem interested in the female teachers he worked with, and he was also very leery about dating someone in the workplace. That always seemed to backfire on people.

Even one of his students had once gotten into the act, telling him her mom was single and thought he was hot. Hollis had made a note to check her out at the next parent-teacher meeting, but nothing had ever come of it. Both shied away in the end.

Thus as the weekend moved along and Monday morning rolled around, Hollis thought again and again about what Wil Stevens had said. Had some part of him been so devastated by his failed marriage that his heart had become hardened to women? Had Wil released that blockage so that Hollis could feel good about dating again?

Hollis had no idea.

What he did know was that the rest of Wil's message had intrigued him immensely. He had never thought much about past lives, although he had always been open to the idea. He had enjoyed his visit with Simon, and though it had only been a few days since his regression, the mark on his leg hadn't bothered him at all. He had gone back to that life easy enough. Now he wondered if he could do it again by returning to a life as a monk or a rabbi. *Maybe I was a Pope*, he thought, and laughed out loud.

By the time school let out that Monday afternoon, Hollis had decided to see Simon Taylor once again. Friday was an early release day for the school, so when he returned home Hollis called Simon's office and made an appointment for two o'clock Friday afternoon.

Hannah Kent had been thinking along the same lines. Her tarot card reading with Madison had suggested a new love interest in the months ahead, and she kept wondering if it might be Stephanus, her lover from Pompeii.

He kept popping into her thoughts as she went through her daily routine. Whether she was washing the dishes, driving through town, or redecorating a customer's living room, Stephanus would enter her mind and Hannah would suddenly lose track of the next ten minutes. It was scary sometimes, wondering how you'd arrived at your destination when you couldn't even remember which roads you'd taken.

The other item that made her consider going back to see Simon was her dreams. They were suddenly pleasant. The nightmares seemed to have stopped altogether. Oh, she had one night where she had dreamt that she was falling off a cliff, but that had been the only bad dream she'd had in the last few weeks.

Hannah had been intrigued by her regression with Simon and was wondering what other lives she may have lived. She figured there must have been some happy lives in there somewhere, and while meeting her soul mate had never been a particular goal of hers, perhaps it would be fun to see if Stephanus showed up again in another life.

Hannah decided to pay another visit to the doctor. She took out the daily planner that she carried with her at all times, checked her schedule for the coming days, then picked up her cell phone and made an appointment.

Simon had been debating long and hard about finally resuming his psychology practice. While he loved doing the regression work, he was beginning to think that he wasn't fulfilling his prime reason for being on the planet. He was meant to be a psychologist, just as Nora had been destined to be a nurse. It was what they excelled at and why they were here. He could hear Melinda's voice in his ear saying, *It's time for the pity party to end, Simon. Get back to work.* He agreed.

That Friday morning he decided to break the news to Grace. "I need to talk to you about something," he said to her.

"I'm not doing a regression, if that's what you're thinking," said his secretary, shaking her head as she did so.

"I would never ask you to do such a thing," said Simon, smiling back at her. "You'd probably throw something at me."

"So what is it?"

"I've decided to start up my psychology practice, three days a week to begin with, plus some time on Saturdays."

"I'm not working Saturdays," Grace quickly said.

"That's okay," replied Simon. "I can handle Saturdays by myself. That would be for emergency patients who can't wait until Monday."

"What about the regressions?" asked Grace.

"We'll cut them down to two days a week at first, and once the practice picks up we'll just do the regressions once a week. Tuesdays always worked well for me before, but I think if we did them on Wednesday it would break up the week nicely. So we'll start with Tuesdays and Wednesdays, and eventually cut back to just the Wednesday."

"Sounds fine to me," said Grace, "but what about when you're off doing these weekend seminars? What then?"

"Well, let's not get ahead of ourselves. We'll cross that bridge when we come to it."

Grace mulled it over for a moment, then shrugged her shoulders and said, "Okay."

"So now my question to you, dear Grace, is whether or not you feel you can handle my psychology patients? I have to warn you, some of them are going to have some pretty severe problems and may present a challenge to you. Do you think you can handle it?"

Grace gave him a sad smile as a look came over her face that he had never seen before. "I don't talk about this much," she said, "but I know you can keep this under your hat, so I'll tell you. Perhaps you should sit down."

Simon took the seat in front of Grace's desk usually reserved for clients.

"I have four children; Tommy, Greta, Jean and Mary," said Grace. "Tommy is a doctor out in Provo, Utah, happily married with two little girls. Greta has four kids of her own, and she's now raising them alone since her deadbeat husband took off for places unknown. Jean owns a bookstore down in Fort Lauderdale, and yes, she has your book prominently displayed."

She paused for a moment, and Simon knew the reason for this talk was coming.

Grace's face seemed to scrunch up a bit as she finally spoke. "Mary was never right. From the beginning she was a difficult child, never listening, always causing trouble. Thrown out of school in the third grade---THIRD GRADE!---for trying to light a classmate on fire. We had to put her in special schools for problem children, and most of them couldn't even handle her. She had her first meeting with a psychologist when she was six, and they were pretty much constant until she turned fourteen."

Grace paused to take a sip of her tea that had been sitting on the desk.

Simon could see the anguish her tale was putting her through and just sat quietly.

"That's when she ran away from the last institution she was in. I knew I'd be hearing about her in short order because there was no way she could stay out of trouble. It took three weeks before the call came, longer than I thought it would take. She was arrested for breaking a jewelry store window and grabbing some items. She tried to pawn them off, but the pawn shop had already received a police report. Cops arrived while the owner was supposedly examining the items to give her the best deal."

"She spent time in juvenile detention?" asked Simon.

"Not long," replied Grace. "Her mind just seemed to go out on her at that point. Within two weeks they put her in a mental ward. Fourteen years later, she's still in one."

"I'm sorry, Grace," said Simon.

"No need to feel sorry for me," said Grace. "It is what it is. I don't know why the good Lord sent Mary to me or what lessons she was supposed to teach me, and I'm not having one of your fancy regressions to find out, either."

Simon just smiled. Cantankerous Grace was back.

"So when you ask me if I think I can handle my new duties, my answer is yes. It won't be a problem. Just remember—no Saturdays."

"No worries there, my dear."

"And I'm gonna want a raise, too."

Simon couldn't help but laugh out loud. "Done," he said.

Barry Homan

SEVEN

Hollis arrived a few minutes early for his two o'clock appointment that afternoon.

Grace buzzed Simon to let him know his client had arrived, and then she asked Hollis if he would like some water. She used to offer coffee or tea to their visitors, but Simon had recently asked her to offer only water to his regression clients.

"No, thank you anyways," said Hollis. "I had lunch a little while ago and I'm still full."

He took a seat in the waiting room and picked up a copy of a travel magazine that was sitting on the coffee table.

A few minutes later the phone on Grace's desk rang. Hollis heard her say to the person on the other end, "That's okay if you're running late, dear, just get here when you can, and thank you for calling to let us know."

Simon came out from the back room a moment later with a young girl who barely looked eighteen. She thanked the doctor profusely for his time, made another appointment, and left.

Simon turned and noticed Hollis sitting in the waiting room. "Hello, Hollis," he said, "nice to see you again. Has the mark on your leg been bothering you lately?"

"Not at all," replied Hollis. "In fact, if I'm not mistaken it appears as though it may be getting smaller."

"Isn't that something?" said Simon. "Strange how things work out some times. Come on back." He led Hollis back to his office, and after the two of them were seated asked, "So what brings you here this time?"

"I had an interesting meeting with a shaman at one of the local psychic fairs."

"Do tell," said Simon.

Hollis told the doctor about his meeting with Wil Stevens and what he had to say about prior lifetimes of his.

Simon was intrigued. "I've never heard of the man," he said, as he jotted Wil's name down in his daily planner, "but that's not unusual. Sarasota is a hotbed of metaphysical practitioners. I probably don't know two percent of them. Did he seem like he was on the up-and-up to you?"

"Well, I can't say I know enough yet to tell the difference between a real shaman and a fake one, but he was certainly very confident about the information he was telling me. The thing is, I'm not religious at all in this life, and I find it a bit hard to believe that would be the case if I had been so religious in the past. Does that seem right to you?"

"From what I understand, having done these regressions over the past half-dozen years, people come to this planet to learn lessons," said Simon. "Sometimes it may take a few lifetimes to learn one lesson, and other times we may learn numerous lessons during just one life. Perhaps you needed to live multiple lives as a religious person of some sort to fully learn a particular lesson. Now, you've moved on to other lessons that require you to be something totally different."

"Well, that makes sense, I guess," said Hollis.

"So why are you here today?" asked Simon. "Do you hope to go back to one of those religious lifetimes to verify what this shaman said or do you just want to see what comes up?"

"I'd like to verify what he told me, if we could."

"Okay," said Simon, "we'll see what we can do about that. Of course, your subconscious mind may have something completely different in store for you."

"Understood," said Hollis.

"Well then, let's get started." Simon made sure all of his equipment was working properly as Hollis lay down on the couch.

"Ready?" asked Simon.

"Beam me up, Scotty," said Hollis.

Simon took his time as they went through the relaxation techniques, sensing that Hollis was still a little too alert and needed to calm down more. Once he thought Hollis was ready, he began the spiral staircase routine. Again Simon went just a bit slower than normal, but by the time he said "one" he was certain that Hollis was completely relaxed.

"Are you standing in front of the door, Hollis?"

"Yes."

"This door leads to your prior lives. As you enter the area beyond the door it will lead you to a past life of yours. Open the door and walk through, Hollis, and tell me what you see."

In his mind Hollis pictured himself doing as the doctor asked, and then a great smile crossed his face.

"What is it, Hollis?" asked Simon. "What do you see?"

"My great-grandfather is here."

In all his time doing regression work, whether stepping through the door or not, no one had ever spoken of someone waiting for them on the other side. Simon was immediately intrigued.

"How does he greet you?" he asked.

"As if he knew I was coming," said Hollis. "He seems thrilled that I would be doing such a thing. He says he saw me with the shaman and he's come to guide me on my quest."

Simon was just as thrilled as Hollis' great-grandfather. This had never happened before in any of the thousands of regressions he had done. Perhaps he was going to be able to just sit back and listen, he thought for a moment, but he was pretty sure that wouldn't be the case.

"Can your great-grandfather lead you back to a past life, or shall we go through the usual progression?" asked Simon.

"He says you can call him John," said Hollis, "and that the normal channels will not be necessary. He will take me to the first life he wants to show me, but he will let you take over from there."

"Let me know when you are ready," said Simon.

A full minute went by before Hollis spoke. "Sorry," he finally said, "but John had some messages for me, some of which I am not to share. However, he says to tell you that we will explore the two lifetimes today that will verify the words of the shaman. The first recall will be very short, and John says you may lead me through it, as you are very good at what you do. The second one will be much longer. John will guide me through that one."

"I am honored by his confidence in me," said Simon. "Are you ready to begin?"

"Yes, John has brought me back to the first lifetime."

"What can you tell me about this life? What year is it? Do you know?"

"The thirteenth century has just begun. It is 1203."

"You seem pretty sure of that date. Can you tell me how you know?"

"John has told me the date. He says you can verify it easily enough. The Crusaders are coming."

Simon had never studied anything about the Crusades, so this would be a learning experience for him. "Can you tell me where you are, Hollis, and what your name is in that lifetime?"

Hollis nearly laughed as he lay on the couch, his mouth breaking open into a wide smile. "You won't believe this," he said, "but my name is Simon."

The doctor chuckled. This had actually happened to him on a few other occasions. "A wonderful name, is it not?" he said. "Where are you, Simon?"

"I live in Constantinople. It is a fascinating place to be. There are nearly half a million people living here."

"What do you do for work?"

"I am in the army, just one soldier among many."

"And how old are you?"

Hollis thought for a moment, and then said, "John tells me I am thirty-six."

"So you are in the army and the Crusaders are about to attack, is that the situation?" asked Simon.

"Yes," said Hollis, who paused for a moment and then continued. "The army has lined up upon the shore, north of the city, to face our attackers. The Crusaders must come by boat, and we are to repel them and send them on their way. Unfortunately our leaders are weak, and when the Crusaders come charging onto the land we are ordered to retreat, barely putting up a fight at all. We are embarrassed as soldiers, but we must obey."

"So you were outside of the city and now you head back?"

"Yes, but the invaders are very aggressive. They chase after us, and finally our leaders show some bravery and tell us to counter-attack. I fight with great courage, for I have been trained well and have been a soldier for many years. I have a sword and a shield, whereas others who are fighting beside me have only a staff or a dagger. Some just have slingshots."

Hollis had told Simon that this regression would not last long, and Simon had the idea that this battle would be his namesake's last. "Do you die in this battle?" he asked.

"I do," said Hollis.

"As you know, no harm can come to you as you go through this regression. Your soul will leave the body before death occurs."

"That's interesting," said Hollis.

Simon suddenly realized that they had not gone through the death portion during Hollis' last visit and that the idea of leaving the body would be new to him. "Take me through this battle as you look down from above."

"The fighting is all hand-to-hand, except for the slingshots. I manage to kill the first three men who attack me, but one has wounded me in my right shoulder. It is the side that I use to hold my sword, and I must retreat for a moment to try and switch my shield over to that hand. I have trained to use my sword in either hand, but I am just not as good with a sword left-handed, and my right arm has trouble holding up my shield. I return to the battle knowing that I will probably die, for I feel defenseless this way."

Hollis stopped talking. Simon was well aware that sometimes picturing one's own death could be unnerving, so he reminded Hollis yet again that no harm would come to him.

"I am barely back in the battle when the end comes. A Crusader with a staff slams it into my shield, knocking me backwards. I lose my balance and fall, and I also lose the grip on my shield. The pain in my shoulder is immense. He jumps on me and plunges a dagger into my side. I look into his eyes, knowing my death is near. He is grinning from ear to ear, thrilled to be killing me, and then he cuts my throat."

"You are looking down on the scene and watching your passing, correct?"

"Yes. My killer dies a moment later when one of my comrades swings a staff into his head."

Simon had a sudden idea. "His soul obviously left his body also. I wonder, can you see him as you are both looking down on the scene?"

Simon found the answer stunning and heart-warming.

"He is right next to me," said Hollis. "I turn to look at him and he smiles back at me. This time it is a smile of warm and tender love. There is no hatred or animosity as we look at each other. We have simply fulfilled the destiny that was ours. Now it is time to move on. He gives me a final smile and a nod of his head, and then he is gone."

"That's amazing," said Simon. "So even though you have both left your earthly bodies, you still see him in human form?"

"Yes, our spiritual bodies still have earthly form because we have just exited them. However, I can also see right through his spiritual body. You might say we are now Beings of Light."

"Fascinating," said Simon.

"John says it is time for us to move on."

"Is there anything about that life in Constantinople you would like to tell me about before we go? Your parents, perhaps, or whether or not you were married?"

"John says no, for the next tale will take a great deal of time to tell. It is why your next client is stuck in traffic."

Simon, not knowing that his three o'clock appointment had already called to say she would be late, was simply bemused.

"John is going to help me remember, for he was a part of that lifetime also. We were boyhood friends, fellow priests, not related but as close as brothers. It is why he has come, so that I may recount the details precisely to you."

"Is this the next life after your time in Constantinople?" asked Simon.

"No, it is earlier than that. Eighth Century."

"What country are you in?" asked Simon.

It was to be the last words Simon Taylor spoke for a very long time.

"I was born in France, in Upper Normandy, and I came early. My parents were enjoying a quiet walk in the woods, not far from the River Seine, when my mother unexpectedly went into labor. I was her first child—six more would follow—but I seemed to be in a rush to arrive. All mothers should have a labor so short! I probably didn't weigh any more than five and a half pounds, and given the times I imagine I was lucky to live.

"My father cut the cord with his knife—he'd seen it done in his family more than once—and took me to the river where he washed me off. When he brought me back to my mother she was still lying on the fallen leaves of an old oak tree that had served as her birthing bed. My mother fed me where she lay, and after only an hour's time managed to get up so we could make our way home. She folded her tunic into her belt to create a basket shape. Normally she would do this to carry vegetables or whatnot, but on that morning it was how she carried me home.

"They named me Philip after my mother's father. We lived on the outskirts of Rouen in a small village of mostly wooden huts with thatched roofs. The neighbor ladies all gathered around to see the newborn baby. My mother held tight to me, not wanting to give me up for even a second, and even as she talked to those in attendance she was praying to God above to keep me safe.

"I imagine it was then that she promised me to God.

"My brothers and sisters came soon after me, as it seemed my mother was always pregnant. They came in order—boy, girl, boy, girl, boy, girl. All survived until the last one, who perished just four days after being born, although my oldest and youngest brothers would not see their tenth birthdays.

"John was a neighbor of mine in the village. In that life he was called Matthew. He was older by about a year, but by the time I turned five we were inseparable friends. I grew up knowing I would join the priesthood, and I was thrilled and excited about the idea. Matthew was quite the opposite as a young boy. He always mocked the priests who came through our village, imitating them in ways that often had me rolling on the ground in laughter, piety not yet my strong suit at that age. I think his parents sent him to the priesthood as a punishment.

"Our lives were fairly simple back then. For such a small village we were very self-sufficient, and we bartered with our neighbors for what we needed. Everyone wore the tunics like the one my mother had carried me home in on the day I was born. My mother's tunic was blue and hung down nearly to the bottom of her calf. It was made out of wool, and she had a train that hung in the back with which she would cover her head in the rain.

"My father's tunic was brown, made of undyed wool, and hung just below his knees. He had cut slits down each side for easier handling. Unlike my mother's tunic, his was sleeveless. She had sewn sleeves onto it once, but he tore them off within days, saying they were always in his way.

"I was twelve when the time came for me to leave the village and begin my studies as a monk. I had known since an early age what my parents plans were for me, so it didn't come as a surprise. The real shock was having Matthew join me on the day the abbot came to claim us. I think his parents just wanted him out from under their roof. He was a rambunctious child, always getting into trouble of one sort or another. Nothing serious, at least most of the time, yet I guess they had had enough. They probably knew that I would be leaving soon and simply decided to send Matthew along with me. It was a wonderful surprise for me, as I had dreaded the thought of being apart from my best friend forever.

"We walked with the abbot to the Abbey of Saint Wandrille, a Benedictine monastery founded a century earlier. I guess it was six or eight miles away, maybe more, but we were used to walking everywhere back then so it was not a problem.

"Matthew hardly said a word for the first part of the journey. I think he was in shock, having no idea that his parents were even thinking of sending him into the priesthood.

"I spent my time listening to the abbot. He was telling us about the abbey, what a typical day would be like, what my training would consist of. I knew right away I would love it. While I enjoyed the time that Matthew and I spent together, I was in fact a child that delighted in being alone. Perhaps it was because I had so many brothers and sisters, and quiet time was rare and hard to find.

"We arrived at the abbey late in the afternoon, and I fell in love with the place immediately. The structure was beautiful, the grounds and gardens gorgeous, and while Matthew thought our private rooms where we would sleep and pray were like prison cells, I thought they were wonderful. We had private rooms because of our age. The monks who lived and worked there all slept in a large dormitory.

"Matthew and I began our education the next day. We joined a classroom that already had four other boys in it. We were taught reading and writing, some basic math, including how to handle money and make change, and of course we studied the Bible. It didn't take long for me to determine that the priesthood was where I wanted to be. Matthew had a much harder time at first and, quite frankly, I believe he came very close to being sent home more than once.

"John is laughing as I say that, and says, 'How true, how true'.

"However, after years of complaining about the place, Matthew came to me one day and said, 'You know, Philip, I like it here'. It was a shock to me, and at first I thought he was putting me on, but the look in his eyes told me otherwise. Matthew had found his calling. He had always been a loquacious child, so I guess it was only natural that preaching would come easily to him. It took him time to fall in love with the Word of God, but once he did the die was cast. I would hear thousands of sermons from hundreds of priests over the course of that lifetime, but few were as talented as my best friend.

"I also found my calling at the abbey, or perhaps I should say my calling found me. It turns out I had a talent for writing. Not the story telling kind, but simply in the writing of the words. My teachers would marvel at the beauty of my letters as I put them to paper. By the time I was actually old enough to take my vows and become a monk it was common knowledge that I had the most beautiful handwriting of anyone at the abbey. For a while it seemed I was the secretary for all the other monks in attendance. Whenever a notice needed to be written, the call would go out to *find Philip*.

"That all changed one cold September morning in my twenty-fourth year. We had just finished with our early morning prayers when I was summoned to meet with the abbot. He and I had developed a close bond ever since that day we first walked to the abbey. He was now in his late fifties, and his health was fading rapidly—he would die within the year—but he still took charge of everything having to do with the Abbey of Saint Wandrille.

"'Philip,' he said, 'you have a talent most of us can only dream about. Your writing is the most beautiful I have ever seen, and it's about time we put it to good use. I know you've been helping your fellow monks with every little note and paper they've needed written, but they used to do that for themselves before you came along, and they can do it again without your help.'

"I had heard rumors in the weeks leading up to this meeting, but I had been unsure if there were any truth to them. Now the full extent of the rumors was laid open to me, and I was astounded by the task set before me. The abbot said, 'I want you to use your talents full-time. Beginning tomorrow, you shall make us a copy of the gospels in the beautiful handwriting that only you can achieve. It shall be your one and only job for the foreseeable future.'

"I was stunned beyond belief, and yet thrilled and excited that such a joy was to be mine. All the instruments that I would need had already been provided for and a room had been set up specifically for me. No one was to interrupt me while I toiled in joy unless it was an emergency. I still went to all the prayer sessions, of course. In fact, they were necessary interruptions, giving my eyes a while to rest and my hand a few moments to relax, for as much as I loved the work, it was hard on the eyes, hands and back. I was told once that most calligraphers worked no more than six hours a day, their bodies unable to withstand any more than that. Yet I commonly worked eight to ten hours a day, and to be honest I don't think anyone's life could have been more delightful than mine.

"I wrote the gospels in the Old Latin Translation, slowly at first, not wanting to make a mistake because of my haste. But as time moved on and I became more proficient, I could write the average line of prose in a minute or so, and the work moved more quickly.

"I had just started the Book of Mark when the abbot died. It was a time of great sorrow for all of us in Saint Wandrille, for he was beloved by all the monks, and we were never to see his like again. I stopped working for two weeks while I mourned, and I spent many hours during those fourteen days with my friend Matthew. It was good to catch up with him, for I had seen him only at prayers and meals for some time now. He was preaching regularly at the Abbey, and also going around to the local villages to share the gospel. He had even gone back to our old village, where I'm sure many of the folks who had known him as a child were shocked beyond belief by his turnaround.

"As it turned out, my time with Matthew was also about to end. Within a month he would be transferred to an abbey southeast of Paris. They were in the midst of a battle with typhus, and almost two-thirds of their monks would perish from the ordeal. Matthew was one of a dozen monks from all parts of France sent to help replenish the abbey.

"I would rarely hear from Matthew after that."

Hollis paused momentarily and Simon, fascinated by this amazing tale and not wanting to interrupt, waited patiently.

"John is telling me that as Matthew he lived for another forty-two years at that abbey and ended up dying of food poisoning.

"As for me, I went back to my work on the gospels. In time I finished my first copy and was asked to do it again, this time with more drawings to accompany the work. As the years went by I finished five books of the gospels, each one more beautiful than the last. The work was never tedious or boring to me, but instead was always a joy to my heart.

"I had started my sixth version of the gospel on the day I died. I was in the middle of Matthew, chapter six, verse four: *That thine alms may be in secret; and thy Father which seeth in secret himself shall reward thee openly.*

"Before I could finish the sentence my Father did reward me. I died of a sudden, massive heart attack, my spirit leaving the body seconds before the attack took place.

"I was discovered when it was apparent that I hadn't shown up for prayers. I am honored to say that my death was received in the abbey much as the death of the abbot had been;

with great sadness. I had spent so much time alone over the previous years that perhaps I did not know how much I was loved by the other monks, but I realized it all as I watched their outpouring of sorrow from above.

"This was my life which I have now shared with you. John tells me it is time to return to the present, for while my current life is totally different from the one I have just recounted, there are interesting trails to travel and connections to be made.

"John says goodbye."

Simon brought Hollis out of the regression. "What a wonderful recounting of that life," he said.

"Thanks to John," replied Hollis. "I believe he filled in many details of the story that I myself probably would not have remembered."

"That was a first for me," said Simon. "I've never had a regression where someone else joined in, as it were. You must have been as surprised as I was to find someone standing behind the door waiting for you."

"Oh, it was a surprise all right. I believe he passed away about three weeks after I was born, and of course I have no idea if he ever saw me or not. Yet as soon as he introduced himself to me I felt as though we were old friends, and of course that turned out to be the case, didn't it?"

"Indeed. So I gather we have satisfied your wonder about your past life as a monk and your time fighting the Crusaders," said Simon. "Interesting lives indeed."

"Yes, thank you," said Hollis.

The two men arose simultaneously.

"Thank you for coming in," said Simon. "You have proven to be an excellent subject, so please feel free to come back anytime, and if you wish to make another appointment today just talk to Grace on your way out."

"Thank you," said Hollis again, as he shook the doctor's hand. He turned and left the room. Entering the front of the office, where Grace was sitting at her desk applying nail polish, his attention was pulled to a young lady sitting in the waiting area. *What an enchanting woman,* he thought.

"Making another appointment?" asked Grace, diverting his attention.

"Not right now," said Hollis, as he stole another glance at the girl.

"Anything else I can do for your?" asked Grace

Hollis realized Grace was wondering what he wanted, since he was still not moving. "No, thank you," he said, and then he headed for the front door.

"Well then, have a nice day," said Grace

Hollis left, but not before taking one more look at the girl, wishing that she would just look up for a moment. His attraction to her was instantaneous. She was obviously younger than him, maybe by ten years, yet he felt a connection to her. *Nothing I can do about it now,* he thought. He opened the door and exited the doctor's office.

Grace had been watching Hollis checking out the girl. "Men," she mumbled, shaking her head.

Hollis was halfway to the elevator and out of earshot when Simon entered the front office and looked into the waiting area.

"Hannah," said Simon, "come on in."

EIGHT

"How are you?" asked Hannah as she sat on the chair in front of the doctor's desk.

"I'm doing well," replied Simon. "I was happy to see your name on my appointment calendar this morning. What brings you back?"

"Well," she said, a provocative little smile caressing her lips, "this may sound funny, or even foolish to you, but I went and had my cards read ..."

"Tarot cards?" asked Simon.

"Yes, tarot cards. One of my best friends reads them, so I went to see her after my late night visit with you. I wanted to know if maybe my Stephanus from Pompeii was going to show up in this life."

Simon just smiled. *Love and soul mates always bring them back*, he thought.

"The reading seemed very positive," continued Hannah, "so I thought maybe I'd come back to see you and find out if he shows up in any other lives of mine."

"You regressed very far back last time. I believe that as far as we could discern Pompeii was your closest lifetime to the present, and that was almost two thousand years ago. Perhaps we should try to find something closer, such as your last lifetime."

"That's what I was thinking," said Hannah. "I went to those other lives because of the nightmares I had been having."

"How's that going, by the way?"

"Those dreams have stopped, thank goodness. I believe having the regression was just what I needed. All I occasionally have now are dreams of falling, but they don't really scare me much compared to the other ones."

"That's good," said Simon. "So let's try to take you back to a more recent time and see if your Stephanus shows up."

"Sounds good to me," said Hannah.

Simon had her lie on the couch that Hollis had just vacated.

"Wow," she said. "I just got some kind of energy buzz."

"The imprint of the man who was here before you, no doubt," said Simon. "Energy is an interesting subject. Did you ever go into a theater that had just emptied and suddenly get a headache? It happened to me once. It wasn't my headache, because I was feeling fine a moment earlier. The person sitting in that seat must have had one, however, and his energy was still there, even though he was gone. I just moved one seat over and the headache disappeared immediately."

"Really? I've never heard of such a thing."

"As I said, it's an interesting subject. You might want to look into it sometime."

Simon began the regression, taking Hannah through the usual steps to relaxation. When he finished and asked her to open the door at the bottom of the stairs, he wondered if anyone from Hannah's past would show up, but no one did.

Simon had been wondering ever since he had first starting using the doorway if he could skip the age regressions in the client's current life and go directly to the past life. It had just happened with Hollis' regression, but that may have been because of his great-grandfather being there. He decided to try it now with Hannah.

"As you pass through the doorway this time I want you to

go directly to your past life. You can do this easily, Hannah," he said, hoping it was true. "Tell me what you see."

As it turned out, she had no difficulties at all in going back immediately.

"I see a field of flowers; daisies, pansies, sunflowers. It's beautiful."

"Are you walking by this field of flowers?"

"Yes, it is on a hillside that I am passing. No wait, I am not walking, I am bicycling. I am almost to the top of a hill, and then I can coast down the other side. The wind is blowing a bit and my hair …"

"What is it, Hannah? Why did you stop?"

She let out a small laugh. "I am a boy."

"That's not uncommon," said Simon. "Do you know where you are going? Perhaps you could find out what country you are in."

"There is a town at the bottom of the hill. That is my destination. I can tell you that it is summer; quite warm." She paused for a moment before continuing. "I have arrived in the town. My parents were waiting for me to return. I was just out joyriding."

"Can you tell how old you are?"

"I must be about fourteen, fifteen years old," said Hannah. "Ah, my father has just called to me. My name is Roberto. I think I might be in Italy again."

"Look at the stores and buildings around you to see if you can verify that," said Simon. He waited patiently while Hannah surveyed the vision she was seeing.

"Ah, no," she said after a while, "although my family is from Italy, we are now in Germany. The town is called Colmar. My father has bought a local vineyard and the home that comes with it."

"Who is with you besides your father?"

"Well, my mother, of course."

"No brothers or sisters?"

"It doesn't appear so. I don't see anyone else around, although they may be off exploring as I was."

"Any sign of Stephanus from your Pompeii lifetime?" asked Simon.

"No, not yet," said Hannah. "We are going to inspect the farm now. It is the first time my mother and I have seen it."

"Let's move ahead a little bit, maybe a year or so. How is life on the vineyard going for you?"

Hannah lay quiet on the couch as her mind processed the information. It took her a few moments to do as the doctor had asked, but eventually she said, "Life is good. The land is perfect for growing grapes, and our new home is quite large for the three of us. I do not have any siblings. My father says the wine will be spectacular when it is ready for bottling. He is very pleased."

"What are your duties around the house?"

"I help in the vineyards, of course. Father is teaching me all he knows so that when the time comes, hopefully many years from now, I can take over the business."

"Can you describe how you look to me?"

"Certainly. I have bronze colored skin, darkened by all the time I spend in the sun. I am about five foot ten, and I probably weigh about 150 pounds. The work helps keep me in good shape. My mother says she loves my brown eyes. She calls them a golden brown, whatever that means."

"Do you have a girlfriend?"

"No," said Hannah, "but I have seen a girl in the distance on three occasions that I am drawn to. I hope to meet her soon. As a man might say nowadays, she has big bazookas."

"You mean she is well endowed," said Simon, attempting to withhold a chuckle without much success.

"Yes, most definitely," said Hannah. "She must live nearby, since I have seen her on a wagon which passes by here on occasion, although never close enough to say anything to her."

"Let's move ahead again to the day that you finally meet her, if you do."

Simon had just a moment's wait this time as Hannah

suddenly grew excited.

"I see her!" she exclaimed. "I have been sent into town to buy supplies, and she is in the store when I enter. She wears a kerchief on her head and is holding a basket with which she is shopping.

"'Good morning', I say to her as we meet in the middle of an aisle. She turns to look at me, and … oh yes, it is the eyes of Stephanus. He is now a girl, and I am the boy."

"Does this first meeting go well?"

"We talk for a few minutes—enough time for me to find out her name and where she lives."

"What is her name?" asked Simon.

"Anne Festa. She is Italian also, but her family moved here when she was a baby. She is older than me by a few years, but I think we have a connection."

"How long is it before you see her again?"

"Nearly a month," said Hannah. "I think of her all the time, and my mother notices. She says I have suddenly become daft, and she thinks I must be dreaming about a girl. When I tell her she is right she just shakes her head. Later she will tell my father, and he asks me many questions. Who is she? How do I know her? What are my plans?" When I tell him that she shops every Saturday for her family, he agrees to let me go into town to see her as long as my work is caught up."

"Tell me what happens when you see her again?" said Simon.

"It is magic. I think she has been thinking about me also. We both arrive in the town at almost the exact same moment, and when I go up to talk to her she seems happy to see me.

"We walk to the bakery together, and I buy some bread and cheese with money my father had given to me for just such a purpose. I know he could tell how much I was smitten. I suggested to Anne that we take a short walk to the nearby woods and have a little picnic.

"She was happy to oblige me. We sat outside and talked for nearly an hour. She was a seamstress, a trade she had learned as a little girl from her mother and aunt. She agreed to meet me again the following week, and I suggested we go on another picnic. She said that would be fine and that she would bring the food from home next time.

"We fell in love quickly after that, but we were both so busy we rarely had time to spend with each other at first. Eventually, however, both our parents knew they couldn't keep us apart much longer. She was anxious to get married so she wouldn't end up like her aunt, who was what they call a spinster. It took longer than we had hoped, but eventually it all worked out."

"Tell me about your life together," said Simon. "How did it all play out?"

"We married in 1887. Anne was twenty-one, and I was about to turn eighteen. She came to live on the farm with my family, and they quickly fell in love with her also. She was beautiful. Five-foot five---nearly half a foot taller than my mother!—and she had long shapely legs that I just adored. Her hair was jet black, which she usually cut short, much to my dismay, and she had light hazel colored eyes that just sparkled.

"In time she opened up a shop in town, what we would now call a boutique, and her expertise with a needle and thread became legendary. She was always busy."

"Did the two of you have children?" asked Simon.

"We had three children over the next few years, two boys and a girl, and they came in that order. They were all healthy, thank God. Michel, Pasha and Danielle were their names. Eventually we built our own home about a hundred yards from my parent's place, and I did take over the farm from my father just before the crazy times hit."

"Crazy times?" asked Simon.

"The war," said Hannah. "World War One. The region of Germany we lived in had once belonged to France. It would return to France after World War I, be taken over again by the Germans in World War II, then return to French control after the war."

"What happened to you when the war broke out?" asked

Simon.

"It started out okay, but when the German troops marched into France they drank a lot of our wine as they passed through, paying for almost none of it. Then of course the war took a turn. Retreating German troops trampled our fields as they sought to stay alive, and the allied troops chasing them did much the same. We had a few lean years after the war ended, although the French allowed us to stay on our land and never gave us much trouble. Suddenly we were living in France instead of Germany, although we hadn't moved an inch."

"And your life with Anne was still wonderful?"

"Oh, it certainly was. We both worked long, hard hours to make our vocations successful, but at the end of the day we only desired to be with each other."

Hannah suddenly laughed.

"What's so funny?" asked Simon.

"One day we were home alone. It was the middle of the day, the children were all gone. What we were both doing home at that time of day I have no idea, but we decided to use the time to make love. It was nothing like our usual dalliances, quiet so as not to wake the children. This was hot and heavy, with lots of moaning and screaming. Anne was on top of me, those big breasts swaying up and down, when all of a sudden … the bed broke.

"It was an old bed, to be sure, but it had always held our weight without a problem. But I guess our movements that day were too much for it, because suddenly one side sort of caved in, and then the rest of the bed just plopped down. We laughed like crazy once we both realized neither one of us was hurt, and then we finished our lovemaking lying on the floor."

Simon wasn't quite sure how to follow up on that story. "Let's move on to the end of that lifetime. Which one of you crossed over first?"

"I did," said Hannah. "It was 1930. I was working in the fields—I never left that farm once I moved there as a boy— and I was bitten by a snake. Snakes in the fields were common, of course, but this was an asp viper, very deadly. I called out to a fellow worker, and eventually I was brought back to the house where I was treated. Unfortunately the treatment was not done properly, or maybe it just came too late. I died before the day was out.

"Anne was heartbroken. Her mother had already passed and her father had moved back to Italy. She eventually moved back to Italy to be with him when it became apparent another war was coming. Anne died of pneumonia in 1943 just after her seventy-seventh birthday."

"You say you died in 1930, yet you've mentioned the Second World War and talked about your widow. How do you know what happened after you died?"

"I don't know. You asked me the questions and the answers were just shown to me. It's like watching a movie."

"Can you also tell me what happened to your children after you passed?" Simon asked.

"Michel took over the farm after I died, but he left and moved to America when the second war broke out. Pasha moved to Italy when his mother did and lived through the second war, but then was killed when he attempted to stop two men from robbing the local market. Danielle had moved to England with her husband. She died in a bombing raid during the war, a son of hers also dying in the attack."

"Besides Stephanus from Pompeii, did you recognize anyone else?"

"My parents in that life are together again. They are an aunt and uncle of mine now. Pasha was my adoptive father in this life. What a shame I can't tell him what I've discovered. I do not know anyone else."

A bell went off in Simon's head and he took a quick look at his notes. "You mentioned that your son in Pompeii was your adoptive father in this life, so Pasha was with you back then also, correct?"

"Yes, he was my son in both instances."

"You also mentioned after your regression to Pompeii that your mother there was now an aunt. Is your mother in

Germany the same person?"

"Yes, my mother in Pompeii was my mother in Colmar."

"You never saw your father in Pompeii, but he could be the man who was your father in Colmar and is now your uncle."

"I don't know," was all Hannah could say.

"Is there anything else from that lifetime you wish to convey to me?" asked Simon.

"No," said Hannah, and a moment later Simon brought her out of the regression.

Simon stopped at Genuine Thai on the way home that night. The small hole-in-the-wall restaurant sat in the corner space of a strip mall that Simon passed every day. It had quickly become his favorite eating establishment shortly after he moved to Sarasota. Although his small home town in South Carolina had never had a Thai restaurant, he had developed a taste for the wonderfully aromatic and delicious food on his many travels with Nora.

Sanjay, the jovial owner, greeted him as he entered. "Doctor Simon, how nice to see you again. Long time since last visit."

"Hello, Sanjay," said Simon. "Yes, it's been too long. My taste buds need some waking up."

"This way," said Sanjay, grabbing a menu from the front counter.

The small restaurant had a dozen booths, six against one wall and six on the opposite side. Tables and chairs took up the middle of the room. Every booth and table contained a candle in an odd assortment of glass holders, and each booth had a framed picture of Buddha on the wall.

Sanjay led Simon to a booth in the back of the restaurant. "Ellen be right with you," he said, as he placed the menu on the table.

Ellen was Sanjay's wife, a tall American beauty with blond hair and cream colored skin. She and Sanjay made a strange looking couple, his wife being nearly four inches taller than him, but the love they shared was obvious whenever Simon saw the two of them together.

Ellen came over to his booth almost immediately with a pot of jasmine tea.

"Hello, Simon," she said, as she poured the tea into the small round cup. "You're looking well tonight." She knew about Simon's struggles, having waited on him many times over the past few months. Some nights he was a man of few words, but on other occasions he had opened up to her about the passing of his wife and how hard it had hit him.

"Thank you, Ellen," said Simon. "I had a good day today. Feeling a bit energized."

"It shows," she replied. "Would you like to start with an appetizer this evening?"

Simon took a quick glance at the menu and said, "I think I'll try the Curry Puffs. I've never had them before."

"Need a minute for the rest of the order?" she asked.

"Yes, please," he said, and Ellen left to place his appetizer order.

He gazed at the menu which he practically knew by heart. He usually ate here at least once a week, although it had been over two weeks since his last visit. He decided to stay with the curry theme for his main course, and when Ellen arrived a few minutes later with his appetizer he ordered the Seafood Curry, a combination of shrimp, scallops, calamari and fish in what the menu described as a delectable coconut red curry sauce.

He ate the Curry Puffs slowly, his mouth warming more with each bite, as he thought back over his day. The morning regressions had been mediocre at best, and he doubted he would see any of those clients again. However, the afternoon sessions of Hollis and Hannah had been totally different, and the fact that Hollis' great-grandfather had appeared to help with the regression was a mind boggling first for Simon.

He was lost in thought when Ellen brought out his dinner. "Here you go," she said, as she moved his empty appetizer plate out of the way and set down his meal. "Lots on your mind tonight?" she asked.

"Interesting day," he replied. "Good things."

"Nice to see you smiling," said Ellen. "I'll bring you some more tea in a bit."

He watched her walk away, the sway of her hips captivating him for a moment, and he knew Sanjay was a lucky man. On another day the thought would have sent him into an instant depression, his loss of Nora rushing into his brain, but tonight he returned to Hollis and Hannah as he dug into his meal. Neither one had made another appointment, but Simon hoped he would see both of them again.

He devoured the Seafood Curry, and Ellen noticed when she brought him a second pot of tea. "Hungry man tonight, huh?" she said. "Doesn't look like there's going to be any leftovers to take home."

"It's delicious," said Simon. "I guess I was hungrier than I thought."

"You really look happy tonight," said Ellen. "It's nice to see."

Simon could hear the heartfelt tone of her voice and appreciated the comment. "Thank you," he said, and was surprised when his voice almost cracked.

He arrived home a half hour later and realized he was whistling as he rode the elevator to the fourteenth floor. He entered his condo and made a vodka martini, which he then carried out to the balcony. He thought he should have a talk with Nora.

The night air was calm as he walked to the railing.

"Hi Nora," he said as he looked to the heavens. "I had a good day today; some very interesting developments. A third party came through during one of my regressions. Maybe you know that already. Were you watching?"

He took a sip of his drink as he gazed upon the Big Dipper. The night sky was unusually clear, and Simon was aware that he could see more stars than usual. He paused for a while longer as he determined what to say next.

"I think I've turned a corner," he finally said. "I miss you so much, Nora, but I have to move on. I don't think I could ever love anyone else the way I loved you. You were my true love, my soul mate. But you're over there, maybe already making plans for your next life, and I'm down here still having to live this one."

A tear slid down his cheek, and he paused for a moment to wipe it away.

"I have to move on, Nora, whether I want to or not. It's time. Just stay with me, okay? Watch over me and help me out when I need it. I love you, Nora."

The wind chimes remained quiet as Simon put his drink on the table, sat down, and quietly wiped away the tears that kept coming.

NINE

Simon awoke the next morning feeling more at peace than he had felt in a long time. His talk with Nora had been cathartic, and for the first time since her death he began to feel whole. Yes, he still missed her and knew he always would, but he was still young, and may not even be half way through this life yet. It was time to move on, and he finally felt ready to do so.

"Just help me as I go," he said as he glanced skyward, but he said it with a wistful smile.

Twenty minutes later he was just finishing his breakfast while thumbing through the morning paper that was delivered to his door. As he was about to set the paper aside, he noticed an ad on the last page.

PSYCHIC FAIR
10-6
VENDORS
READERS
AURA PHOTOGRAPHY

It was a rare weekend in Sarasota when there wasn't a psychic fair, as the area was a hotbed of metaphysical happenings. Seeing the ad, Simon immediately thought of the shaman that Hollis had been to see. He went to his briefcase, found his daily planner and opened it up. He suddenly recalled the name of Wil Stevens a moment before he saw it.

The ad had a phone number at the bottom if you needed more information. Simon punched in the number on his cell phone.

The lady who answered sounded a bit stressed out but tried to cover it. "This is Louise. How may I help you?"

"I was wondering if Wil Stevens was going to be at your fair today."

"I believe so, but let me check my sheet," said Louise.

Simon heard the rustling of papers and a muttering of "where is that sheet" while another voice in the background asked Louise a different question.

"Ah, here it is," Louise finally answered. "Wil Stevens will be at table 27, which will be on the far left as you enter."

"Thank you," said Simon, and a frazzled Louise muttered something unintelligible as she hung up the phone.

The fair was on the other side of Sarasota and was in full swing by the time Simon arrived. He parked in a space near the door that was just being vacated, entered the building, and was immediately greeted by a short, plump lady looking rather odd in a T-shirt and jeans.

"Hi there," she said. "Welcome to our fair."

"My pleasure," said Simon, noticing her nametag said Judith.

"Admission is free, and here is a list of our vendors and readers. On the back is a little diagram showing where each one is located."

"Thank you, Judith," said Simon.

He entered the hall and slowly walked around the room. These fairs were different from the conferences that he often spoke at. Most of the items on sale at those were books or CD's of the various speakers. Here at the fair a person could find almost anything, both new and used.

Simon walked around the entire room, making sure to

check out the spot where Wil Stevens was set up as he passed. He finally ended up in front of a break area where sandwiches and drinks were being sold. He purchased a coffee, leaned against a wall, and was surveying the scene around him when he heard a woman's voice call out.

"Doctor Taylor, how are you?"

Simon turned to see a beautiful woman, tall and well proportioned, with long black hair and stunning emerald eyes. She looked familiar, but he couldn't place the name right away.

"Maria Vasquez," she said. "I came to see you about three months ago for a regression."

"Of course," said Simon, and when the name finally hit home he said, "I have a new client because of you. Thank you very much."

"Because of me?"

She had the most beautiful smile, and her voice gave away her Spanish background. "You met a man in a bar during a girl's night out," said Simon.

"Oh my goodness, he actually went to see you?" said Maria. "I never thought he would really go. Were you able to explain the mark on his body?"

"I believe we did," said Simon. "He even came back to see me again just yesterday."

"Well, I'm happy I could help. Do I get a commission?" she asked, and they both laughed. "So what brings you here today?" asked Maria.

"Oddly enough, Hollis did."

"Oh yes, Hollis. That was his name," said Maria.

"Yes. He told me about a shaman that he had been to see, and I discovered that the man was here today. I thought I'd check him out, maybe go see him."

"Do you mean Wil? He's a friend of mine," cried Maria. "Oh, you must go see him. He's fantastic."

She waited while he finished his coffee and then led him over to see the shaman. Wil was in the middle of a reading for a customer, but when he saw Maria coming towards him he gave her a small wave.

There was a signup sheet on his table. Maria glanced at it and said, "One other person is waiting to see him. It's going to be another half hour before he's free, but I'll put your name down."

She picked up the pen attached to the clipboard and mumbled "Doctor Simon Taylor" as she wrote the name. Then she looked up at him and said, "We have some time. Shall we stroll around and see what we find?"

He kept to himself the fact that he had already walked the entire fair as they slowly ambled around the room. Maria knew a number of the vendors and frequently stopped to chat with them, introducing Simon as she did.

"So tell me," he asked after they had nearly completed his second loop around the room, "how was your regression? I can't say that I remember offhand."

"My regression was very interesting," said Maria, the hint of a smile forming on her face.

"So did you get anything out of it?"

She gazed at him for a long moment, their eyes locking, and then she gave him the most beautiful smile he had seen in a long time. "I did," said Maria, and she left it at that. "It should be just about time for your visit with Wil. In fact, I notice he's waving at us."

Simon turned to see Wil Stevens standing in front of his signup table, and he and Maria headed that way.

"Hi, Wil," said Maria, and she gave the shaman a long hug. "I'd like you to meet a friend of mine, Doctor Simon Taylor."

The men shook hands, and Wil said, "A pleasure to meet you, doctor. What brings the two of you here today?"

"Oh, we didn't come together," said Simon.

"I found him looking lost in the break area," laughed Maria, "but he said he was here to see you."

Simon noticed a look pass between the two of them but couldn't imagine what it was for.

"Well," said Wil, "your time is now. Come on back to the

massage table, take off your shoes and have a seat."

Simon did as asked, placing his shoes under the table before sitting down. He did not see or hear anything as Wil turned to Maria.

"Does he …?" whispered Wil.

"No," said Maria, "and let's keep it that way."

"I understand your thought process, but I remind you that time is a precious commodity that tends to speed up as we get older. Don't waste too much of it."

"You forget my situation," said Maria, her voice barely audible as she stole a glance at Simon.

Wil gave her a raised eyebrow but said nothing more. He turned and approached the doctor. "So why have you come here to see me today?" he asked.

"A client of mine came to see you last week. I gathered by the way he spoke about you that he was impressed, and since I've never met a shaman before, I thought I'd stop by."

"You speak at spiritual conferences all over the country. You've never met a shaman at any of them?"

"Can't say that I have," answered Simon.

"Well …," said Wil, but he let the thought go. "Give me your hand and let's see if I can impress you."

Simon extended his right hand and Wil took it in a handshake grip. Simon always thought he had large hands for a man, but Wil's hand swallowed his up, and when the shaman cupped his left hand over his, the doctor's hand seemed to disappear altogether.

"I know your story, in large part thanks to Maria, so I won't try to amaze you with what you already know about this lifetime. She's tried a hundred times to have me read your book, but I haven't circled around to it yet."

Simon stared at the man, saying nothing, but simply trying to take in the moment. Wil was tall and well built, his blond hair flowing in all directions. His face could best be described as rugged looking, large like his hands and well-worn, making him look older than he probably was.

"I will say you're at the beginning stages of healing, but I believe you have realized that already," said Wil. "Let's see what we can find from your former lives."

"You make retrieving past lives sound so easy," said Simon. "Perhaps you should have my job."

Wil smiled. "I only give you bits and pieces of information, not entire stories. Hopefully what I can tell you will help you understand why you are who you are in this lifetime."

Wil gazed into space as he was gathering his information, but he looked directly at Simon as he spoke. "This is certainly not the first time you have helped people. I have a clear picture of you walking through the woods, studying flowers and plants for their medicinal purposes."

Simon had always kept an aloe plant in his home because of its healing powers, although his current abode did not yet have one.

"You were also a doctor in the Far East many centuries ago," continued Wil. "I'm thinking Japan, but that's only a guess."

"Haven't spent any time in the Far East," said Simon.

"I think you've spent a great many lives below the equator; Africa, South America, Australia. You loved Africa, went back there many times."

"I went on safari there with … my wife," said Simon. "We loved it."

The hitch in his voice was obvious, and Wil didn't need to be a shaman to know the pain of Simon's loss was still near the surface, even if he was beginning to move on.

"Your need to be a healer comes from there, for you saw much fighting among the tribes where you lived, and a great deal of needless killing." Wil paused for a moment before continuing. "Unfortunately you were a part of that back then. You led a tribe that attacked another village. You did it for food and plunder and the joy of the battle." He noticed Simon wince. "Don't be ashamed. It was simply the times you lived in. We've all been there."

Wil stared at the ceiling for a long moment before continuing.

"Ah, here's a happier time. You were a carpenter. Wait, not just a carpenter, but a wood carver. You did amazing things with wood; statues of birds and animals in amazing detail. My guides are showing me Brazil; I'm guessing seventeenth or eighteenth century."

Wil let go of Simon's hand. "That's enough of that for now, I think. Lie down and get comfortable," he said.

Simon did as requested. "So I help people now because I once hurt people, is that it?"

Wil walked to the front of the massage table and placed his hand on Simon's forehead. "You have carried a great sense of remorse with you for many lifetimes now. It's not uncommon. We've all been through it, for when has civilization not been at war with each other? When we pass to the other side we go over the life we have just lived, study it to see what we have learned, where we could have done better. Then we choose a new life to put what we have learned into action and to learn something new. You will forgive yourself when this life is finished. Your remorse will be lifted, and your need to be a healer over and over again will come to an end. You've started the turn to spirituality in this life. My guess is that will be the focus of your next incarnation."

"How do you get all this information, and how can I know that it's real?"

"I suppose you could have a past life regression done," said Wil, smiling broadly. "Other than that, I'm afraid you have to trust your gut instincts. What do they tell you? Did my words ring true, or do you think I was just making stuff up?"

"I'll have to think on that, I guess."

"No, no thinking. What was your thought the second I gave you the information? What did you think before you started thinking? How did my words feel to you? That is what matters."

Simon lay on the table, somewhat perplexed, and said nothing.

"As to how the information comes to me, it is mostly in visions; sometimes very cloudy, sometimes clear. Yours came through quite nicely, I must say, and I think it's because you needed to know. It's important. Events are shaping up for you in the future that you need to be aware of. This was just the opening step to that process."

"Are you getting images of my future now?"

"You have much life to live," said Wil. "Now be still and let me heal this body of yours."

Simon closed his eyes as the shaman moved his hands to various parts of his body; forehead, heart, stomach, legs, knees and feet. Wil remained quiet the entire time, not speaking until he was finished.

"As I said earlier, you have begun the healing process. I've released some of the pain you've been holding on to and the tension that accompanies that. You had a small blockage in your left thigh that I took care of. I actually saw the vein bubble up as I released it, which I don't often see. You should feel a little more energetic in the coming days. I suggest drinking lots of water for the next week."

With that, Wil waved his finger in a circular motion, signaling Simon to sit up.

Simon put his shoes back on, stood up, and immediately had to hold on to the side of the table. He felt dizzy and light-headed.

"Easy there," said Wil, reaching out to take the doctor by his arm. "Sometimes it takes a moment for the equilibrium to come back."

Simon turned and stared into the shaman's eyes. "An interesting day," he said.

"I hope you find that it helps you," said Wil. "You should be okay now."

The dizziness had already passed, and Simon wondered if Wil's touch had cured it just like that. Or maybe he was still just over-thinking everything. He placed a bill in Wil's donation jar, shook hands one final time, and turned to go.

"See you again," said Wil.

"You know that for a fact?" asked Simon.

Wil just smiled.

Maria was waiting for him in the lobby. "How did it go?" she asked.

"The man is an interesting character, that's for sure," said Simon. "I think I need time to process it all."

"He's really very good at what he does," said Maria.

They headed for the exit together as Simon said, "Probably so, but … it's different, you know."

"Not that much different than what you do," she said. "Wil tells people about their past lives, you bring people to their past lives."

"But when I do it, it's the people who remember their own past life; much like you did when you came to see me. It's your own memories. With Wil, I just have to take him at his word. Not sure I can do that."

"Well, I hope he helped you in some small way. I'm parked over there," she said, pointing off to her left. "It was nice seeing you again, doctor."

"Do you think you'll be back for another regression?" he asked.

"I was thinking about that while you were with Wil," replied Maria, as she began to walk away. She turned to look back at him, smiled, and said, "I may just do that."

Simon gave her a small wave and then headed for his car.

Maria Vasquez arrived home from the fair to mayhem. Her husband, Alfonso, was in a foul mood, which was not unusual. It seemed lately he spent most of his time like that.

"Where you been?" he shouted at Maria as soon as she walked in the door. "Quick trip to the fair, you said. You've been gone over two hours."

"I ran into some friends of mine," she said. "What's so important that you needed me here for?"

"Don't talk to me in that tone of voice, woman," Alfonso sputtered. "A woman's place is in the home. You should be here, taking care of your family."

"What, you can't take care of a three-year-old boy for a couple of hours?"

Alfonso stared at her long and hard. Maria was sure she was about to receive the slap across the face that she had grown accustomed to, but it didn't come. Finally, she asked, "Where's Enrique?"

"In his room, where I sent him," said Alfonso. "Boy likes to sass me, just like his mother."

"You better not have hit him," cried Maria.

"He needs to learn some respect for his father," Alfonso yelled.

"Respect is earned," said Maria. "Has he earned your respect?"

She saw the fire flare in his eyes, and quickly moved towards Enrique's room before her husband exploded. The boy was lying on his bed, tears still in his eyes and a red blotch noticeable on his cheek.

"Enrique," she said as she entered the room, and the boy ran into her arms, crying "Mami, Mami!"

The downfall of the marriage of Alfonso and Maria had been going on for some time now, although few knew about it except for Maria's closest friends. They had been married just over four years ago in Puerto Rico at the home of Alfonso's parents. At no time during the two years that they had dated had Alfonso shown a predilection for anger, but as soon as the marriage was official it became obvious that he thought the man should run the family and the woman should knuckle under to his demands.

The first time he slapped her was on their honeymoon. She had been taken aback by his sudden anger, which she had not seen before. Her attempt to put her foot down at such outrageous behavior was quickly thwarted, and over time she had learned not to push her husband too far. She had hoped that having a son would help to change him, but it seemed to have had no effect. Alfonso loved the boy but had little patience with him.

The family moved to the United States when the factory that Alfonso worked for opened a plant just outside of Sarasota and offered to make him a department manager. Maria had hoped that the move and the extra money it brought them would help change things, but it hadn't worked out that way. She spent her days with Enrique, who was a precocious little boy with an infectious smile.

She had wanted to get a part time job, but Alfonso wouldn't hear of it. "I make the money in this family," he had told her more than once. "You just keep your skirt on and raise the boy."

Lately she had begun to think that her husband was having an affair, although she had no proof of that. In her mind it didn't matter. Her marriage was a disaster, and she knew she couldn't stay with the man much longer.

The problem was how to get out without being hurt.

TEN

Simon arrived at his office the following Wednesday looking forward to a day of regressions.

Grace was already in the office. "Only been here ten minutes," she said, "and already I've had two calls for new psychology patients. It seems as though your schedule is going to fill up fast. I've penciled them in for tomorrow; hope that's okay."

"That's fine, Grace," said Simon. "I'll leave the scheduling to you."

While the morning was busy, nothing spectacular happened in any of the regressions, although all of the clients had seemed happy with the results. The final regression of the morning, a young and obviously nervous man, had actually ended early, and Simon used the extra time to enjoy a leisurely lunch at the deli around the corner.

Upon his return to the office, Grace informed him he had more time to kill. "Your one o'clock was just in a fender-bender on I-75," she said. "She won't make it in today."

"Is she alright?" he asked.

"Said she was fine; the car, not so much."

"Well, I'm sure I must have some paperwork I can catch up on," said Simon.

He walked back to his office and sat down. He was

debating what to do when the memory of Maria Vasquez popped into his head. He had enjoyed seeing her at the fair and had thought of her more than once since then.

Grace entered the room with a pot of tea and saw him staring into space. "Is that how you do paperwork?" she said. "I guess I've been doing it wrong all these years."

Simon smiled at her and said, "Just daydreaming."

"Like I couldn't tell that," said Grace. "What's her name?"

"What?" said Simon, a quizzical look on his face. "What makes you believe I was thinking of a woman?"

Grace poured him a cup of the hot steaming beverage and simply replied, "Drink your tea, Romeo." Then she turned and headed for the door, laughing and shaking her head as she went.

Simon took a sip of tea and then decided to get Maria's file. Even though he had all of his client's regressions on audio, he still kept written back-up files. The file contained the questionnaire they had filled out plus notes he had written about the person and the regression.

He found Maria's file, sat back down, and took out the paperwork. She had been in the first week of February, just three weeks after he had opened his Sarasota office. She had regressed easily and skipped quickly through a time as a man in seventeenth century Egypt. From there she had moved to a life as a woman on the reservation of the Cherokee Indians. Her name had been Leotie, which she said meant Flower of the Prairie.

Simon began to remember bits and pieces of the regression as he read. The tribe lived in northern Georgia, and Maria had been married to a medicine man. The Cherokees of that time were not the typical Indians as portrayed by old western television shows and movies. They had fought with the British in the American Revolution and had taken on many of the European customs. Maria had been born in 1800. She and her husband, who was ten years her senior, lived in a log cabin and had four children, three girls and a boy.

Simon didn't remember all of her tale, but he did recall that she and her family had been part of the infamous Trail of Tears, where the Cherokee had been forced off their land and moved to what is now Oklahoma.

Simon checked his watch and noticed he still had some time before his next appointment. He decided to find the audio version of Maria's regression and listen to some of it. Once he had it set up, he fast-forwarded through the early portion, then clicked PLAY.

"… had to go. The white man had already taken about ninety percent of our land. Now they were pushing us off what little we had left. We resisted as best we could, but eventually they removed us by force.

"Some of the tribe traveled by water, but Gawonii and I were in one of the groups that traveled by land. We had some wagons, but many of us had to walk. It was extremely difficult. Many were already sick from the internment camps we were forced into before leaving. They were overcrowded, sanitation was poor, and a drought had exacerbated the situation.

"Once we started the journey the weather turned bad. People were dying nearly every day from exposure and starvation, and before long diseases were running rampant through our group. Gawonii tried to help as many as he could, but he had not been able to bring many of the herbs and medicines that he used, and he found little during our daily travels. He was beside himself with despair, and when I began to get sick it simply made it worse.

"Winter hit before we could cross the Mississippi. We were forced to stop and wait for better weather, and I knew then that I would not survive the trip. Most who had died were infants, young children or the elderly. I was none of those, yet I was always small in stature and probably never weighed more than one-hundred and fifteen pounds. My body was disappearing in front of my eyes."

"Is that where you died?" Simon had asked.

"Yes."

At this point Simon had told her to look down on her final moments from above and describe it as best she could.

"Gawonii is cradling me in his arms, tears running down his cheeks. We had enjoyed a wonderful marriage, and he will miss me terribly. I look at him and tell him that the Great Spirit is calling to me. My final words are 'help who you can,' and then I cross over."

Simon had brought her out of the regression at that point and heard his voice on the tape say, "That was an interesting story you told, Maria."

"Have you heard that story before?" she asked.

He remembered the moment now because the question had surprised him. No one had ever asked him that after a regression. "I've probably heard dozens of stories from people who had once belonged to Indian tribes, although most have been in the western United States," he had replied.

Just then the buzzer on his desk went off, signaling that his next client had arrived. Simon put Maria's folder and audio back in their proper places and prepared to return to work.

Hollis Brown had been thinking about the girl in Simon's office for the past two weeks, yet he wasn't sure why. He saw many beautiful women on the streets of Sarasota, even worked with a few at school. He thought the girl he saw sitting in the waiting room was attractive, although from what he could tell she didn't appear to have much in the breast department, and she hadn't even looked up at him as he left the office.

So what was it about her that kept her popping into his mind every few minutes?

He had no idea, and no clue as to what he could do about it. He had thought about calling the doctor's office and just asking for her name, but he quickly eliminated that. Surely the names of all the doctor's clients were privileged information. Besides, he was pretty sure that the secretary had noticed him checking out the girl, so calling her to ask who the girl was would probably earn him a stalker label.

He also thought about making another appointment in the hopes of running into her again, but what were the odds of that happening?

He finally decided it was just one of those times where you pass someone on the street and think you know them from somewhere, even though you're sure you've never met them before. He needed to just forget her, yet for some reason he was having a hard time doing that.

He was suddenly interested in dating again, however. It seemed to be an urge running through his body. He found it hard to believe that the touch of a shaman could have anything to do with his feelings, yet he had no other explanation. Had his heart been hardened by his divorce? Had Wil Stevens really unblocked his heart so that he could love again?

He had never paid much attention to the metaphysical world; had always considered himself a down to earth type of guy. If someone had told him a year ago that he would be having a past life regression and visiting a shaman he would have laughed. Yet the regression had felt real to him, and the spot on his leg, while still there, did seem to be fading a bit. If his past life as a woman were true, was it possible that the impressions Wil had received simply by holding his hand could also be true?

Hollis didn't know what to think.

The thought of dating again appealed to him, however, and since the girl in the doctor's office was not available to him, he had to look elsewhere. While dating someone in the workplace wasn't always the best idea, he had noticed for quite a while now that one of the secretaries in the school office seemed to brighten up whenever he entered the room. Amy Mason was tall, blond, and in the words of one of Hollis' fellow teachers, a knockout.

Hollis decided to take the plunge.

Amy was delighted when Hollis asked if she'd like to get a coffee after work. She had always thought he was a handsome man with a level head on his shoulders, his decreasing hairline notwithstanding, but all her past attempts to catch his attention had seemingly gone unnoticed. She had no idea where the sudden invitation had come from, but the yes came out of her mouth so fast it was almost embarrassing.

They met in the parking lot after school, hoping they wouldn't draw too much attention to themselves.

"How about we go to Mabel's Place?" asked Hollis. Mabel's Place was a local favorite in downtown Sarasota that served all sorts of flavored coffees and homemade goodies.

"That's fine," said Amy. "I'll meet you there."

They waved goodbye to each other just in case anyone was watching, both knowing school gossip could be a dangerous thing. Amy even called out, "Have a nice day."

Ten minutes later they arrived at Mabel's in separate cars. They ordered their coffees, bold flavor for him and hazelnut for her, and they agreed to share a cranberry orange muffin. Then they found the most secluded table they could.

Amy got right to the point as soon as they sat down. "So what made you ask me out after all this time, Hollis Brown?"

The use of his full name and the humorous way that she said it made him smile. He decided to play along and said, "A shaman made me do it."

It was obviously not the reply she was expecting, but it did get the conversation started.

"Umm … a shaman?"

Hollis took her through the events of the past few weeks, starting with his first visit to Simon concerning the spot on his leg. "Sorry I can't show it to you at the moment," he said.

"Hopefully soon," Amy replied, a sensuous smile coming over her, which she followed up with a tongue roll over her upper lip.

Hollis momentarily lost his train of thought as a trickle of sweat broke out on his forehead. "Yes, that would be nice," he finally said, not having any idea if his response was appropriate or not. He managed to continue his story, telling her about his visit to Wil Stevens and his second visit to Simon.

When he finished, Amy said, "You don't honestly believe

any of that could be true, do you?"

"Well …," he began to say, but Amy interrupted him.

"I mean, come on. Those people are just charlatans who are out to take your money. You can't possibly believe those stories?"

"I have no reason yet not to believe them," said Hollis defensively. He was a bit disappointed by her lack of willingness to consider the subject, but he didn't want to get into an argument with her. He decided to move the conversation in a different direction.

"So tell me about yourself. How did you end up at Bay Crest High School?"

Amy Mason's story turned out to be much like his. She had been married at twenty-one and hoped to start a family immediately. When it didn't happen, she and her husband went to be tested just in case anything was wrong. It turned out he was sterile and would never have children, and over time it drove a wedge between them that they couldn't resolve. They divorced when Amy was twenty-six.

She'd had a few flings since then, but nothing that ever became serious. She was hired at the high school three years ago, and she'd had her eye on Hollis from the moment she'd seen him. In another month she was going to be turning thirty, and the urge to be married and have kids was still strong in her. As she sat talking to Hollis, she wondered if he would be the one to help her reach her goals.

"This has been nice," said Hollis, as they finished their snack and prepared to leave.

"It has," said Amy. "I think we should do it again, don't you?"

Hollis was surprised and happy that Amy had made the suggestion before he could. "Absolutely," he replied. "It's supposed to be a nice weekend. How about we go to the beach on Saturday?"

Amy immediately knew which bikini she would be modeling for Hollis that day. A Star Trek fan, the words *resistance is futile* came into her mind, and she let out a giggle.

"What, the beach idea is funny?" said Hollis.

"No, that's a great idea," she said. "Will I get to see this disappearing spot on your leg then?"

"You will."

"Then I'm in," said Amy.

She gave him her address and they finalized their plans. Hollis thought it would be a great day at the beach. Amy thought it would end up in the bedroom.

Amy was right.

Whatever hopes Hollis and Amy had of keeping their relationship secret were washed away that day at the beach. A dozen Bay Crest students saw them together, most of them ignoring Hollis as they stared at the skimpy string bikini that Amy was wearing. By the time Monday's school day was nearing an end the news was common knowledge, and Hollis and Amy were thankful the school year only had a few more weeks left.

The love affair that started after their day at the beach took off like a raging wildfire. Both of them had been missing sexual companionship for so long they attacked it with vigor when it finally arrived. It helped that Amy had the largest assortment of sexy lingerie that Hollis had ever seen.

"I've been dying to wear some of these items forever," she told him one night, as she modeled a see thru bra while wearing white thigh-highs and nothing else.

"I think you forgot the underwear," said Hollis, as he gazed at the open area between her legs.

"Nope, didn't forget," she replied. "Just didn't think they were necessary."

They made love on her couch that night, showered, and then repeated the performance in her bedroom. "My God," Hollis said when they were finally sated, "you're the best thing that's ever happened to me."

"I was thinking the same thing about you," said Amy.

The relationship blossomed as May turned into June. The

school year ended and Hollis, who often taught some summer school classes, decided to take a pass this year so he could spend the time with Amy.

They split their time equally between her house in Sarasota and his condo in Bradenton, and it was a rare occurrence when they said goodnight without making love.

As Amy's birthday approached, Hollis said, "We should do something special to celebrate your big event. After all, turning thirty is a milestone."

"Did you have anything in mind?" she asked.

"Maybe we should take a trip together," said Hollis.

"I've actually been thinking about that," said Amy. "Where would you like to go?"

"Well, I've never really traveled much," he said, "so anywhere would be good for me. Did you have anything in mind?"

"Do you have a passport?" she asked.

"I do, although I've never used it."

"Well, I've been looking online for some last minute bargains that we could take," said Amy, "and I think I've found a pretty good one. How would you like to go to Nassau?"

"The Bahamas? Sounds great."

"If we book the airfare and the hotel at the same time, we can stay at a great hotel on the beach for about $1100. That's just $550 apiece."

"I can handle that," said Hollis.

"We'd have to leave on Monday and fly back July third. Is that doable for you?"

"Let's see," said Hollis, a big smile appearing as he grinned from ear to ear. "A week in the sun with a hot, sexy lady who wears skimpy bikinis during the day and skimpier lingerie at night; can I do that? Why yes, I think I can."

Amy laughed, then arose and went to him. She sat on his lap and gave him a big hug.

"It'll be great," she said, and then she gave him a long, hard kiss. "I'm going to make the reservation right now, and then you and I are going to have a little oral extravaganza."

Hollis Brown had never been happier.

Hannah hadn't seen her sister in nearly two months, so when Jessica called inviting her to a July 4th backyard barbecue Hannah quickly said yes. She then called Madison to see if she could join them, and Madison said she'd be delighted.

Jessica was born in China, one of a long line of Chinese babies put up for adoption simply because they were born female. Kate and Martin Kent adopted her when she was just six weeks old. Hannah had been four months old when she was adopted a year later. The two girls had developed a close bond from the start, and when their parents died in the car accident and the grandparents took over the raising of the girls, they became even closer. They loved their grandparents, but the kids were products of a new technological age that the older couple would never be a part of.

Jessica was now Jessica Brown, having married Donald Brown three years ago. Average in height and slender, she cut a striking figure as she moved across the backyard in a short summer dress.

"Hannah, my goodness, it's been too long," she said, as she gave her sister a hug.

"Hey Jess, you look wonderful. How are you?" replied Hannah.

"Oh, you know, overworked and underpaid," said Jessica with a laugh. She turned to Madison and said, "Oh good, it's the tarot girl. Did you bring your cards?"

"I never leave home without them," said Madison.

"Great," Jessica said. "I need to know when all this work I'm doing is going to start paying off."

Her husband entered the backyard carrying a plate of chicken and hamburgers that needed grilling, and another round of greetings took place.

Don and Jessica ran their own catering business out of their home. It had taken some time to get off the ground but was finally beginning to show a profit. They had a small staff that worked for them full time, plus a number of on-call employees. Hannah had even helped out on one occasion, serving as a waitress when they were short staffed.

The Sunday afternoon sun was beating down with temperatures in the low 90's as they prepared to eat. Fortunately the picnic table was under an awning and in the shade. They spent their time catching up on each others' lives, from catering near disasters to tarot card non-believers.

"Hannah, have you met your man from Pompeii yet?" asked Jessica.

"Not yet. Madison told me it was going to be a while. Wait," said Hannah, suddenly thinking back, then looking at her friend, "that was a three month reading back in the beginning of April, so my three months must be just about up."

By this time the strawberry cheesecake had been devoured and everyone was ready to move inside to the air conditioning.

"Madison, would you do some readings for us?" asked Jessica.

"Sure," said Madison. "It's the least I can do in exchange for this great meal."

Don set up a card table in the living room while Jessica made a fresh batch of iced tea, and then the four of them took seats all around.

"No one feels the need for a private reading, I take it?" said Madison.

"No secrets in this family," said Hannah.

"Okay then, who's first?"

The other three looked at each other for a moment before Don said, "I'll go first."

Hannah and Jessica stared at each other, a bit surprised, since they both knew that Don was more than a little skeptical about such things.

Madison took her cards out of her purse. This was not the larger set in the pine box that she used in her home but a smaller travel set of cards. She explained exactly what she would do as she shuffled the cards, mostly for Don's benefit, as she had read for Jessica and Hannah more than once.

"So Don, what is your question?" she inquired when she was ready.

Don asked what the future held for their catering business in the next three months.

Madison mixed, cut and laid out the cards, and then went through each card in the layout. The reading showed that things would be touch and go for a while longer as far as money went, but that an event was coming up in the not too distant future that would cause the business to suddenly expand.

When she finished, Madison said, "I don't see any delay in the cards, so I would guess this event will happen by Columbus Day."

"We can hold out till then," said Don.

Jessica was up next. "Donald and I are ready to start a family," she said. "I want to know if a pregnancy is in my future."

"Really?" cried Hannah. "You guys are ready to make me an auntie?"

Jessica grinned, her eyes sparkling as she looked at her sister, but Don immediately threw in a cautionary note.

"I'd really like to get the business going full blast first, but ..." he trailed off, and the girls could read between the lines. Jessica was ready *now*.

Madison shuffled again and laid out the ten-card Celtic Cross as she always did. After a moment, she asked, "Are you sure you're not pregnant already?"

"What?" said Jessica and Don in unison.

"You have the Empress here in your fourth position. The Empress is the Mother card, and the fourth position is the recent past. You may be pregnant already and not even know it yet. If not, I'd have to say the answer to your question is a resounding yes. You will be having a little bambino soon. There is really nothing negative in any of these cards, and you have the Nine of Cups here in the ninth position. The Nine of

Cups is the minor arcana wish card, and in the upright it gives your wish a positive yes."

Once again Madison went through each card with them. Hannah could tell her sister was beside herself with joy. After a ten minute discussion about the pros and cons of having a child at this point in time, the table moved on to Hannah.

"What's your question, sis?" said Jessica. "Wait, let me guess. Where is Mister Right?"

Hannah laughed along with everyone else at her sister's teasing. She then turned to look at Madison, furrowed her brow, and said, "Yeah, Madison, where is my lover from Pompeii? And you'd better not make me wait another three months for him either."

The group of friends all laughed again.

"Okay," said Madison, "a three month reading for Hannah and her long lost lover."

She shuffled the cards, mixing them as always so some were upright and some reversed, and then cut them and dealt them out.

Madison stared at the cards for a long while, not speaking.

"Something wrong?" asked Hannah.

"Not wrong," said Madison, "just unusual. You have five major arcana cards, which means that things are happening on a karmic level which are out of your control. That could be a good thing, since you're looking for your karmic lover. However, we have both the High Priestess and the Moon in the reading, which tells me there is a great deal going on that you don't know about. I believe you had the Moon reversed last time, if I remember right, and I told you the Moon was better in reverse. Now we have it in the upright, which can be a little more difficult."

"Are you saying I won't meet him in this three month period either?"

"No. In fact, you have the Three of Wands here in the sixth position, which shows your ship coming in. In your case I would have to say that your karmic lover, your soul mate, will be showing up shortly. However, there's a lot swirling around you that indicate the meeting may have its ups and downs."

"I guess that's to be expected," said Hannah, "considering we don't know each other in this life yet?"

"Like any good relationship, it may take some time," said Jessica. "I'm sure you'll work it out in the end."

Madison went through every card in the layout with Hannah and tried to assure her that things would be fine. "The guides know what they're doing," she said. "If you're meant to be with …"

"Stephanus," said Hannah.

"Yes, Stephanus. If you and he are meant to be together again, you will be. He's coming, Hannah. Get ready, and listen to your gut instincts. The Moon upright is a great time to increase your psychic abilities, and when this long lost lover of yours shows up, your gut will tell you. Pay attention."

Hannah saw the smiles around the table and tried to look happy. Inside, however, a sudden nervousness was running through her veins.

ELEVEN

Eight days later Simon Taylor arrived at his office before Grace, which was unusual. He checked the appointment calendar on her desk for the day's regression clients. Most were first time visitors, although he was surprised to see the name of one returning client.

The switch back to his psychology practice had gone surprisingly well. Fellow doctors who were overwhelmed with patients had transferred a number of people to him, and Simon's patient list had grown quickly. He was beginning to think he would have to cut back to just one day for his regression clients much sooner than he had anticipated.

Grace came in as he was puttering around in the back room. "Oh, it's you," she said, as she opened the door and looked in. "I thought maybe we were being robbed. What are you doing here so soon?"

"I was up early and decided to come on in. The coffee should be just about ready," he said.

"I could smell it when I walked through the door. Thank you," said Grace. She returned to the front of the office, poured two cups of the aromatic brew, and brought one to Simon.

Grace was pleased to see her boss looking so well. He seemed to be more relaxed and happy with life lately. The loss of his wife would always be with him, of course, but he was coming out of the funk he had been in ever since Grace had known him, and he was getting on with his life. Not always an easy thing to do, as she knew all too well, but something that had to be done.

Grace still wasn't convinced that all these past lives people came up with when they came to see the doctor were real. She transcribed his notes for him, however, and had read some pretty interesting tales over the course of the past few months. Some of them made her think more deeply about the subject than she had ever intended; mostly concerning Mary, her poor lost soul of a child.

Simon had told her during one of their many chats that each person chooses the basic outline for their lives before they are ever born. "There's more than enough food to feed everyone on the planet," he had said, "yet hundreds of children die of starvation every day. Why do so many come to the earth plane to live in poverty and die of starvation? I think it's because we, the human race, have not yet learned how to share, not learned how to treat each other as equals."

Had Mary chosen to come to this planet to live a life of mental illness? Why would anyone do that? Was she working out her own karma, or was she here to teach her mother a lesson of some sort? Grace had been thinking about these questions and many more like them for some time now, but she had no answers.

Perhaps it was simply a way to help her cope with the countless patients who were now coming to see the doctor every day in his practice. Grace loved the job, and she was compassionate and understanding of all who came in. Most days she was too busy to get too heavily involved in her own problems.

But regression days always made her think of Mary.

"Your two o'clock is here," said Grace.

"Show him in," said Simon, and a moment later Hollis

Brown entered. Simon immediately noticed the big smile on the man's face and the hop he seemed to have in his step.

"Doctor," said Hollis as he held out his hand, "how nice to see you again."

"You also," said Simon. He shook the offered hand and then motioned Hollis to sit. "To be honest, I didn't expect to see you again."

After seeing the name on the appointment calendar, Simon had taken out Hollis' folder and refreshed himself about his prior visits. "Still have that spot on your leg?" Simon asked.

"I do," said Hollis, "although it seems to fade more and more each week."

"How interesting. I hope you'll let me know if it should ever disappear completely."

"I'll do that," said Hollis.

"So what brings you here today?" asked Simon.

"Well, I've met someone, and we've really hit it off quite splendidly. To be honest, it's the best relationship I've ever been in and I couldn't be happier."

"So you've come to try and find confirmation that she is your soul mate, is that it?"

"It is," said Hollis.

Simon had been a bit surprised when he had first started doing regressions about how important the soul mate question was to people. Many were sometimes confused or perplexed when they realized that their soul mate didn't have to be a spouse, but could be a brother, sister, aunt or any number of other people in their current lifetime.

Jill Palmer had found three lifetimes where her soul mate was also her husband or lover. She had also been married to a husband who cheated on her in her current life, only to find out she had done the same to him in a past life. Yet when Jill fell in love after her regressions with Simon had ended, she had never come back to find out if he was *the one*. Her reasoning had been simple. She loved him, and if he wasn't her lover from her past lives that was okay. She was happy now, and that was all that mattered.

"I was going over your file before you came in," said Simon, "and oddly enough it seems you only recognized two people in your past regressions. Part of that was due to the fact that the first regression was so short, and then it appears I never asked you whether you recognized anyone after the time your great-grandfather took you through. That story was so compelling I think I just forgot to ask."

"That was a wonderful regression," said Hollis.

"So let me ask you now," said Simon. "Aside from Matthew, who we know was your great-grandfather in this life, do you recall recognizing anyone from your life as a monk who you know in this lifetime?"

"I remember thinking my father then is my father now," said Hollis, "but my mother then is now a grandmother of mine. That's different."

"Not really," said Simon. "It happens a great deal of the time. Anyone else?"

"Not that I recall," said Hollis.

"Well then, let's get started."

Hollis walked the few steps to the couch and lay down while Simon checked his equipment to make sure it was all functioning properly.

"Ready?" asked Simon, and Hollis nodded yes.

The regression proceeded in the usual manner. When Simon told Hollis to open the door and walk on through, no one was waiting on the other side. Simon was not surprised, but he did feel a tinge of disappointment that John would not be joining them, and he imagined that Hollis felt it too.

"You're looking for a prior life where you are with your soul mate. Go back through your memory banks and see which life comes to you. Take your time if necessary," said Simon. "There is no rush."

Hollis found a past life almost immediately. "I'm a woman," he said, and after a short pause he added, "I've been here before. Yes, this is the life where I fell on the sharp piece of wood and received my wound."

"That's fine," said Simon. "That was your last life prior to your present one, so it is normal that you would go there again. Let's see if we can go back to when you were younger."

Simon took a quick look at his notes to be sure he had his information correct.

"You lived on a farm when you were a teenager. Your name is Anne, and you thought you were in Canada. Try to go back to your time as a teenager and see if you can gather more information."

Simon waited patiently as Hollis attempted to make sense of what he was picturing in his mind.

"I see the farm that we live on. Our home is quite nice. There's a fire in the fireplace that keeps us warm. My father has just come inside and is standing in front of it rubbing his hands. He says it is cold outside and the wind is biting."

"Do you recognize your father as someone you know now?" asked Simon.

"Yes, he is my uncle Jack, who was the first born in my father's family."

"That's good, Hollis. You're doing fine. Can you tell me what year it might be, and whether or not you are definitely in Canada?"

"Well, I'm not quite sure where we are. My mother and I are sitting in rocking chairs. She is mending some socks that have holes in the toes and I am reading a book."

Simon took another quick glance at his notes. "You said before that your mother in this prior life is now your Aunt Doris; is that correct?"

"Yes, she is my aunt now."

"Is Doris married to your Uncle Jack?"

"No," said Hollis, "she is his sister now."

"Let's move ahead a few days if you have to in order to find out where you are," said Simon.

"Okay," said Hollis, who paused only momentarily before continuing. "I am riding in a wagon, going into town to buy supplies. My father feels I am old enough to go by myself now, something he would not let me do until recently." He hesitated for a moment before resuming. "It is not Canada. I believe we are somewhere in Europe."

"Try to narrow it down when you can, Hollis."

"I am in the town now looking at the signs in the store windows." A moment later Hollis added, "Ah, I remember now. This is Germany."

"Excellent, Hollis," said Simon. "Can you tell me what year it is?"

"Not yet. What my father doesn't know is that the real reason I wanted to go into town alone is because I am meeting a boy. We meet in town every Saturday; have been doing so for the past few weeks. We are neighbors, but this is the only time I get to see him. He is waiting for me by the market."

"When you meet him, is he someone you recognize in your current life?"

A deep furrow appeared on Hollis' forehead. "No, I do not recognize him."

"That's okay. Does this relationship with this boy continue?"

"Yes. We try to keep it secret for a while, but our parents soon realize something is going on. He finally admits it to his parents, and then our families meet each other."

"You say you were neighbors. Didn't the families know each other already?" asked Simon.

"I don't know. The farms were very large and kept both families quite busy. They may have seen each other in town, as Roberto and I did, but I do not believe they knew each other very well until he and I met."

"So this boy's name is Roberto?"

"Yes."

"Okay, why don't we move forward a few years and see what has transpired. Do you and Roberto marry in this lifetime?"

"Yes, he and I do marry. It is a wonderful relationship. I move in with him and his family. His father owns a vineyard, a very large vineyard. They are wonderful people and I am happy to live with them. Roberto takes very good care of me. We love each other very much."

"Can you tell me yet what year it is, or perhaps the name of the town you live in?"

"Yes, the town is called Colmar."

Colmar? The name rang a bell in Simon's mind, although why it did he wasn't exactly sure.

"Tell me about your life in Colmar, your life with Roberto," said Simon.

"We had a very strong marriage. I was older than him by a few years, and I wanted children as soon as possible, but it took some time before it happened."

"How many children did you have in all?" asked Simon.

"We had three children, two boys and a girl. Thank God they were all healthy. I taught my daughter to sew, just as my mother had taught me. When she was older she worked in my store that I opened in town."

"You opened a sewing business in town?" asked Simon.

"It was a store for women mostly. We made dresses, hats, scarves and blouses, but we also did repairs for both men and women."

The story was sounding more familiar to Simon by the minute, like one of those tips of the tongue moments that just wouldn't come. "Tell me about your children," he said.

"My daughter who worked with me in the store was Danielle. She was the youngest, a very bright and lively child."

"And the boys?"

"The oldest one is named Michel; sort of the strong, silent type. The other was Pasha, who ..."

"What is it?" asked Simon, when Hollis stopped talking.

"It was Pasha who was driving the day I was hurt, the day I received the spot on my leg."

"You did say he was your son back then. Now you know which one it was."

Suddenly it all clicked in Simon's mind. *Colmar, a seamstress store, Pasha.* He'd heard this story before, and not from Hollis. It had been over two months ago, but it only took him a moment to remember, because he had been surprised the other client had known what had happened to her children even though she, as a man in that prior life, had died.

Hannah Kent.

"How long did you stay on the farm with his parents? Did you ever move to a place of your own?" asked Simon, as he quietly arose and went to find Hannah's folder.

"No, we stayed on the farm. Roberto took over the vineyard from his father and made it a huge success."

"What happened to your husband and children? Did they live long, happy lives?" asked Simon. He was opening Hannah's file as he asked this, and he quickly found what she had said concerning the fates of her children.

"Roberto and I had been married over forty years when he died suddenly. Michel took over the farm after that, but he sold it for pennies on the dollar when the Second World War broke out. He moved to America—he thought they would certainly win the war—and he stayed there as far as I know."

"What about Pasha and Danielle?" he asked as he returned to his seat, trying to quell the excitement that was surging through him.

"Danielle had been married and had moved to England with her husband. They had one son that I know of."

"You don't know what happened to them?"

"No. I died before the war was over. I had moved to Italy; that's where Pasha had been taking me when I was hurt."

Simon rapidly perused his notes on Hannah's regression in Colmar. "Tell me," he finally asked, "what was your last name before you married Roberto? Do you remember?"

"My last name?" Hollis thought for a moment before answering. When he did, a chill went through Simon like he'd never felt before.

"Festa," said Hollis. "My name was Anne Festa. Then I married Roberto and became Anne Borrelli."

"Hollis, do you recognize any of your family, or Roberto's family, as people you know now?"

"Danielle is my sister Vivian. I can see it plain as day. And Michel …" Hollis started laughing.

"What is it?" asked Simon.

"Michel my son is now Terry, my younger sister. No wonder she's such a tomboy."

"Do you recognize Roberto or Pasha?"

"No, I've never seen them before."

"There is a lady you are dating now in your current life; have you seen her in your Colmar life?"

"No," said Hollis, a look of dejection suddenly overtaking him.

"Let's go back to your life on the vineyard." said Simon. "Perhaps she will show up at some point."

Hollis spoke for another fifteen minutes about his life on the vineyard with Roberto, but he never recognized Amy in any of the faces he saw.

"What did you do after Roberto passed over?" asked Simon as the regression neared its end. "Did you meet someone else?"

Hollis waited a long time before finally answering. "I grieved mightily when Roberto died. We loved each other very much. I stayed on the farm with Michel for a few years. He had never married, had never seemed interested in girls. Living on the farm always reminded me of my husband, however, and was very painful. My father had moved to Italy after my mother died, and eventually I decided to go stay with him. That is where Pasha was driving me when I hurt my leg."

"And you still haven't seen your current girlfriend anywhere in this regression?"

"No," said Hollis."She is not here, and I have seen enough. You may bring me back."

Simon did, and the dejection that Hollis felt only deepened upon his return.

"Well crap," he said, "that didn't go as planned. I was sure I would see Amy in my past life."

"Amy is your girlfriend now?"

"Yes, and it's a fantastic relationship. I can't believe that she could not be my soul mate, if there really is such a thing."

"Yet you stated that your relationship with Roberto was very deep and very loving. Perhaps you will meet up with him down the road."

"Do people usually recognize each other from one life to the next?" asked Hollis.

"Not on a conscious level, no. However, on a subconscious level there seems to be some sort of cellular recall. It is said humans use only a small portion of their brain; some say no more than ten percent. Sometimes I think all the past lives we've had and all the people we've met are stored somewhere in that part of our brain we don't use."

"So even if I met this Roberto in this life I wouldn't recognize him?"

"That's an interesting question. From what research and regression work I've done, I've noticed that one of the two people involved often will have an instant attraction, while the other one may not."

Hollis sat up on the couch and just stared at the doctor. He was quiet for a long time as he tried to process all that he had learned. "Well," he finally mumbled, "it was a great marriage, but I don't know that person now. I guess you don't always meet up with the same people every lifetime after all, huh doc?"

As he arose to leave, Hollis shook hands with Simon and said, "I don't think I'll be back again. It's has been interesting, but …"

"I understand," said Simon.

He watched Hollis leave. Now he completely understood Jill Palmer's thinking about not returning. *Smart move, Jill,* he thought. *Smart move.*

Grace could tell by Hollis' gloomy face and slumped shoulders that he was dejected as he left the office. She was therefore extremely surprised a moment later when Simon came into the room beaming.

"What's up?" she asked. "He left the office looking as though you just told him he had cancer, and then you come out looking like the cat that swallowed the canary."

"Something amazing just happened, Grace, but he has no idea what, and I couldn't tell him."

"Why not?" she asked.

"It has to do with another client," said Simon. "I had to uphold the doctor-client privilege."

"So this guy just regressed to a life where another client had already gone, and they knew each other?"

"You're too smart for your own good, my dear," said Simon. His three o'clock appointment entered the office at that point, cutting their conversation off.

"Would you like me to type up your notes for you?" asked Grace, a twinkle in her eye.

Simon realized he still had Hollis' folder in his hand. "No thanks," he replied. "I think I'll take care of this one myself."

"Party pooper," said Grace.

Simon arrived home just after seven that night, set down the bag of Chinese take-out he had picked up on the way, and made himself a martini. He carried the drink out to his balcony, sat down on the lonely chair, and said, "Nora, you won't believe what happened today," as he stared out over the bay.

He had not had an easy time concentrating on his last two clients of the day. The fact that two of his clients knew each other in a past life, as husband and wife no less, yet had apparently not met in this life, was both exciting and exacerbating.

Grace had asked him as they closed up the office if the doctor-client privilege applied to his regression clients, as they weren't really patients.

Simon thought for a moment that she might have a point, but realized it was a fine line that they would be walking with that interpretation. He needed to think on it in a calm manner and determine a course of action, or perhaps take no action at all. After all, Hollis was apparently very happy in his current relationship. Simon didn't think he had a right to interfere with that.

The first thing he needed to do was be one hundred percent certain that the two lives in Colmar did, in fact, match. He had brought home the folders of both Hannah and Hollis to check not only for matches in their stories but also discrepancies. He had also brought the recordings of their regressions, although his notes were always rather extensive and he wasn't sure if he would need the audio.

He finished his drink and was about to pour a second one before changing his mind. He wanted to get started on his research right away and he wanted a clear head.

Simon grabbed a yellow legal pad, two pens, and the Chinese take-out and set them on the coffee table. He went back to the kitchen for a plate and some chopsticks, doled out the food, and went to work. He placed the two folders side by side and opened them both. The initial regression to Colmar had been by Hollis, although at the time Hollis thought he might be in Canada. Simon started there, eating as he read.

The regression had been fairly short, since Hollis was simply looking to find an explanation for the red mark on his thigh. Simon smiled as he recalled how surprised Hollis had been upon discovering he was a woman in that life. He jotted down a few pertinent notes and quickly moved on to the next regression, which had been Hannah's as a boy named Roberto.

Simon refilled his plate with food and brushed off a noodle that he had dropped onto Hannah's folder.

Her regression had been fairly extensive, and as Simon read, whatever doubts he may have had about whether these two clients of his had once been married in a previous life faded completely away. The evidence was simply too overwhelming to ignore. As he reached the end of Hannah's regression, he was once again taken by the fact that she could recall events that occurred after her passing.

At the time Simon had been intrigued. Most of his clients

were able to describe their death scene as they floated over their bodies, and Jill Palmer had once relayed how her adopted father had reacted even though he was hundreds of miles away. As far as he could recall, however, none of his clients had ever gone on to tell what happened to the people in their lives years after their own passing.

Simon wondered if Hannah's guides had been giving her the information while she was in the meditative state. Simon had received messages from guides on occasion which they felt he needed to hear. Usually the client didn't remember relaying any of those messages upon awakening. Perhaps in this case they were giving him a heads up that something unusual was heading his way.

Hannah's parents in that life were now her aunt and uncle, and Pasha had been her adopted father, now deceased. Simon had no idea how old Hannah's father had been when he adopted her, but it was obvious that he must have returned to the earth plane very quickly after dying as Pasha shortly after the war. While it was not the first time he had come across such a rapid turnaround, it was very unusual.

Simon brought his dish, chopsticks, and empty boxes over to the sink and set them down, and then he decided to pour that second martini. He brought the drink back to the table, set it on the coaster, and prepared to go through the final regression of interest, which had been Hollis' visit this afternoon. However, as his eyes scanned between one folder and the next, a shocking revelation became apparent to him.

"There's no way!" he shouted to the empty room.

Hollis and Hannah had back-to-back appointments on May 5th. He was leaving as she was coming in. Had they seen each other? Did they speak? A chill passed through Simon for the second time that day.

Fifteen minutes later Simon completed his review of the regressions, confident beyond a doubt that Hannah and Hollis had once been Anne and Roberto Borrelli.

Hollis had recognized Danielle and Michel as two of his current sisters. He had not recognized Roberto or Pasha as people he knew, and Simon was sad when thinking that Hollis would never get to meet Pasha in this life.

Suddenly a new thought struck Simon. Hollis and Hannah had appointments back to back, and that was the time that Grandfather John had appeared. Had he, knowing that Hannah was the next client, stuck around for her regression as well? What if he were the one who gave Hannah the information about what had happened to her children?

Simon could only wonder.

The information that had come through Hannah about the fates of her family after her death, together with the fact that Hannah and Hollis had had adjoining appointments, made Simon certain that the couple's guides were trying to get them together again. The problem was, Simon didn't know if he could, or should, interfere.

As he went to bed that night his mind kept repeating over and over again, *What to do? What to do?*

TWELVE

Hollis drove home after his appointment with Simon. He was extremely disappointed that the regression had not gone as he had hoped it would. He called Amy, told her he was feeling a little under the weather, and said that he was just going to stay home and go to bed early.

"You want me to come over?" she asked.

"No," he replied, "I'll be fine. Probably just need some rest."

"See you tomorrow then. Why don't you come by around noon and take me to lunch?"

Hollis agreed, and then they said good night.

He did not go to bed early, however. A thousand thoughts were going through his head. He was madly in love with Amy and was sure she felt the same way about him. Although they had only been dating for eight weeks, he had already started imagining what being married to her would be like. If there were such a thing as soul mates, Hollis thought that Amy must be his.

The regression had not raised doubts about his relationship with Amy. It had, in fact, made him question the validity of the regressions. He tried to convince himself that nothing he spoke of during his regressions could possibly be true, but instead everything must simply be a figment of his imagination. Even if the regressions did hold some semblance of fact, maybe Roberto had not been his soul mate in his German life. Maybe it had been another relative whom he had not seen, or a friend who lived next door.

Hollis walked from room to room, sat on his couch, lay on his bed, and then walked some more. No answers came to him. He was sure that Amy was the one for him and the regressions didn't hold the answers. As the clock neared midnight he decided to take a warm shower and go to bed. He was just drying off, his mind finally beginning to slow down, when he ran the towel down his leg.

The spot on his thigh had completely disappeared, and the wheels in Hollis' mind started spinning again.

Amy knew something was wrong within minutes of seeing Hollis the next day. "Are you okay?" she asked. "You look like something's still bothering you."

Hollis tried to flash a bright smile for her but knew it was a feeble attempt. "I'm fine," he said. "I just had some trouble sleeping last night."

"You still sick?"

"No, I guess I'm just a bit out of sorts from a restless night. I feel much better now that I'm with you," he said, and that part was certainly true.

Amy smiled. "I missed you last night. It was lonely without you."

"Me too," said Hollis, and his mood began to lift as he gazed into her eyes. Regressions be damned, this was the woman he loved.

They stopped for lunch at a downtown sports bar. "I've been dying for a cheeseburger," said Hollis, "and they're really good here." Amy ordered an Oriental salad, and they both asked for iced teas.

After the drinks arrived, Hollis said, "I know you don't think too highly about psychics and all, but I want to ask you something."

"If you must," she said, a questioning look coming over

her.

"Do you believe in reincarnation?"

"What? No," she said. "Where did that question come from?"

"You don't believe in it?"

"I've never given it that much thought," she said, shrugging her shoulders. "You know I don't believe in all that new age mumbo-jumbo. Why do you ask?"

He debated where to go from here. Should he tell her about his recent visit to Simon or should he just forget it?

"Well?" she said, when he didn't respond right away.

"I've told you before about seeing the doctor who does past life regressions. He's actually quite famous; has a book out on the subject, although I've never read it."

"I'm surprised that you're even bringing the subject up," said Amy. "Why are you? Do you want to go see this guy again?"

"Actually, I saw him yesterday," said Hollis.

"What? Why in heaven's name would you do such a thing?"

Hollis could see that Amy was startled by his admission and none too happy. He was pretty sure that she considered him a sucker for believing in such things, but he decided to plunge ahead.

"Well, I went to see him because I was hoping to find you in my past life."

"Oh, I see," said Amy, obviously perturbed, "having me in this life isn't enough for you?"

"You know it is," he replied. "I'm sure you're my soul mate and we are meant to be together. I just wanted …"

"What? Confirmation?" asked Amy.

"I guess so," said Hollis, suddenly wishing he'd never brought the subject up. "I've recognized other people in my life during regressions. I thought I'd find you, now that I know you."

"I'm guessing that wasn't the case," said Amy.

"No," Hollis replied sheepishly.

"Listen, Hollis, you need to stop going to see these people. They're just taking you for a ride. You're wasting your money on them."

He stared at the table, not wanting to face her.

"You have me here in this life, right now. I would hope that would be enough for you."

"It is," he said, finally gazing at her with puppy dog eyes. "I'm sorry."

"Stay away from those people, and let's not bring this subject up again, okay?"

"Okay," said Hollis.

He had never been what one would call a spiritual being before meeting Maria Vasquez in the bar. His mind had been opened, however, by his visits to the doctor, and the mark on his leg was most certainly gone. He wanted to keep exploring the metaphysical world, although he was pretty sure he was finished with regressions. However, in the future he knew he could never discuss the subject with Amy.

"I'm sorry," he said again. "I do love you. I believe it was fate that brought us together, since I don't believe in coincidence."

"Really? I think coincidence happens all the time. How else can you explain some things?"

"Well, I think everything happens for a reason," said Hollis. "You and I worked together for a long time before we ever went out. Why was that? Why was that day the time chosen for us to suddenly be together?"

"Hey, I was ready to go out with you long before that," said Amy, the edge in her voice a strong signal that she was still mad. "You just didn't seem to be getting the messages I was sending."

"I just think there is a synchronicity to life," said Hollis. "Everything happens at a particular time for a particular reason."

The waitress brought their food out and set it before them. "Getcha anything else?" she asked.

"No," said Hollis, while Amy just shook her head.

Hollis bit into his burger as he wondered where to go next with the conversation, but Amy beat him to it.

"You weren't really sick last night, were you?"

"I was upset about the regression. My mind was all over the place."

"That's what those people do to you," said Amy. "They put crazy thoughts into your head so you can't think straight. Just stay away from them."

"Okay," he agreed for the second time. "So what shall we do today?"

"I think we should head back to your place," said Amy, her tone finally softening, "so I can show you once again just what you have in me, and I do mean *in me*, if you get my drift."

Hollis understood perfectly well, and he suddenly relaxed for the first time in almost twenty-four hours.

Three days later, Hannah was following her GPS as she drove out to Longboat Key. Florence had called her last night and asked Hannah to meet her at a condo there. It was a Sunday morning, an unusual time for Florence to ask Hannah to work. Whenever something came up on a Sunday, Florence usually handled it herself.

The condo was in a six-story building on the Sarasota Bay side. Florence was waiting for her when she arrived. "Good morning," she said. "I hope I didn't disrupt any plans."

"Not at all," said Hannah. "My life outside of work is pretty drab at the moment."

"And shame on all the local men for that being the case," said Florence. "A lovely girl like you should be turning the suitors away."

Hannah just smiled and thought once again how much she loved working for this woman.

"Here's what's going on," said Florence. "We have a gentleman who lives in 4C, a good friend of mine whom I've known for many years. His wife passed away about three months ago, and while he loved her very much, he never liked the way she decorated. He wants us to redo his place for him."

"Great," said Hannah.

They took the elevator up to 4C, knocked on the door, and were let in by an elderly gentleman wearing tan slacks, a white shirt and a dark brown sweater.

"Hannah, I'd like you to meet my good friend Gene Kincaid," said Florence. "Gene, this is Hannah Kent, my associate I was telling you about."

"Pleased to meet you," said Gene, as he shook Hannah's hand. "Florence has nothing but nice things to say about you."

"Thank you," Hannah replied, happy to know that Florence liked her as much as she liked her boss.

Gene immediately took over the conversation. "Here's the thing," he said. "My late wife Pam did all the decorating and almost never asked for my opinion. I loved her dearly and never said a word, but the truth is I can't stand the way this place looks. Too much stuff everywhere, hardly room to move in spots, and all put together in a mish-mash that makes no sense to me."

Hannah gazed around the condo and had to agree that it was overburdened with furniture and absolutely garish in places.

"I want most of it gone," continued Gene. "I've already marked the pieces that I want to keep, and I want a condo that's open and clean and has just one theme to it, not a couple of dozen like it has now."

"I'm sure Hannah can do that for you," said Florence.

"What?" said Hannah, caught off guard.

"Oh, did I forget that part?" said Florence, a twinkle in her eye. "This is going to be *your* assignment."

Hannah was thrilled. She had worked side by side with Florence for months now, doing her own work but always getting Florence's okay. Now it appeared she was to be left on her own, and not in some two room apartment on the poor side of town but in a half-million dollar condo. "Oh Florence, thank you," she said.

"Think you're up to the task?" asked Gene.

"Yes sir!" exclaimed Hannah.

They began a tour of the five room condo. When they were finished, she said to Gene, "You mentioned a theme earlier. What did you have in mind?"

"Well, I've been thinking about that," he said. "So many places down here have these beach themes, of course, but I'm not interested in that. My wife and I used to travel quite extensively in our younger days, and I was always partial to the Far East. I'd like an Oriental theme to my home. It can be a mixture of Japanese, Chinese, Indian; Shinto, Buddhist or Hindu. Mix and match any way you like. Think you can do that?"

"Yes, we can do that," said Hannah.

"*You* can do that," corrected Florence. "This project is all yours."

"I'm leaving this afternoon for two weeks," said Gene. "I'll be visiting my son up in Wisconsin. That's why I needed you over here this morning. You have a twenty thousand dollar budget at your disposal. I've already given the check to Flo here. Do whatever is necessary; paint the place, change the rugs, donate this stuff somewhere, or keep some of it if you want. Just have the place ready when I get back. Okay?"

Hannah's head was spinning with so many thoughts going through it at once. "Okay," she mumbled.

"Here's a set of keys for you," said Gene, and he handed them to Hannah. "The car service is picking me up at 3:00 this afternoon. After that the place is yours. Don't let me down."

"I won't, sir," was all she could think to say.

A few minutes later Hannah and Florence were standing outside again. "You can do this," said Florence, noticing the trepidation in Hannah's face.

"Are you sure? It's an awfully big job."

"And it's the only job you have for the next two weeks," said Florence. "I'll take over whatever else you have going on. My plate is actually quite clean at the moment, so it won't be a problem. I will give you one suggestion though."

"What's that?" asked Hannah.

"He has beautiful hardwood floors under those rugs. Get rid of all that carpet and use them. And you should probably come back here at 3:30 and get to work," said a laughing Florence.

"I was thinking that myself," said Hannah.

She arrived back at the condo that afternoon to begin the renovation of Gene Kincaid's condo. First she took another tour of the rooms, making note of all the items Gene had marked as keepers. These she gathered together, putting them all in a corner of the kitchen for now. They included a two-foot high sitting Buddha, a pair of Oriental wall hangings, two Chinese table lamps, and six figures of Indian gods and goddesses, of which she recognized Ganesh and Kali.

"Hi there," she said to the Kali statue. "I was once named after you in a long ago lifetime." Then she laughed.

There was a knock on the door just as she was setting the statue down. When Hannah opened it she was surprised to see Don Autry. Florence had a stable of workers whom she regularly called whenever a job warranted it. Don was the flooring expert.

"What are you doing here?" asked a surprised Hannah. "It's Sunday."

"Flo called. Said you had a big job ahead of you and could I possibly work today. She pays triple time for Sunday, so who am I to say no? Who were you talking to just now?"

Hannah laughed again as she showed Kali to Don. "I was once named after this goddess many lifetimes ago."

Don gave her a sideward glance, eyebrows raised, and said, "Really." It wasn't a question as much as a statement that she may have a screw loose.

"I'll tell you about it someday," said Hannah, "but right now we have work to do."

Don took a quick glance into the living room. "Flo said the carpets have to go and the hardwood refinished. I take it we won't be using a dumpster on this job, so I'll just toss the carpet in the back of my truck."

"Okay," Hannah said, and they went to work.

The next two weeks flew by. Not only were the floors redone but the rooms were painted, the lighting fixtures all changed, and Hannah hung Oriental artwork on the walls. As she was going through the kitchen one day, Hannah realized that Gene was a tea drinker; there wasn't an ounce of coffee in the house. That afternoon she spent nearly five hundred dollars on a Japanese tea set and tossed out all of the mugs that were sitting in the kitchen cabinet.

An auction house came and took everything Hannah decided was no longer needed. She spent hours shopping for just the right accoutrements that would turn Gene's residence into an Oriental dream home. She turned the second bedroom, which appeared to have become a catch-all for everything that didn't go anywhere else, into a meditation sanctuary, complete with an altar of sacred items, a running fountain, and a miniature Zen garden.

Florence came by two days before Gene's return to see for herself what Hannah was doing. She was stunned when she saw the meditation room.

"My God, Hannah, he's going to love this!" she cried out. "How did you know he meditated?"

"I saw some tape sets that he had, one of which he had just purchased. It still had the receipt with it, so I brought it back to the store and exchanged it for the CD version. Then I purchased a new CD player for him. Truth be told, I didn't know anyone still sold tapes. I figured we needed to get Gene into the 21st century."

"How's the budget looking?" asked Florence.

"We'll make it, and even though he said to just get rid of everything, the auction house will be sending him a check after they sell his stuff. Heck, some of those items were beautiful and costly. For all I know he may even get his money back."

"Not after he gets my bill," said Florence, a wide smile on her face.

Florence was waiting outside for Gene Kincaid to arrive home on Sunday afternoon while Hannah nervously walked from room to room making sure everything was perfect. She thought she had done an excellent job of transforming his home, but you never knew how the client would feel until he saw it.

She walked to the front door when she heard the *ding* of the hallway elevator, and a moment later Gene and Florence entered the condo

Gene Kincaid took two steps, stopped dead in his tracks, and stared at his new surroundings. He saw the tea set displayed on the kitchen island, the Chinese paper lanterns in his living room, and the Japanese wall hangings he had saved in the hallway leading to the back rooms.

Hannah couldn't tell from the surprised look on his face if he was happy or furious.

"Where did you put Buddha?" he asked.

"Follow me," said Hannah, and she led him to his new meditation room. The two-foot tall Buddha statue was in the corner.

"Oh my," said Gene, as he stepped into the room. He turned to Hannah, a huge grin finally breaking out on his face, and said, "This is wonderful, my dear."

Then he gave her a great big hug.

Hannah showed Gene the final two rooms and then led him out into the living room. The three of them sat down as Florence asked, "So Gene, what do you think? Has my girl done right by you?"

"It's amazing," he said, "better than I had even hoped. I thought you would have the Buddha statue here in the living room, sort of as a centerpiece, and yet it's perfect where you put it. And all the carpeting is gone, thank goodness. My wife loved carpets for some reason, but these floors are absolutely gorgeous, don't you think?"

"I do," said Hannah. "You do have this one rug, however." Hannah had found a Persian rug that she thought would be amazing in the center of the living room. She had spent nearly two thousand dollars for it, less than half of the retail price, because the store was going out of business.

"I saw that when I first came in and couldn't believe my eyes," said Gene. "It's stunning, absolutely stunning."

He made jasmine tea for them with his new tea set. As they sat around the living room, Hannah explained how the renovation had gone, where she had found some of his new items, and how she had upgraded him to a CD player.

"You may have to show me how to use that," Gene said, and they all laughed.

An hour later he showed them to the door as they prepared to leave. "I'm going to enjoy the place by myself for a few weeks," he said, "and then I think I'll have a little party, what do they call it …?"

"A housewarming," said Florence.

"That's it, a housewarming party. I will expect the two of you to be here."

"We'd be delighted," said Florence, and Hannah agreed.

Barry Homan

THIRTEEN

Simon arrived at his office ten minutes late the following Wednesday and was surprised to see Maria Vasquez in the waiting room.

"Good morning," Grace said as he entered. "You're late." She handed him a cup of freshly brewed coffee as she nodded at Maria. "She was waiting at the door when I arrived."

Simon set the cup down on Grace's desk and went to see Maria. "How are you, my dear?" he said.

"I'm okay," she replied, in a voice that stated she was anything but. "I came to make an appointment, but your secretary said that you had an opening first thing, so I took it. I hope you don't mind."

"Mind? Of course not. I'm happy that you're here. Come on in," he said, and Simon led Maria into his office. "Have a seat while I get myself situated. Would you like some coffee?"

"No, she already asked me," said Maria.

The question reminded Simon that he had left his own coffee on Grace's desk, but a moment later his efficient secretary entered the room with his brew in hand.

"Forget something?" she asked, a Cheshire cat grin on her face.

Simon gave her a sheepish look and muttered, "Thank you." He put away a few files that he had brought from home, cleaned up some work he had left out on his desk, and then looked at Maria. "What's wrong?" he asked.

"It shows, huh?" Maria looked down at her hands in her lap before slowly turning her gaze to him. "I've left my husband. My son and I are living with a girlfriend of mine."

"I'm so sorry to hear that," said Simon.

"He is an abusive man. It's been an unhealthy relationship for a long time. I had to get a restraining order against him because he kept driving by the house where we are staying. Everything is okay now, however."

"He's not bothering you anymore?"

"I think his anger got the best of him. He exploded at work one day and hit an employee of his. The company fired him, and just yesterday he moved back to Puerto Rico."

"Can you move back to your home?" asked Simon.

"No. The house was just in his name and he's already sold it. Besides, it had too many bad memories for me. I need to find a job so I can get my own place."

Simon felt bad for the young woman sitting in front of him. She still had a radiance about her, even as all this sadness oozed from her pores.

"So what brings you here today?" he asked.

"My first regression with you was very interesting. I ..." she paused, wanting to choose her words carefully, "...saw some people I knew, and I wanted to see if they were in other lives with me." She stopped for a moment, and then added, "Or maybe I just want to get away from this life for a few minutes."

"Understandable," said Simon. "I don't recall, did your husband show up in that life?"

"No," she replied a bit forcefully. "He was simply a mistake I made in this life."

Simon gazed at Maria. Her black hair had grown longer since he had last seen her, now hanging well over her shoulders. Her emerald eyes were tinged with sadness at the moment, yet they were beautiful at the same time. She wore a light summer dress that accentuated the curves of her body, and her shapely dark brown legs were absolutely gorgeous as far as Simon was concerned. Why anyone would want to harm this woman was a wonder to him.

"Let me get your file," he finally said. It had been three months since he had looked through Maria's file after seeing her at the fair, but her story about the Trail of Tears came back to him immediately upon opening her paperwork.

"Let's see," he said after sitting back down, "your last life that you spoke about ended in 1839. It's quite possible you had another incarnation after that and before your current one. Would you like to try for that period, or shall we just see what comes up?"

"I suppose my most recent life would be interesting," said Maria, "but I'll be happy with anything."

"Shall we begin then?" he said.

He went through the process he had done a thousand times before, wondering all the while if Maria would be able to relax enough to come to a meditative state. However, when they finally reached the point where he asked her to find a life in her past, Maria had no trouble.

"Tell me what you see?" said Simon.

"I'm a dancer, I guess," she said. "I'm on a stage with others who are dressed like me. I think it's a nightclub of some kind."

"Tell me about the nightclub. Do you know what city you are in or what year it might be?"

Maria lay on the couch as still as could be, but Simon saw her eyes wandering about under her closed lids, as though she were checking out the scene in front of her.

"Oh my!" she suddenly cried out. "I'm a flapper!"

Simon knew the term was popular during the Roaring Twenties and Prohibition and surmised that Maria had indeed found her most recent past life. He was about to say something when Maria continued on.

"I dress as a flapper for my job, but it's also who I am. I love to dance. The Bunny Hug and the Charleston are my favorites. When our dance is finished I go out and sit at the tables with the guests. The men love this new brand of women, what with our short skirts and our hair up in a bob. They offer me a cigarette and a drink, and I accept. Gin is my favorite, but I am careful not to drink too much. I'm looking for a mark."

"A mark?" said Simon.

"A guy with a nice bankroll; someone we can rob once I get him alone."

Simon was momentarily surprised, although he had heard numerous stories from people who had led unsavory lives. "We? Who is the other person you are talking about?"

"It's …." Maria stopped, as if taking the time to make sure she had her information right. "It's my brother. He is the one who was my husband in my Cherokee life."

"Tell me what your name is."

"I am Lucille. My brother's name is Randall."

"Do you know what city you are in, Lucille?"

"No, not yet. We move around a lot so as not to get caught."

"You said you were looking for a mark. Tell me what happens," said Simon.

"I move from table to table. It is part of our job to interact with the customers; get them to buy more drinks, you know. I do this until I find a man flashing money, and then I settle in at his table. Tonight the man I find is a fat-cheeked, overweight tub decked out in a suit that looks two sizes too small for him. He's loud and boisterous, smoking a god-awful smelling cigar, and I wouldn't give him the time of day under normal circumstances."

"But you've noticed he has a bankroll," said Simon.

"Yes. It's probably the only way he can get a woman to sleep with him."

"And you and your brother are planning to rob him?"

"Yes, we have done this many times. I will hint to the man that he has a shot with me, and of course he will ask me up to his room. My brother is watching from the bar, and when the man and I head upstairs my brother will follow. He gives us about ten minutes alone, enough time for the man to make out with me a bit and begin undressing. Sometimes the mark might be a handsome man and I will actually want to have sex with him. In those cases I will give my brother a sign, and he will wait until I have had time to enjoy myself."

Simon, for one of the rare times in his life, didn't know what to say.

"Tonight my brother gives me the sign, kiddingly of course, knowing that I would never want to sleep with this overweight pig."

"What happens?" Simon managed to say.

"It all works out," said Maria. "Randall enters the room waving a pistol just as the man is about to take his drawers down. I act surprised, and to make it seem more real I hand over the rings I am wearing. Randall takes my rings and the man's bankroll and departs, and then I run out, telling the man that I am going to get the police."

"Does it work?" asked Simon.

"It always works," said Maria.

"Let's see if we can start at the beginning," said Simon. "I assume you are in the United States. Go back to your younger years and tell me about yourself."

Maria took a moment before starting. "I was born in Dubuque, Iowa. My father was a policeman, a stern and uncaring man who ran a strict household. My brother was two years older than me, but we were like two peas in a pod. We loved each other dearly, and when we were old enough to do so we ran away."

"How old were you?"

"I was fourteen at the time, my brother sixteen. We had been working in town and were supposed to turn our pay over to our father, but we had been holding back a little each week, saving it up until we had enough to run."

"Where did you go?" asked Simon.

"We went to Wisconsin at first, thinking that our father would not look for us there. We thought he would think we would head for someplace like Chicago."

"Did you stay in Wisconsin long?"

"We started in Madison and stayed there for nearly two years, working menial jobs and just trying to survive. Then we went to Milwaukee. It was there we started robbing people."

"Tell me how it happened?"

"I started dating a man. He was in his early twenties and seemed like a nice guy. We had some fun and he showed me a good time. It was obvious he was well off, but eventually he became a drag and I decided to end it."

"Do you remember the man's name?"

"Preston something," said Maria. "I can't remember his last name. My brother and I were still struggling at the time, and one day I just had this bright idea to rob Preston. He had never met Randall—my brother had a night job back then—so I told Randall my idea and he thought it was great."

"How did it go?" asked Simon.

"Like clockwork," said Maria. "I had slept with him plenty of times by then, so I figured once more wouldn't hurt. I went to his home, which was a small apartment in town that he rented, and I managed to coax him into bed. He was actually a pretty good lover. I had unlocked the front door when Preston wasn't looking and Randall had snuck inside. He listened to me making love to Preston, and later told me it sort of turned him on.

"He entered the room when he heard my code words— 'Oh, that was great'—and he pointed his gun right at Preston. That's when I learned it was best to rob a man while he's naked," said Maria, a huge grin breaking out on her face.

"Did Preston have much cash on him?"

"More than we'd hoped. It turned out he had a Mason jar hiding in his kitchen. Preston's gun scared him so much he gave it up almost without asking, which was funny because the gun was just a toy. We ended up with more than $60, which was a fortune to us back then."

"Did you leave Milwaukee at that point?"

"We did. We moved around a great deal after that. Randall bought a real gun with the money we stole, and we just pulled the same scam over and over. Eventually we did make it to Chicago. Now that I think of it, that is where my job as a dancer was."

"Let's move back to that Chicago period. What was it like to be a flapper? It was a pretty exciting time, wasn't it?"

"Oh my God, it was so much fun. We were rebels, of course. Women weren't supposed to wear skirts so short, or smoke, or drive cars. Old society looked down on us, aghast at what we were doing. We were called all sorts of names, and I guess they thought most of us were prostitutes. We did enjoy sex, of course, but not for money." Maria paused for a moment and then let out a small giggle, saying, "Except when we robbed them."

"Were you in Chicago during Prohibition?"

"Oh yes, but it was never a big problem. You could always find alcohol if you wanted it."

"Did you ever rub elbows with any of the famous gangsters of that period?"

"Not personally. I used to shop at one of the local florists that was run by some mob boss, but I don't remember his name. I think it was a front for a bootlegging scheme."

Simon glanced at his watch and noticed it was nearly the top of the hour.

"Let's move on to the end of that lifetime. Tell me what's happening."

Maria did not answer at first, although a frown appeared on her face. "We ended up in St. Louis," she finally said. "I had turned fifty by then, and my looks were gone. I'd put on a lot of weight and I had some health issues from all the drinking I had done over the years. Neither Randall nor I ever married. We stayed together the entire lifetime."

"Who passed first?" asked Simon.

"I did. I think my liver just gave up one day," she said, and a smile appeared back on her countenance. "I didn't mind. It had been a good life."

169

"Were you ever caught for all the robberies you had pulled?"

"Never. Randall was with me when I passed. I had been bedridden for some time and my passing was not unexpected. Still, he took it hard. I have no idea what he did once I was gone."

"Maria, I'm going to bring you back now. I will count from one to three, and when I say three you will open your eyes and be back in the present, fully aware. You will be able to remember all that you have told me. Do you understand?"

"Yes," said Maria.

"One, two, three," said Simon, and Maria's eyes slowly opened. She took her time sitting up, and she remained on the couch for a few moments.

"Well, that was interesting," said Simon.

"Indeed," she said, slowly raising her head to stare at the doctor. "One never knows what one will find, I guess, when one has a regression."

"You said your brother Randall was also your husband in your Cherokee life. Do you recognize that person yet in your current life?"

"I know who he is," she said, and left it at that.

Simon had a feeling she didn't want to discuss it any further and let it go. "I hope this regression has helped you in some way. While we may have learned that you had an unsavory side, I'm sure you had many good qualities about you too."

Maria gave him a larger smile than he expected. "I'm well aware we all have a dark side to our prior lives," she said. "I think this one was actually pretty interesting, and I verified what I came here to know."

With that, Maria arose and said, "Thank you, Simon." Then she headed for the door.

Two nights later Simon was relaxing on his balcony while watching a bright orange sun sink below the horizon. It had been a hot, steamy day, but as the sun set a westerly breeze picked up and helped offset the day's heat.

He set his glass of chardonnay on the table and glanced up at the wind chimes that always made him think of Nora. Nearly a year and a half had passed since her death. He still thought of her often, yet occasionally a day or two would now pass where she wouldn't enter his mind. The terrible nightmares had also become less frequent of late, perhaps another sign that he was moving on.

He supposed that somewhere down the road he would marry again, although he had no hopes that such a marriage could possibly be as rewarding as his life with Nora had been. Many of his patients had been in similar circumstances, and he often had to guide them through some very rough waters.

Who will guide me? Simon wondered.

The survivor group in Willis had tried to help him get through the initial shock, but after moving to Sarasota he had not sought out another such group. The overwhelming sadness that he felt every time he attended the meetings was almost too much to bear.

He had talked to a local colleague on several occasions after opening his practice. Doctor Paul Tracy was an elderly gent in his early seventies who had an office down the hall from Simon's. Semi-retired, he worked three days a week. Paul was a transplanted New Englander who had a down-to-earth way of looking at things, and Simon appreciated the directness of his approach.

"You can't bring the flower back to life after it's been picked," Paul said one day. "You just have to move on."

He never tried to tell Simon everything was rosy, never said things would work out for the best. He simply reiterated the same things Simon always told his clients. Life can be hard sometimes, things happen that we don't see coming and can't understand, but it will get easier with time.

The ageless Time heals all wounds, thought Simon. He wondered if it really would. He picked up his glass and took a good long swallow. It was time to think of something else, so he turned to the other item that had been on his mind for over three weeks now.

Hannah and Hollis.

He had been thinking about them daily ever since realizing that they were in each other's regressions and were very possibly soul mates to each other. He would love to get them together, tell them how their stories coincided, and be the matchmaker they needed him to be.

If they were patients of his in his psychologist role he would not be able to interfere, because the doctor-patient privilege would prevent it. Hannah and Hollis were not seeing him as a psychologist, however, but as a regressionist, and therefore he felt there was a grey area there. The major problem he saw was that Hollis was already with someone else, and Simon didn't think he had a right to interfere with that relationship.

He had spent the last few weeks racking his brain in an attempt to come up with a solution, but the truth was he may never see either of them again if they never came back for another regression. He had considered calling both of them in an attempt to schedule back to back sessions, but there was no guarantee both would agree. He also debated bringing them in at the same time for a meeting, but once again Hollis' relationship with Amy put the quash on that.

What was driving Simon crazy was the fact that he really *wanted* to get Hannah and Hollis together just to see what would happen. Would they hit it off right away? Would one of them fall in love at first sight? Would there be no reaction at all? Simon was desperate to find out, as much for him as for the two past life lovers. It would be the first major break-through in his regression work since the Jill Palmer story. He simply didn't know what to do.

He picked up his wine glass, drank the rest of his chardonnay, and headed to the kitchen for a refill. When his phone rang he almost didn't answer it, not wanting to disrupt his quiet evening alone. However, it could be an emergency with a patient of his, so Simon set down his glass and picked up the receiver.

He didn't know it at the time, but it was synchronicity calling.

Barry Homan

FOURTEEN

Gene Kincaid had just greeted two guests to his housewarming party and was about to close the door when he saw Simon exiting the elevator.

"Doctor Taylor," said Gene, "how nice of you to come."

"My pleasure, and from now on you'd better call me Simon."

"Simon it is. Come on in."

The loss of his wife had not been a shock to Gene. She had been ill for a long time and he had known her passing was near. However, he had still felt the need to talk with someone about it after her death became a reality, and he had turned to his good friend Paul Tracy. Unfortunately, the part-time psychologist had been under the weather that week and had suggested that Gene go down the hall and see Simon instead.

Gene had seen Simon three times in the month after his wife's passing. Simon never brought up his own tale of woe, although Gene did eventually hear about it from Paul. He felt comfortable talking with Simon, however, and found his mood lifted after each visit. Once he decided he no longer needed to see Simon as a patient, he had called the office and invited Simon out to dinner.

Although Gene was more than thirty years older than him, Simon felt a connection with the man, no doubt in part due to their shared loss of a loved one. Besides, he had not made many friends yet since his move to Sarasota, had not even tried to do so. Thus Simon had taken Gene up on his offer, and the two men had met for dinner on a second occasion also.

Simon entered the condo and was immediately moved. The living room was sleek and stylish, and he quickly picked up on the Oriental feel to the place. "Very impressive," he said.

"Let me show you around," said Gene.

Gene pointed out a few details in the living room, made a tour of the kitchen, and was about to take Simon down the hall to the bedroom when they ran upon Florence coming out of the master suite.

"Ah, Florence," said Gene, "I'd like you to meet Doctor Simon Taylor."

"A pleasure," said Florence.

"Florence has been a friend of mine for many years, and it was her company that did all this wonderful renovation."

"You've done a marvelous job," said Simon.

"It wasn't me," said Florence, "but let me introduce you to the young lady who did do this." She led them to the meditation room, where Hannah was just putting away her cell phone.

"Sorry," said Hannah as she turned to face them, "I … Simon?"

Simon stared at her a moment before he managed to utter, "Hannah?"

She was wearing a cream colored designer dress that hugged her body and matching high heel shoes. The sequins on her dress shone brightly in the light. She looked nothing like the waif that had knocked on his office door so many months ago, and Simon could barely believe the transformation.

"You two know each other?" asked Florence, but her question was drowned out as Hannah screamed, "Oh my God!" and gave the doctor a big hug.

"What are you doing here?" asked Hannah.

"Apparently I've come to see the amazing work that you have done," said Simon, who suddenly remembered that Hannah was an interior decorator. "And it is amazing. Is this a meditation room?"

"Yes," said Gene, standing behind Simon. "I never asked Hannah to turn this room into a meditation room for me, but she saw tapes and such that I had and determined that I did indeed meditate. It's a practice that I have been doing for years, but when Pam was alive there was no one place for me to go and meditate. I usually just sat on the couch and did it whenever she wasn't home."

"So how do you two know each other?" asked Florence a second time.

"I went to see Simon one night because of these horrid nightmares that I had been having my entire life," said Hannah. "They were coming more frequently, and I had reached the point where I didn't want to fall asleep anymore."

"I'm a psychologist," said Simon, "but I also use hypnosis to do past life regression work."

"Really?" said Florence.

"I knew he had moved to Sarasota," continued Hannah, "and I just barged in on him. He was kind enough to do a regression right away for me, and you'll never guess what we found out."

"Do tell," said Florence.

"I used to live in Pompeii and …." Hannah turned to look at Simon.

"Herculaneum," he said.

"I can never recall that name," said Hannah. "Anyway, I was there when Mount Vesuvius erupted, and that's where my nightmares were coming from."

"That's quite astounding," said Gene. "Let's finish the tour, and then we can talk about this some more."

More guests had arrived by the time Simon's tour of the home was finished, and Gene and the two ladies were tied up for another hour. Simon took the opportunity to slowly check out every detail of the living room. He was impressed with everything Hannah had done for Gene's home. She obviously had a talent for decorating and put a great deal of thought into her work.

It was nearly ten o'clock before all the other guests had left and the four of them were alone. They sat in the living room, Florence and Hannah on the couch, the two men in chairs on either side.

"Now," said Gene to Simon, "tell me more about this regression work of yours."

Simon spent a few minutes telling the three of them how he had begun using hypnosis to help his patients quit smoking or lose weight, and then one day a young lady with back pain from an unknown cause slipped back into a past life.

"It turned out she had been struck by a car in her previous life and had carried that pain with her into this life," said Simon. "Since I had always thought reincarnation was possible, I began doing regressions, and in time I published a book on the subject."

"Past Life Memories," said Hannah. "I've read it a couple of times. It's very good."

"Thank you," said Simon.

"I had been to one of his weekend conferences before," continued Hannah. "It was in Memphis a few years ago. It's why I went to see him here. My nightmares were becoming worse and I figured they must be from a past life."

"And did it help?" asked Gene.

"It seems to have." She looked at Simon and asked, "It's been what, four months now?"

Simon wasn't sure but it sounded about right. "I think so," he said.

"I haven't had a nightmare since then."

Gene and Florence were obviously impressed.

"I've never really thought much about reincarnation," said Gene, "but I will tell you this. I've always had this love affair with the Orient, as you can probably tell, and Pam and I traveled there on more than one occasion. But one day we were in this small town just outside of Bombay, or whatever they call it now, and it was like I had just been there yesterday. It seemed I knew what was around every corner before I got there. I remember Pam asking me once how I knew that, and I couldn't answer her. It was strange."

"Perhaps you should try a regression," said Florence.

"Oh, at my age I guess I'll be finding out soon enough if there's life after death," said Gene.

"So how do you know Simon?" Hannah asked.

"I went to see him a few times after my wife died." His smile sagged just a bit, and it was obvious to everyone that the loss of his wife still hurt.

A short while later, as Simon arose to leave, an idea of how he could resolve his dilemma of Hannah and Hollis formed in his mind. He would simply follow Gene's lead.

"Hannah," he said, "I love what you've done with this place. It's first rate all the way. How would you like another job?"

Hannah's face lit up in obvious excitement. "That would be wonderful," she said, "but I think you need to go through my boss."

"I don't think that will be a problem," said Florence, obviously pleased. "Why don't you call the office in the morning and we can set something up." She took out one of her cards from her purse and handed it to Simon.

"Thank you," said Simon. "I'll do that. My place is pretty empty and drab at the moment. I haven't done much with it. It needs a lot of help."

"We'll be happy to work with you," said Florence.

Simon left a moment later. His mind was not so much on the renovation that would take place in his condo as it was on the special party he would throw when it was done.

Simon called Florence's office at ten the next morning and was surprised when Florence herself answered the phone. "Secretary have the day off?" he asked.

"No secretary here," said Florence. "I prefer to handle

things by myself. I've been going over our schedule here, which has suddenly become pretty jammed up, as I imagine yours is. I suggest we get together some night after work, say around seven."

"That would be fine," said Simon. "What night were you thinking?"

"How about Wednesday?" asked Florence. "That would work for me."

"Wednesday it is."

"Okay, great. Let me have your address and I will see you then."

Simon gave her his address and then asked if Hannah would be coming.

"Actually, Hannah is pretty tied up with other jobs right now, so I think you're stuck with me."

"That's fine," said Simon, although he was a little disappointed. "See you at seven on Wednesday."

Hannah had been working on a nearby computer when the call came in. "Was that Simon?" she asked.

"It was," said Florence. "I hope you don't mind that I'm doing the job at his place."

"Not at all," laughed Hannah. "I have enough work to keep me busy. Maybe while you're with him he can talk you into a regression."

Florence had been surprised by all the talk about regressions and past lives the previous evening. She wondered why Hannah had never mentioned anything about it before. *If I'd found out about a life in Pompeii during a volcanic eruption I'd have been telling everyone about it,* she thought. Perhaps it was because Hannah hadn't been working with her that long at the time and didn't want to seem like a kook.

In any event, Florence was looking forward to seeing Simon Taylor again. He was handsome, single and currently unattached. She had been attracted to him from the first moment, which was the real reason she had chosen to take on Simon's renovation herself.

Hannah had told her on the ride home from Gene's last night about the death of Simon's wife. It had been a year and a half ago, so maybe he was ready to begin dating again. Even though Florence figured she was ten years older than Simon, she thought she might just give it a shot.

Florence had been pregnant and married at sixteen. It was a high school one night stand that had no possible chance of succeeding, but the parents on both sides had demanded they give it a try. A second baby came two years later, but the stress level was more than either could handle. They divorced before the new baby was a year old, and Florence moved back in with her parents. She managed to get her high school diploma through night school, and then a fortuitous turn of events changed everything for her.

Uncle Billy, who lived on the other side of the country, won two million dollars on a lottery ticket and wanted to share it with his family. He sent Florence's father a check for one hundred thousand dollars, and her dad decided right away that his little girl should go to college. It changed her life.

She achieved her degree in interior design and worked in the business for fifteen years before finally opening her own shop. She married again, this time to a college professor who loved her and her two children. It lasted eighteen years—the happiest times of her life—until a raging case of B cell lymphoma took him from her.

It had taken her a long time to get over her husband's passing, so Florence knew what Simon was going through. She would have to move slowly at first to gauge his interest and to validate her interest in him, but she hoped there was a chance it could all work out.

She was fifty-two and hadn't slept with a man since her husband had died. The thought of doing so sent shivers through her body.

The next morning Hollis Brown parked his car in the school parking lot, took a box of items from his trunk, and headed for the front door. It was the first day for teachers to begin setting up their classroom for the start of the new school year. He saw Amy's car parked over in the corner and knew she had been here for a half hour already.

They had been dating now for almost three months. The initial infatuation period was winding down and they were settling into a normal routine. They were still finding out new things about each other, of course. Just last night Hollis had discovered Amy had an aversion to Brussels sprouts. He had made dinner for them and had the sprouts as his vegetable.

"Oh my God, get them off the table!" she had cried.

"What?" he had asked, thinking at first that an ant or some other creature had attacked their meal.

"Those!" She pointed at the dish holding the offending items as she turned her head away.

Hollis had started laughing. "You're afraid of Brussels sprouts?"

"Just get rid of them," she said, still not turning to face them. "I hate them with a passion."

He brought the dish back into his kitchen and quickly opened a can of corn, which he heated in the microwave and brought back to the table.

"This better?" he asked.

By now Amy had a sheepish look on her face. "Sorry," she said. "I just never took you for a Brussels sprouts guy."

She explained that she had been forced to eat them as a child and couldn't stand them. Her goal as an adult was to never see them again if at all possible. Hollis then informed her that he had an aversion to lima beans, and they made the decision to eradicate both items from all future meals.

Hollis thought the relationship was going as well as could be expected after three months. He knew from past experiences of his own and his friends that the three month mark was oftentimes a splitting up point, but he didn't see that happening to them. They did have their differences, but who didn't. Amy was more of a fish person and loved being in the water; Hollis liked red meat, had never learned to swim, and avoided the water for the most part. Amy tended to drink vodka or gin; Hollis drank wine, which Amy wouldn't touch.

If there was one thing that bothered him about the relationship, it was Amy's penchant for jealousy. There had been tons of beautiful women in skimpy bikinis in Nassau, and Hollis enjoyed looking at them. Amy had become upset with him more than once.

"What?" he had asked. "You're not checking out all the handsome guys that are looking at you?"

"I don't need to," she had replied. "I'm with a handsome guy, and I'd like it if he kept his eyes on me."

It had continued even after they had arrived back home. Amy would get upset if he happened to glance at a pretty girl as they drove by in the car. He had never met anyone who reacted in this manner, and at times he found it hard to deal with.

The one big fight they had in their first three months together had been over her jealousy. They had gone to a bar located down the street from Amy's house and found a table near the wall. Hollis had gone up to the bar to order their drinks. As he waited, a girl sitting to his left had begun chatting with him. It was completely innocent stuff, yet when he returned to the table Amy was furious.

"Did you get her number?" she had asked, and it had taken off from there.

The next day was just the second time since they had started dating that they hadn't seen each other.

To this point, however, the good parts of their relationship more than offset their differences. Overall, the trip to Nassau had been an exciting adventure that both thoroughly enjoyed, although Amy had been a bit peeved when she had to go snorkeling alone. Everything else, from the sunbathing to the afternoon shopping trips to the nighttime partying, had been spectacular.

What continued to amaze Hollis more than anything, however, was the sex. Amy was a tiger in the bedroom, her penchant for sex dazzling to behold. Every night a new position, a new toy added to their repertoire. After years of having almost no sex at all, Hollis now rarely had a night off. His eyes had been opened to the countless ways one could have fun in the bedroom, things he had never even imagined, and he thoroughly enjoyed it, although he did occasionally long for a simple missionary position.

However, after one particular night of passion, the other problem in their relationship suddenly raised its ugly head. Hollis had mumbled, "I'm making up for my time as a monk."

"What did you say?" asked Amy.

Hollis immediately knew he had made a mistake as soon as the word *monk* was out of his mouth, and he tried to cover it up. "Nothing important," he said.

"Your time as a monk?" said Amy, as she rolled away from him on the bed. "You're talking about that reincarnation crap again, aren't you?"

He had been careful not to bring up any metaphysical topics since their last discussion. However, he had not stopped investigating the subject. Carefully hidden in his bedroom were four new books he had purchased since that night; two dealing with near death experiences, one about channeling, with the fourth one being a reincarnation novel. He always made sure they were well out of sight when Amy came over.

Hollis supposed it was the one big thing they would never agree on. He didn't like the fact that he had to hide things from her, yet he knew that any attempt to discuss some of the topics he was interested in would draw her rage.

Her anger on that particular night had eventually abated, and things had been fairly smooth since then. He wasn't about to leave Amy over the jealousy or reincarnation issues, but he wondered if circumstances somewhere down the road concerning the two matters would eventually come between them.

Hollis saw Amy in the office as he entered the school. He gave her a quick wave before making his way to his classroom on the second floor.

He always enjoyed the start of a new school year. He may have been a monk or a warrior in his past lives, but he was certain that teaching was what he was meant to do in this one. While many of his colleagues often complained about the hassle they had to put up with each day, Hollis enjoyed the challenge. It was a thrill to see a student who had never made an effort before suddenly perk up and take an interest. His reputation as a teacher who made classes fun had grown over the past few years to the point that kids who didn't get into his class were bummed out.

Hollis unpacked the box of supplies he had brought with him and put them away. Nowadays it was up to the parents to supply the school with all the little items needed to make it through a day, but he knew that not all the parents of his students could afford to spend their money on school supplies.

He had been working for twenty minutes when Ted Osterman, who had the room across the hall, came in.

"Hey there," said Ted. "Welcome back. You and Amy are still an item, I hear."

"Hello Ted," said Hollis. "Yes, we are still dating."

"It can be dangerous to date someone at work," said Ted, eyebrows rising. "Breakups can be very messy."

"We knew that when we starting going out with each other. We just take it a day at a time. Right now things are great."

Hollis finally managed to change the subject, and after catching up on all that was new in Ted's life, the two men went back to work.

Unfortunately for Hollis, the same conversation would come up another half dozen times that day.

Barry Homan

FIFTEEN

Florence Davidson arrived at Simon's condo just after seven on Wednesday night. She took about five steps after he ushered her in, stopped dead in her tracks, and said, "Wow, when you said you hadn't done much with the place you weren't kidding, were you?"

Simon could only give her a foolish grin as he shrugged his shoulders and replied, "I'm afraid not. Would you like a glass of wine?"

That would be delightful," she replied. "White if you have it."

He poured two glasses of Chardonnay and handed one to Florence. "Let me show you around," he said, "although that shouldn't take long."

She was shocked that he had been living here for nearly a year and yet had done so little to the place. It looked to her as though someone was just moving in. The kitchen was missing many of the usual appliances that one normally finds, the living room was sparse, and the second bedroom was nothing but a storage area. The master bedroom and bath were the only places that looked lived in. Both were neat and orderly, and Florence imagined that Simon had just cleaned, knowing that she was coming.

"It's a nice night out," he said when the tour was finished, "why don't we sit on the balcony?"

Florence immediately noticed there was only one chair next to the table, and the thought struck her that this man may not be ready to date just yet.

Simon also realized the problem and said, "Oh, be right back," and then he went and retrieved the second chair from his storage room.

When they were finally settled in Florence said, "You have a beautiful view from here."

"Yes, I come out here often at night. We can catch the sunset in a little while."

Florence gazed at the view a while longer before finally asking, "So what did you have in mind for the place?"

Simon had thought about that ever since seeing Gene's place. "Well, I'm open to your ideas, of course, since you are the expert. Gene's place was beautiful, but I'm not into that Oriental style myself. I'm more of a modern, contemporary guy. Stainless steel in the kitchen, comfortable sofa and chair in the living room, wooden coffee table, not glass. I'd like something that says Florida without being too beachy, if you know what I mean?"

"You don't want living room lamps with grass-skirted hula girls as a base, I take it."

"Lord, no."

"No signs all over the house proclaiming your love of sand and surf?"

"No, thank you," said Simon, a chuckle coming from his smiling face. "I think you understand."

"Let me show you some things," said Florence, and they made their way back into the living room.

She withdrew a design book from her briefcase and they spent the next twenty minutes going over different styles and ideas. Simon quickly eliminated the rustic and eclectic styles among others, and it became obvious that he was indeed leaning towards a simple contemporary style. He pointed out some sofas that appealed to him, and by the time they were finished Florence had a pretty good idea of how she would proceed.

"When will you start?" he asked.

"I have some projects I need to finish up this week," she said. "Why don't I begin Monday morning? That will give me some time to set things up and give you some time to unpack or remove those boxes you have in your second bedroom."

"You mean my storage closet?" said Simon.

"Whatever you want to call it," replied Florence. "Just have it ready on Monday so you can tell me if there's anything in there you would like to display."

"Okay," he said, "will do."

"Now what would you like me to do with that room?" asked Florence. "Do you want it as a guest bedroom, or perhaps you would like me to set it up as an office for you?"

Simon hadn't really thought about what he should do with that room. "Well," he finally said after a momentary pause, "I don't think I need a second bedroom, and I really should have some office space here at the house, so why don't we go with that."

"That'll be fine," said Florence, and she jotted down a few more notes on her pad.

Simon went to the kitchen and retrieved the bottle of wine while Florence put her things back in her briefcase. "Let me refresh your drink," he said as he poured, not waiting for an answer.

"Just in time for the sunset," said Florence. She looked out over the water as the bright yellow sun began turning to orange. "What a beautiful sight."

"I never get tired of it," said Simon.

I could get used to this, thought Florence, but her instinct told her now wasn't the time to hit Simon up for a date. They quietly watched the finishing touches of daylight, and then she drained her glass and prepared to leave.

"Should I get a hotel room for a week so you can more easily work here?" asked Simon, as he led her to the door.

"That shouldn't be necessary," said Florence, "assuming

you'll be working every day; unless, of course, you want to be surprised."

"I think I'd like to be surprised," he said. "Let me get you a key."

Simon retrieved the spare condo key from his bedroom nightstand. "I'll go through everything this weekend and have it ready for you, and then I'll book a room at the Ritz. Will one week be enough?"

"That will be fine," said Florence. "We're not doing any painting or remodeling, so that should be plenty of time."

He brought her down to the parking garage and showed her where she could park. "I'll let the condo people know you may be arriving with a truck on some days. It won't be a problem."

They rode the elevator back to the first floor and said their goodbyes. As she prepared to leave, Florence put her hand on his arm and gently ran her fingertips down its length.

The gesture surprised him, and as he watched Florence depart Simon realized he had goose bumps.

He went through the boxes he had stored in the bedroom first thing Saturday morning. He had saved very little in his hasty exit from South Carolina; most of it had some connection to Nora.

The hardest box to go through was the one with the eight photo albums in it. Nora loved taking pictures whenever they went on vacation, and putting albums together was always one of her first projects when they returned home. She always labeled the covers; Maui, Rome & Pompeii, Paris and Wine Country, Ireland, St. Petersburg & Moscow, African Safari, Bali, Tahiti.

He spent two hours poring through the photos. Tears came more than once. He was not ready to store the memories of his wife in a closet, so after repacking the box, he placed a note on it that said, *My bedroom, but inconspicuous.*

The next morning he packed a small suitcase and moved

into the Ritz.

Eight days later Hannah sat fidgeting at her desk. For some reason her mind kept straying from her work, and every time she looked up at the clock another fifteen minutes had gone by. She was supposed to be working on a living room design for a new client but was getting nowhere, and her two o'clock appointment with the lady was now only three hours away.

She had spent an enjoyable weekend visiting with her parents, driving up Saturday morning and returning Sunday afternoon. Last night she and Madison had taken in a movie, and Hannah had kidded her friend about the fact that another three month reading was half gone and still no Mister Right had arrived.

"He isn't here yet Madison," she said more than once. "Where is he?"

Madison had reassured her that her guides and angels did not lie, and if the cards said he was coming than Hannah could believe it.

"Remember though," Madison reminded her, "they did say there might be a problem. Just be patient, okay?"

"My sex drive is running out of patience," Hannah had replied, a wry smile, but no laughter, on her face.

Florence jarred Hannah out of her latest reverie. "I have to run out for a bit," she said. "Man the phones for me, okay?"

"Sure thing," said Hannah.

Florence had finished Simon's condo on Saturday, and from everything Hannah had heard the doctor had been well pleased with the results. Hannah had hoped to be asked to help on the project, but Florence had done all the work herself. By the time the project was finished, Hannah thought she knew why.

Her boss had a crush on the doctor.

While she hadn't invited Hannah over to help, Florence had spoken repeatedly about the job with her. Every time she talked about Simon her face would light up, and she had said on more than one occasion, "Do you think he will like it?" or "I hope he'll be pleased."

Hannah had never seen Florence acting like this with any other customer. At times it seemed as though she were a giddy schoolgirl. She wondered if the doctor had noticed.

Fifteen minutes later the phone rang. "Designs by Florence, this is Hannah speaking."

"Hannah, hello, this is Doctor Taylor. How are you?"

"Simon? I'm fine, thank you. How do you like your new place?"

"Florence did a wonderful job," he said, "very nice indeed. Is she there?"

"I'm sorry, she just stepped out a little while ago," said Hannah. "Can I take a message?"

"I can just tell you," said Simon, "since it involves you also. I'm going to have a party at my condo and I want you both to be there. I was thinking maybe not this Saturday but the following one. That would be September 9th. Hopefully everyone's calendar will be clear that day so they can all come."

"It's a housewarming party, I take it?"

"In some respects, yes," said Simon, "but I'm basically inviting a number of regression clients for reasons I can't go into now. Is that date okay with you?"

"Of course," said Hannah, "and I'm sure Florence will be delighted to come also." She wanted to ask something more about how he and her boss had gotten along but thought better of it.

"Great," said Simon. "I'm leaning towards 7:00, but perhaps you and Florence could arrive a bit earlier so I can show you around. How's that sound?"

"That sounds terrific," said Hannah. "I'll tell Florence as soon as I see her."

She stared at the phone for a minute after hanging up. *Why regression clients?* she wondered.

Hollis Brown was in the shower when Simon called him

that night. He was dripping wet as he grabbed his cell phone from the bathroom sink. "Hello," he said.

"Hollis, this is Doctor Taylor, how are you?"

Hollis was surprised to hear the doctor's voice and wondered what he could possibly be calling for. "I'm fine, doctor, how are you?"

"Very well, thank you," said Simon. "I hope I'm not disturbing you."

"Not at all," said Hollis, as water dripped onto his carpet. "What can I do for you?"

"I'm having a party at my condo on Saturday, September 9th, for a number of my regression clients. I am very much hoping that you can come."

Talk about an invitation from left field, thought Hollis.

"Are you still there?" asked Simon.

"Yes, sorry," said Hollis. "I guess you caught me off guard. Is there a particular reason you're doing this?"

"Yes," said Simon, "but I'm afraid I can't go into details, other than to say it's quite important to me that you be there."

"Should I bring a guest?"

Now the pause was on the other end of the line. Hollis waited for the answer.

"I believe it would be best if you came alone," said Simon.

A moment later, a naked Hollis was traipsing through his kitchen looking for a pen and paper. Once he found both, he wrote done Simon's address, noted the date and time of the party, and said goodbye.

"That was strange," he mumbled, as he put his phone back on the bathroom sink and re-entered the shower.

Twenty minutes later Hollis was sitting on his couch watching television. He had originally planned to have dinner with Amy tonight, but another one of her jealous outbursts had caused him to cancel.

The start of the school year had gone as well as could be expected. The incoming freshmen were the only ones who looked lost, and of course the upper classmen generally pointed them in the wrong direction. He and Amy had worked hard to keep things professional while at school, and things had run smoothly until today.

There was a teachers' lounge on the first floor that was also used by the secretarial staff. Hollis and Amy ate lunch together there whenever possible. Hollis had arrived first this morning and noticed that MaryEllen Borgeault, the new French teacher, didn't seem to be feeling well. He had gone over to her and asked, "Are you all right?"

She was twenty-six years old and perhaps a bit overweight, yet quite attractive, with auburn hair cut short and light blue eyes that Hollis assumed to be contacts.

"Just a little jittery, I guess," she said.

"That's certainly understandable," he replied. "High school kids can do that to you." He spoke with her for a few minutes more, hoping to help her relax and get through the day. Finally, he smiled at her and said, "It gets easier," and then he turned around.

Amy was twenty feet away and staring straight at him, a look of anger written all over her face.

He walked over and sat at the table she was standing by, hoping to avoid a scene. "Nervous new teacher," he said. "Let's have lunch." Amy turned around and went back into the office.

The explosion occurred in the parking lot after school once everyone else had left.

"If you're not happy in this relationship, maybe you should get out," yelled Amy to start the conversation.

"I am happy," he replied, "but this jealous streak of yours is over the top. I saw that she didn't look well and just tried to make her feel better, nothing more."

"It looked like more to me," cried Amy, her face contorted in a rage he couldn't understand.

"You're being ridiculous," he said, which simply infuriated her more. "I can't live my life not talking to other females."

It continued on for another few minutes that seemed like hours to Hollis. He tried to get her to be reasonable, but everything he said just seemed to make her angrier.

Eventually he had given up and driven away. They hadn't talked since, and Hollis had no idea if they were still a couple or not. He thought he was in love with Amy, but if love came with such a high price tag then maybe he was mistaken.

She finally called at ten o'clock. "I'm sorry," she said. "I guess you're right. Sometimes my jealous streak just gets the best of me."

They spoke for twenty minutes and attempted to smooth things over, promising to try harder to make their relationship work. They both said "I love you" before hanging up, and Amy said, "I'll be thinking of you as I lie in bed."

He imagined it was a subtle hint that she would be playing with one of her toys, a little reminder that it could be him she was playing with … if he'd just stop flirting with other women.

Whether or not that was what her words were meant to convey, that's the way Hollis took them. He went to bed having no idea what their relationship held in store for them.

September ninth was a typical Florida day. The temperature hovered in the low 90's until the daily four o'clock thunderstorm hit, dropping them back into the 80's and clearing out some of the humidity for a while.

The caterer and bartender Simon hired arrived at six and set everything up in the kitchen. The guest list was small, fifteen in all if everyone came, twelve of whom were regression clients. Simon wandered around the condo making sure everything looked okay, as he had already done a half-dozen times before.

He was very pleased with the work Florence had done, and for the first time since he had moved here it actually felt like home. The furniture he had purchased for the living room such a short time ago was gone, replaced by a contemporary style that was much more comfortable. In fact, his bed frame was about the only item Florence had kept.

Florence and Hannah arrived at 6:30 so Hannah could see the work her boss had done before anyone else came by.

"It's gorgeous," Hannah said upon first entering. "A bit on the subtle side, which suits your personality, I think."

"I think you're right, my dear," said Simon. "I'm very happy with the way it turned out."

Hannah walked out onto the balcony and was thrilled by the view. "It never gets tiresome," she said, "no matter how many times I see the bay or the gulf in the distance. I love the view, and the sunsets in Florida are simply amazing."

"I hope we get to see one tonight," said Simon, "but it looks like those clouds may block it out."

The guests began arriving shortly before seven. Eleven clients of the twelve invited showed up, including Hannah, Hollis and Maria Vasquez. Each of them came alone, as Simon had requested, except for Maria. She had asked to bring Wil Stevens with her, and Simon had acquiesced. He had also invited Grace and Gene Kincaid; thus, when everyone was there, he had fourteen guests in all.

He had debated long and hard about how to go about the evening, and he had changed his mind more than once. One day after work, still up in the air about what he would do, he noticed Paul Tracy's light on down the hall and decided to get a second opinion.

Paul Tracy had been a psychologist for nearly fifty years, but he had never used hypnosis on anyone and had certainly never been involved in regressions. He was therefore intrigued as Simon presented his problem to him.

"So let me get this straight," he said. "You have two regression clients that you think were married in a previous lifetime, but they don't know each other in this life, and you want to try to hook them up?"

"Whether they hook up or not in this life is not really what I'm trying to do," said Simon, "but I think they should have the opportunity to meet each other. I mean, I'd love to see what happens."

"So the first hurdle you need to clear is the ethical question, right?"

"Right, and obviously if they were patients of mine I would have to stay out of it. But these are people who came to me not as patients but as regression clients. I'm not really so much their doctor as I am their hypnotist."

"I'd say it's a bit of a fine line you're walking there," said Paul.

"I agree. However, I have decided to go along with my party, which will bring them together. My real question at this point is how do I go about it? Do I say anything to the group to give them a hint that two of them might know each other, or do I just let nature take its course and see what transpires?"

"If you tell them, I would assume that they'd spend their time talking with each other about all their regressions, trying to see if anyone matches. They'd be sure to find each other that way, I would think. And you say one of them is in a relationship?"

"Yes, the man is; at least he was the last time I saw him, which was about two months ago."

"Then I think that would be interfering with his free will in a way you probably shouldn't get involved in," said Paul.

In the end, Simon had agreed. He would bring Hannah and Hollis together and then let fate take over.

"If I could have your attention," he called out, and his guests quieted down. "I'd like to thank you all for coming tonight. I'd like to begin by introducing Florence Davidson, who did all the decorating that you see here. She is the owner of Designs By Florence, and I hope if any of you ever need such services you will think of her first. I think she did a wonderful job."

Florence gave a quick wave as the guests politely clapped.

"Some of you have asked why this seems to be a party for regression clients. Perhaps it is my way of saying thank you to all of you for the wonderful past-life stories you have told me. Many of them have been truly amazing, and if I decide to write another book I may be asking to use your stories in it. So please feel free to mingle, have a good time and perhaps trade some stories with each other."

He hadn't intended to add that last part, was in fact trying desperately not to give them any clues, but when push came to shove he simply couldn't help himself. He immediately knew he had made a mistake, but he couldn't put that genie back in the bottle now.

He was upset with himself, but a part of him couldn't wait to see what would happen.

SIXTEEN

Hollis accepted a glass of merlot from the bartender and turned to survey the room. He thought it was strange that someone would hold a party where basically no one knew each other.

Amy had not been pleased when she found out he was going to a party without her. He told her a doctor he knew was having a small housewarming party and had asked him to come alone. Fortunately she hadn't asked too many questions.

"Make an appearance, have a drink, and then get your ass back here," she had said, her harsh tone making her displeasure known. "I'll make it worth your while."

He'd told her he would try to get back soon, but he understood what she was really saying. *No flirting. I'm the best sex you'll ever have.* Hollis knew that last part might be true, but he was no longer sure it was worth it.

His gaze settled on a stunningly attractive woman standing by the balcony. She looked familiar, but he couldn't place her at first. It took him another minute to realize it was Maria Vasquez, the woman he'd met in the bar. He also recognized the man she was talking to. It was the shaman. *Guess I do know some people here after all*, he thought.

It had been four months since Hollis had seen the shaman and the name didn't pop into his head. However, since it was at least someone he had met before, Hollis headed in that direction.

"Hello," he said as he approached the couple, "I hope I'm not interrupting."

"Ah, it's the monk," said Wil, and the two men shook hands.

"You remember after all this time?" asked Hollis.

"I saw you standing over there earlier as Simon was speaking," said Wil. "It came to me after a few minutes."

"I'm sorry, I forget …"

"Wil Stevens," the shaman said, "and this is my lovely friend Maria Vasquez."

"Yes, we've met before," said Hollis.

Maria gave him an inquiring glance, obviously not remembering him from the night in the bar over five months ago, and he filled her in on the details.

"Ah, yes," she finally said. "How nice to see you again. Simon has told me that it was our talk in the bar that brought you to him."

"It was, and then it led me to Wil also. It's been an interesting few months," said Hollis.

He turned to Wil and said, "I want you to know that after seeing you I went back to see Simon again. He regressed me back to the very lives you told me about. In fact, my great-grandfather appeared to me during the regression and helped verify what you had said."

"I'm delighted to hear that," said Wil, obviously pleased with the news. "As you can imagine, I don't often receive confirmation of what I tell people."

"Has Simon regressed you?" asked Hollis.

"No, but like you he has been to see me. I am here simply as a friend of Maria's."

Hollis returned his gaze to Maria, who looked lovely in a yellow dress and sandals. "So how many times have you seen Simon?"

"I've been to see him twice," she said.

"I owned a vineyard in Germany in my last life," said Hollis. "What did you do?"

"I was a thief," she said, and laughed when she saw the look on his face. "It was a good life, very interesting to say the least. In this life I am very honest."

They chatted for a few minutes more, and then Hollis' gaze suddenly settled on a young lady across the room.

Hannah had been talking with Simon about the work Florence had done. He seemed happy with the outcome, but she realized it didn't seem to be the reason he had invited everyone. She decided to ask him about what had been puzzling her since his invitation.

"Why regression clients, Simon? Why not invite your friends?"

Simon looked at her, a wry grin on the corner of his mouth, but said nothing.

"There's something you're not telling us," she said.

He gazed into her eyes for a moment longer before answering. "Truth be told, I haven't really made many friends since I've moved here; haven't really tried to. The loss of my wife was very hard on me, as I'm sure you can imagine. I suppose I'm just beginning to recover now. It's been difficult."

"I understand," said Hannah. She waited a moment before continuing. "But you said on the phone you couldn't tell me why you were inviting regression clients, which means you've done it for a reason."

He smiled as the thought *Dangerous ground, tread lightly* passed through his mind. "A reason, yes, but I still can't tell you why." he said.

Gene came over to talk to Simon a moment later, and Hannah wandered into the kitchen to get a glass of wine. "Merlot," she said to the bartender, and then she turned to scan the room.

Hollis watched Hannah standing in the kitchen as the bartender poured a glass of wine for her. As she turned back in his direction he looked away, and then quickly looked back again. Something about her was familiar. He soon realized she looked a great deal like the woman he had seen in the waiting room of Simon's office, but he wasn't sure. She had been dressed casually that day. Tonight she looked radiant in a flowing red dress, a gold chain around her neck, and red high-heeled shoes.

Hannah gazed around the room, saw a man across the way staring at her, and quickly looked away. She looked back a moment later to find the man heading her way.

"Hello," said Hollis, as he arrived by her side. "I take it you're a client of Simon's also."

"I am," she said.

He had the bartender top off his glass and then he turned back to Hannah. "My name's Hollis Brown," he said.

"Hannah Marie Kent," she replied. "Pleased to meet you."

"Sounds like a family name passed down through the generations."

"I wouldn't know about that," said Hannah.

Across the room, Simon Taylor smiled. He had been trying to keep an eye on the two of them while attending to his other guests.

Grace noticed his sudden interest in the couple across the room and sidled up next to him. "Something's going on," she said. "I can see it written all over your face."

Simon gave her a quick Cheshire cat grin and said, "I think the evening is about to be a success."

Hollis was drawn to Hannah immediately, just as he had been that day in the office. Her smile lit up the room, and she had an innate beauty about her that wasn't enhanced by makeup. "I think I've seen you before," he said, "in the doctor's office. You were in the waiting room reading a magazine. I saw you as I was leaving."

"Really? I think you must be mistaken. I haven't had an appointment with Simon in, oh gee, four months now."

Hannah looked at this man who seemed so interested in her. He was obviously older than her, maybe even by ten years. The thick black glasses he was wearing were out of style, she thought, but they actually looked pretty good on him. He was dressed casually in tan pants, a short sleeved brown shirt and brown loafers.

"It was a Friday as I recall," said Hollis. "School let out early that day. I think my appointment was at two." He took a pocket calendar out of his wallet. "Here we go; May fifth. I remember it now. You would have had the three o'clock time slot."

Hannah gave him a non-committal stare when something else popped into his head.

"You were held up in traffic and arrived late."

"What? How …?"

"You remember, don't you?"

Hannah was perplexed. "Well, there was an appointment I had that I arrived late for, but how did you know that?"

Hollis explained to her how his great-grandfather had come through during his reading and told Simon his next client was hung up in traffic. "I'm sure it was you," he finally said.

By now they had ambled into the living room. Hollis was enchanted by this young lady, and when thoughts of Amy moved into his mind he quickly dismissed them.

Hannah was similarly intrigued by his seeming interest in her, but neither one of them had yet jumped to the idea that this could be a past life connection.

They sat on the couch as Hollis continued to regale her with his story about fighting the Crusaders and being a monk in France. Hannah listened intently and realized that she felt at ease with this man. As Hollis finished his tale, she turned to retrieve her glass, which she had set on the end table. As she did, she noticed a framed picture by the glass and did a double take. She picked the frame up and looked closer.

"What is it?" asked Hollis, but she temporarily ignored him.

She saw the doctor standing across the room talking with

his secretary. When he glanced in Hannah's direction, she motioned to him to come closer, and as he did she asked, "Simon, is this what I think it is?"

Simon turned and looked at the picture. "It's a picture of my late wife, Nora."

"Yes, I realize that," said Hannah. "She was very lovely. But what I meant was, is this Pompeii?"

"Oh, yes," he said, suddenly remembering why she would be interested. "It was from a vacation Nora and I took there. We went there twice, actually, as I may have told you after your regression."

Hollis looked at Hannah. "You were in Pompeii?" he asked.

"Yes," she replied, and now it was her turn to regal him with her life from nearly two thousand years ago.

Simon, delighted with what was happening, stood by to help her fill in any missing details.

Hannah spoke for nearly ten minutes about her regression to Pompeii. She told Hollis about her nightmares and how she barged in on Simon after hours, and she spent a good deal of time speaking about Stephanus.

As she spoke, she realized this was the longest she'd talked to a man who wasn't a friend or a client in a long time. He appeared to be genuinely interested in her story, and talking to him--this man who was a complete stranger--came free and easy to her. The fact that he remembered her from a quick glance as he was leaving Simon's office blew her mind. There were a couple of younger men in attendance that she might have approached tonight instead of this man if given the opportunity. Now she was glad he had made the first move.

For his part, Hollis was smitten. The longer he sat by Hannah's side, the more he wanted to be with her. He couldn't place his finger on why exactly. She certainly didn't have the body that Amy had, but she was cute in her own way and had an outgoing personality. There had been an instant attraction to her in the doctor's office, and he found that it hadn't lessened any here.

However, the thought of Amy did cause Hollis to ask himself what he was doing. He was in a relationship, and yet here he was flirting—yes, that's exactly what he was doing—with this young woman he had just met. He was not the type of man to cheat on a woman and he thought poorly of men who did. Amy was a wonderful person with a great body. They had fabulous sex, better than he had ever experienced before. If it wasn't for her damned jealous streak she'd be the perfect woman for him.

But she did have a jealous streak, and suddenly Hollis thought, *Maybe she's not the perfect woman for me.*

Hannah finished her tale with its gruesome ending.

"What an amazing story," said Hollis. "So tell me, have the nightmares ended?"

"So far so good," said Hannah.

Simon wanted to make sure these two didn't suddenly drift off in separate directions. "You two haven't eaten anything yet, have you? Why don't you go grab some appetizers from the kitchen?"

Maria and Wil had been watching Simon as he made his way around the room chatting with his guests. When they saw Hannah holding up the photograph, Maria mumbled "his wife" to Wil.

"He's still very much attached to her," Wil said.

"Understandable," said Maria, "but he needs to move on. I'm not sure he has yet."

"So tonight's not the night either?"

"I don't think so," she replied, "but perhaps the next step is in order."

"And what would that be?" asked Wil.

Maria just smiled.

"So what do you do?" asked Hollis, after they had both finished nibbling on the appetizers.

"Actually, I work with Florence," said Hannah, pointing

to her boss.

"You helped decorate this place?"

"No," Hannah replied, "Florence did this one all by herself. I think she might have a crush on our host." She pointed to Gene, who was just approaching them, and said, "I did redecorate this gentleman's condo a few weeks ago."

"And a splendid job she did," said a smiling Gene Kincaid. He introduced himself to Hollis and the two men shook hands. They chatted for a moment before Gene turned to go. He winked at Hollis as he left and said, "She'd make a mighty fine catch, young man."

Hollis turned back to Hannah and noticed her blushing. "He seems like a nice man," he said.

"I'm blushing, aren't I?"

Hollis laughed. "It seems so."

"I blush so easily; it's embarrassing," said Hannah.

He wanted to tell her how incredibly attractive she was, but felt that might be a little too forward. Instead, he asked, "So how many times have you been to see Simon?"

"Just twice," said Hannah. "The Pompeii visit was my first one. I went back one more time to see if Stephanus showed up again."

"Did he?"

"He did. I guess he really is my soul mate. I just haven't met him yet in this life. How often have you seen Simon?"

"I've been three times," said Hollis. He pointed out Maria, who was heading to the balcony with Wil. "I met her in a bar one night. She's into all this metaphysical stuff, from what I gathered, and she told me about Simon. I'd had this spot on my leg since I was born, and she told me it might be a carryover from a past life."

"What happened?"

"Well, Simon regressed me to my last life. It turns out I was an old lady traveling with my son to Italy. I had to use the bathroom, so he pulled the car over and I went in the woods, but I fell down and pierced my leg on a stick."

"Really? Where's the mark?" asked Hannah.

"That's the funny thing," said Hollis. "Soon after seeing Simon it started to disappear, and now it's gone."

"No way," said Hannah.

They were interrupted by the sound of Beethoven's Fifth coming from Hollis' phone. He removed it from his pocket and checked the number. It was Amy. "Would you excuse me for a minute," he said to Hannah. "I'd better take this."

"Sure," she said.

She was enjoying talking to this man she had just met. The fact that he had noticed her from across the room and immediately came over to introduce himself didn't hurt. As Hollis walked away, Hannah took both their wine glasses and had them refilled.

Hollis went out into the hallway before he answered. "Hi, Amy."

"Are you still there?"

"Yes."

"I thought I told you to leave early," she said, her voice making it clear she was more than a little perturbed. "Were you not listening?"

"It's an interesting night here," he said. "We're all regaling each other with our past life stories," he added, feeling a sudden need to piss her off.

"Oh God, not that crap," she cried. "Get back here now."

"Actually, I'm having a good time and I think I'm going to stay for awhile."

"Listen Hollis, I've had about enough of you wasting time on this fantasy of yours. It needs to stop. If you don't leave there right now, I think our relationship is in serious jeopardy."

Hollis paused for a full five seconds, his mind seemingly running through a dozen scenarios. Finally he took a deep breath and replied, "Your jealousy has had our relationship in serious jeopardy for some time now. I think perhaps it's time we just went our separate ways."

Amy hung up.

Hollis called her back three times but Amy refused to

answer, so he sent her a text message.

Sorry you wouldn't answer. In the long run I think our differences would overpower the good parts. It's time we both moved on. Let's try to be civil at work.

Hollis shut off his cell phone and returned to the party to find his glass of wine full. "Thank you," he said to Hannah.

She noticed he looked a bit frazzled and his hand was shaking as he picked up his glass. "Everything okay?" she asked.

"It is now," he said.

Now that you're back with me? she wondered. "So, you said you had three visits with Simon. One for your leg, one with your grandfather's help; what was the third one?"

Hollis wondered how he should explain this. He didn't want to lie to this wonderful girl he had met, but he also didn't want to scare her away.

"Umm," he mumbled, the sound escaping before he knew what he was going to say. He looked Hannah in the eyes, and a moment later the truth came out. "I was dating a girl at the time. We broke up about a minute ago."

"Oh my, I'm so sorry," said Hannah.

"I'm not," he replied. "It was time."

Hannah took a sip of wine as she waited for him to continue.

"I went back to Simon to see if she and I were soul mates. I regressed back to the same life where I fell on the stick, but this time I told a much more detailed account of that life. As I said before, I was a woman named Anne."

"Anne? I don't believe you mentioned the name earlier."

"Perhaps not. I lived with my family on a farm in Germany," said Hollis, and he suddenly started to laugh.

"What's so funny?" asked Hannah.

"Well, if my recall is correct, I had really big boobs."

Hannah started to laugh with him but suddenly cut it short. A puzzled look came over her face for a moment, but Hollis had reached for his wine and didn't notice. *Anne, big boobs, Germany? It couldn't be,* she thought. She was sure there must have been many well-endowed women named Anne in Germany.

"I fell in love with the boy on the farm next to ours," continued Hollis. "His family owned a vineyard."

Madison … tarot card reading … he's coming!

She listened for another minute as Hollis explained how they had met. Her stomach started doing flip-flops, and she had to set down her wine glass, because now it was her hand that was shaking. The coincidence was becoming too much for her, and she didn't believe in coincidence anyway. "Oh my God," she finally said, "Was his name Roberto?"

"How did you know that?" asked Hollis, a startled look coming over him.

"And the name of the town, was it Colmar?"

"It was, but how …?"

Hannah suddenly screamed.

Everyone in the room turned to look at Hannah and wondered why she kept yelling, "I'm Roberto!"

Hollis had been shocked when Hannah let out her scream, and it took his mind a moment to understand what she was trying to tell him. "What?" was all he could think to say.

Simon had just started a conversation with Gene when he heard the yell. He made a beeline for the couple, the smile on his face as wide as it could possibly be.

Hannah tried to calm down and explain everything to Hollis. "I'm your Roberto," she cried. "You're my Stephanus from Pompeii."

Hollis stood stock still, as if comprehension wouldn't come.

"How wonderful," said Simon as he arrived by their side. "You two have discovered each other, I take it?"

"You knew?" asked Hannah.

"Of course I did, my dear," said the doctor. He turned to face the others in the room. "If everyone would please gather around," he said, waving his arms to motion them forward. "Many of you have asked me why the invitees were all reincarnation clients of mine. Now you have the answer," he said, as he looked at Hannah and Hollis.

Hannah still had a stunned look on her face but was smiling brightly. Hollis finally realized what Hannah had been yelling about and was just beginning to process it.

"These two lovely people came to my office on separate occasions for a regression," continued Simon, "just as most of you have, and I discovered during one of their visits that they had spent a past life together as husband and wife."

The other guests responded with looks of amazement and words of surprise.

"Unbelievable," said Grace.

"How about that," said a man in the back.

"I didn't feel I had the right to come right out and tell them," continued Simon, "but I did want to give them an opportunity to discover each other, so I came up with the idea of this housewarming party to see if they would pick each other out. I've been watching them closely, and I can tell you that Hollis here made a beeline across the room once he saw Hannah."

The couple looked at each other in amazement as Hannah blushed again.

"As you've just heard from our lovely Hannah's scream, they've discovered their secret."

"Any other couples in here we don't know about yet?" called out Gene Kincaid, and suddenly heads started turning to look at each other.

"I'm afraid not," said Simon. "Now I suggest we leave these two alone for a while. I think they have some catching up to do."

Maria, standing in the back of the crowd with Wil, looked at him and simply shook her head.

The guests returned to what they had been doing before Hannah's scream, and although Simon had said there were no other surprises to be had, reincarnation stories were suddenly being swapped all over the room.

Simon turned back to Hannah and Hollis. "I hope what I have arranged pleases you and doesn't cause any trouble," he said, not knowing that Hollis' relationship with Amy was on the rocks.

"I'm delighted," said Hannah. She looked at Hollis and asked, "How about you?"

"I'd say your timing was perfect, Simon," he said, and then he turned to gaze into Hannah's beautiful eyes.

His smile told her everything she needed to know.

Barry Homan

SEVENTEEN

"I'll leave you two alone now," said Simon. "You have a lot to talk about."

Hollis looked at Hannah as Simon departed. "Is it really true?" he asked. A look of amazement was still etched on his face.

Hannah thought he may be having a hard time processing the information. "I'm afraid it is," she said.

His look immediately lightened. "Oh, don't be afraid," he said. "I'm delighted to know we've known each other for so long."

They were interrupted more than once by people coming over to say how wonderful it was that they had found each other. Finally, Hannah decided it was time for them to go someplace quiet.

"I'm still hungry," she said, "and I've probably had enough wine. There's a cafe down the street from here. How about we continue our conversation there?"

Hollis thought it was a great idea and just shook his head yes. They made their way to Simon and Hollis said, "We're going to head out. I think we need someplace a bit quieter."

"I understand," said Simon. He shook hands with Hollis

and then gave Hannah a big hug. A moment later he watched the couple depart, feeling like a proud parent.

"Well, that was exciting," came a voice from behind him. Simon turned to see Grace. "That day in the office when you looked like you swallowed the canary; it was about this, wasn't it?"

"It was," he replied. "Sorry I couldn't tell you then."

"You're a good man, Simon Taylor," said Grace.

"I do my best," he said. "So what do you think of reincarnation now?" He noticed her eyebrows rise and could swear he saw a twinkle in her eye.

"Well, boss," she said, "you have my attention. I may just have to do a little research on my own."

Florence came by and broke up their conversation. "There you are," she said to Simon. "Interesting evening, huh?"

She had performed a small miracle in his condo as far as Simon was concerned. He was thrilled with everything she had done and had told her so more than once. However, she had been pestering him all night, following him around like a little puppy dog and constantly interrupting his conversations.

Simon wished she would just go away.

The Blue Moon Cafe had just a few customers when Hollis and Hannah arrived a little after nine. He pointed to the sign in the window that showed they closed at eleven and said, "Looks like we just have a couple of hours to catch up on lifetimes."

They took a booth in the corner that was distant from the only other parties in the restaurant. The waiter, a short, curly haired youth named Jim, came right over and plopped two menus on the table.

Hollis ordered coffee, and Hannah said, "Me, too."

"I'm going to have to make you a fresh pot," said Jim. "It will be a few minutes."

Hollis looked across the table at the lovely woman sitting

with him. His head was still spinning from the evening's events. The phone call and break up with Amy, the recognition of the girl in Simon's office, Hannah's scream and Simon's revelation; his mind kept playing them over and over.

"Well, this night turned out to be much more than I expected," he said.

Hannah had been watching him, looking for a clue as to how he must feel. While the suddenness of it all had been stunning to her, she had been waiting for a moment like this for months now. Madison hadn't let her down. She said it would happen, but with complications. She was pretty sure the girlfriend he had apparently just broken up with was the complication.

"I've been waiting for you," she replied. "My friend who reads tarot cards told me you were coming." He gave her a warm and hopeful smile that made her tingle inside.

"That day in Simon's office," he began, "I just wanted you to look up. I kept looking over at you, and all I wanted was for you to look at me." He waited a moment before adding, "I never thought I'd see you again, and then tonight … I was sure it was you when I saw you."

"That would be the day I first told Simon of my life as Roberto," said Hannah.

"Tell me everything you remember of that regression," said Hollis.

"It's funny," said Hannah. "One of the first scenes I saw was of you riding by the farm, and I mentioned how you had big boobs."

Hollis had what Hannah's father would have called a *shit-eating grin* on his face, and Hannah let out a laugh.

"But to get down to specifics, let me see." She made sure she had it straight in her mind before continuing. "My family was Italian and I was about fourteen when we moved to Colmar. My father had bought the vineyard. The regression began with you and me meeting in the town, and soon we would meet on regular occasions and have picnics together."

"I mentioned that in my regression," said Hollis.

"We fell in love and were married," Hannah continued. "I remember the year: 1887. We had three children, two boys and a girl."

The waiter brought a carafe of coffee and filled their cups, and then they took a moment to place their order.

"Do you remember their names?" asked Hollis, after the waiter had left.

"Of course I do," said Hannah, "Michel, Pasha and Danielle."

"It was Pasha who was driving me to Italy when I bruised my leg," said Hollis.

"That fits," said Hannah. "Michel had moved to America."

"How do you know that?"

"Well now, that's interesting," said Hannah. "You see, I died in 1930 from a snake bite while working in the fields, but when Simon asked me if I knew what had happened to my children, the answers came to me somehow. I knew what had become of them, even though I shouldn't have known."

"Freaky stuff, huh?" said Hollis. "So Michel came to the States, Pasha took me to Italy and Danielle …?"

"Danielle died in a bombing raid in England during the Second World War. A son died with her."

"Now, I lived longer than you and I knew Danielle had moved to England," said Hollis, "but I didn't know her fate." He waited a moment and then asked "Have you recognized any of our children in this life?"

"I knew Pasha," said Hannah.

"Knew? Past tense?"

"He was my adoptive father. He and my mother died in a car accident when I was young. I'm sorry you'll never get to meet him. He was a wonderful man."

"That's so sad," said Hollis. "So you were adopted?"

"Another story for another day, perhaps," said Hannah. "I also know my mother and father from Colmar. They are now an aunt and uncle of mine."

"That's interesting," said Hollis, "because I know the other two children."

"You do?" cried Hannah. "Tell me."

"You're not going to believe this, but they are both sisters of mine now. Danielle is my sister Vivian, and Michel is my sister Terry, and let me tell you, Terry is quite the tomboy. I think she wants to be a boy again."

They were both laughing when their food arrived. As he walked away after serving them, the waiter thought they made a rather strange but interesting couple.

They stopped reminiscing about past lives while they ate. Instead, the discussion turned to their current incarnations.

"What do you do for work?" asked Hannah.

"I'm a teacher over at Bay Crest High School."

"Really? What do you teach?"

"Ancient History," said Hollis. He thought she might turn her face up at that, but she surprised him.

"I guess that's what we've been talking about," she said, and once again the couple found themselves chuckling at the irony of it all.

They chatted on as they ate their meal, Hollis slowly pecking at his burger and fries, Hannah ravenously attacking her Crab Cake sandwich and steamed veggies. When they finished, they settled back in their seats and Hollis refilled their coffee cups.

"Ready to get back to tales of long ago?" he asked.

"In a minute," said Hannah, "but I think there's one thing I need to ask you about before we go any further."

Hollis was pretty sure he knew what was coming and just nodded.

"You said you broke up with your girlfriend tonight. Please tell me you didn't do that just because you saw me at the party."

The wry smile could not hide the sadness that showed in his eyes. "No," he finally began, "it had nothing to do with you."

Hannah could tell this was going to be hard for him and

waited patiently for Hollis to continue.

"We started dating back in May just as school was letting out. She works there as a secretary. It took off fast. A month later we took a vacation to Nassau, and I thought I had found the woman of my dreams. But she has this jealous streak that just won't quit. If I just glance at another woman, she's all over me about it. She also can't stand the fact that I believe in reincarnation. Anything having to do with the metaphysical just sets her off.

"Tonight when she called she ordered me to leave the party and go to her, and when I said no she said some things and then I said some things. Her attitude tonight was the last straw. I'd just had enough, so I broke it off."

"I'm so sorry," said Hannah.

"Don't be," he replied. "It was bound to happen sooner or later."

"Any chance you two will make up?"

"I'm pretty sure I wouldn't have made up with her even if I hadn't met you tonight. Now I know I won't."

"We just met," cautioned Hannah. "We may not like each other a week from now."

"I understand that," said Hollis, "but I don't believe it." He looked deeply into Hannah's eyes. "I think there's an attraction here that's unmistakable, and I believe you feel it too. Simon put on this party tonight simply to bring us together because he knew of our connection. I don't profess to know what the future holds for us but ..." He stopped to gaze once more at this lovely woman sitting across from him. "God, you're beautiful," he finally said.

Hannah stared back at him, her body tingling again at his words.

"I would love to get to know you better in this life," said Hollis.

"Me too," was all Hannah could think to say.

Hollis thought it was time to change the subject. "So you lived in Pompeii at the time of Vesuvius?"

"*We* lived in Pompeii," she said, and Hannah suddenly realized Hollis hadn't grasped that part of the connection yet. "It was actually the second time I'd seen you in that regression."

"Really?"

"Yes. Before Pompeii I had seen us as children in a life in India. It was a very short recall. I think we were both about nine years old. I had a large family, lots of brothers and sisters, although I forget how many. You lived in the village also, and I thought I would marry you when we were older. Your name was Ashoka."

"Did we marry?"

"No. A monsoon came during the night and caused a mudslide. My family lived at the bottom of the mountain, and the mudslide wiped us out."

"That's awful," said Hollis. "Did I die also?"

Hannah thought for a moment and then said, "I don't know."

"So you saw me in three different lifetimes; India, Pompeii and Germany."

"Yes," said Hannah. She smiled at him and added, "Everywhere I go I see traces of you."

Hollis had a puzzled look on his face.

"What is it?" she asked.

"Well, if I went back for another regression and I returned to Colmar, I guess I would recognize you now. But I'm pretty sure the other regression that I had did not have you in it. The first part was rather short. I was a Muslim soldier fighting against the Crusaders and I died in battle, as I told you earlier. I didn't even see a woman in that time. Then in the other life that I went back to, I was a monk living in a monastery in France. I'm pretty sure you weren't in that life either."

"Hey, I could have been one of your fellow monks," said Hannah.

"That's true," said Hollis.

"Maybe we don't always show up together, or maybe we

just don't know enough about those two lives to say that for sure."

"This reincarnation stuff is damned interesting, isn't it?" asked Hollis.

The waiter came by before Hannah could answer. They declined dessert, and Jim put their bill on the table. "We close in ten minutes," he said.

They both turned to look at the clock that hung behind the far counter.

"Wow," said Hollis, "that went by fast."

"I'll say." Hannah put her credit card down on the bill and saw Hollis begin to object. "It's a brave new world," she said, "and if you glance at the hot blond by the door as we leave, I won't say a word."

He could only stare at her in wonder before finally mumbling, "I hope you don't turn into a pumpkin."

They left the diner five minutes later. Hollis took an obvious look at the girl Hannah had been talking about, and then said, "Not bad, but I'm think I'm going to stick with you."

They walked slowly to the lot where their cars were parked next to each other. Hollis was unsure what he should do, but Hannah solved the problem for him. "I think a hug is in order," she said.

He held her tight and inhaled the aroma of her perfume. "It's crazy," he said. "I just met you, yet I don't want to let you go."

"We'll take it slow," said Hannah. "Just because we have known each other through the ages doesn't mean we should be together again now." She skipped a beat before adding, "But it sure feels right to me."

"Me too," said Hollis.

She handed him her business card on which she had already written her home phone number. "I usually sleep in on Sunday," she said. "Call me around ten and we'll see what this fairy tale holds in store for us."

They hugged one more time, and Hollis couldn't resist giving her a peck on the cheek. When he drew back she locked eyes with him for a moment, and then she put her left hand behind his head and brought him to her. She kissed him long and hard, and suddenly they heard the blond from the diner yell out, "You go girl!"

When they finally separated, Hannah said, "I thought I could resist, but I was wrong."

"I'm thankful for that," said Hollis, his body shaking with excitement. When he drove off a minute later, he was whistling a Beatles' love song.

Hollis thought of Hannah and the extraordinary evening they had just shared all the way home. A huge smile was still on his face as he parked his car in the garage and entered his condo. He had only taken two steps into his kitchen when he was startled by a light suddenly turning on.

Amy was sitting on his couch in the living room, wearing nothing but a see through negligee and a thong. "I'm sorry," she said. "I know we both said things we didn't mean. Certainly we're still a couple."

He hadn't thought of Amy once on the drive home, and he had never imagined she would use the key he had given her to let herself in. He measured his words carefully before speaking.

"You shouldn't have come here, Amy. I'm afraid our relationship is, in fact, over." He watched as her alluring smile faded and a look of fear overtook her.

"You can't mean that," she said, attempting to remain calm. She arose from the couch and started towards him, running her hand down her body as she said, "Surely you're not going to give all this up. You can have me any way you want me tonight, my darling."

Hollis was still frozen to the kitchen floor. "Stop," he said. "You need to put your clothes on and go home."

She tried one more time, cupping each breast in a hand and shaking them at him. "Are you sure these gals can't change your mind? Where are you going to find tits like this?"

And suddenly Hollis started laughing, which first shocked Amy and then turned her furious.

"What are you laughing about?" she screamed at him.

"You just reminded me that in my last life I had tits like that," he said.

The words and accusations flew fast and furious after that, Amy swearing at him one minute and trying to use her wiles on him the next. None of it worked. Twenty minutes later, fully clothed and no longer with a key to his condo, a totally bewildered Amy left his place for the last time.

EIGHTEEN

Hannah's morning to sleep in turned out to be just the opposite. She awoke at six forty-five needing to use the bathroom and her mind kicked into high gear. She thought of Hollis and immediately had goose bumps all over her body. She had thoroughly enjoyed their time together last night and couldn't wait to see him again. She was thankful that Simon had found a way to bring them together that was planned and yet spontaneous.

She pictured Hollis as Anne Festa, remembering her beauty and how much in love they were. She recalled gazing into the eyes of Stephanus and the wonderful life they had enjoyed. She even remembered the little boy from long ago in India and how she had hoped to marry him one day.

She tried to fall back asleep but soon realized it wasn't going to happen. She slipped out of bed again and ambled into the kitchen to make coffee. She turned on the television and decided to watch the home renovation shows on HGTV. She always found some great decorating ideas from these shows, but this morning she kept gazing at the digital clock on the cable box. The time seemed to be moving not at all.

"Why didn't I tell him to call at *eight*?" she finally yelled to the empty home.

She made a bowl of oatmeal and a second cup of coffee

as she watched her digital clock slowly meander from 9:10 to 9:14 to 9:21. After eating she decided to take a shower and get dressed.

She had just finished putting on her blouse when the phone rang. It was 9:50.

"I couldn't wait any longer," said Hollis after Hannah had answered. "I think I've been sitting by the phone for a half hour now just waiting for ten o'clock to arrive."

"I know how you feel," she replied, and then she told him about her morning.

They wanted to spend their time together, not just talking on the phone, so the conversation didn't last long. Hannah gave him her address, and he said he would be there at twelve.

More clock watching. For the second time that morning it seemed like the longest two hours of her life. Hollis arrived exactly at noon.

"Right on time," said Hannah. "I appreciate that."

Hollis looked at her, wondering how simple green shorts and a flowered blouse could look so good on anyone, and said, "I'm a Virgo. We're very punctual people most of the time."

He led her to his car and opened the door for her as she asked, "Where are we going?"

"I thought we'd start with lunch, if you're hungry."

After determining each other's likes and dislikes, they decided to go to Genuine Thai.

When they arrived, Ellen led them to a table. She came back a minute later, took their order, and brought it into the kitchen. As she handed it to Sanjay, she said, "Young couple in love; can't take their eyes off one another."

They talked only about their current life as they ate, discussing family and friends and jobs they had held. His need to be honest coming to the forefront, Hollis told her about his meeting with Amy at the condo, although he left out the part about how she was dressed.

"Nothing happened," he said. "I made sure she knew it was over."

"You must have been tempted to have a final fling," said Hannah.

"Strangely enough, I wasn't," said Hollis. "I …."

"What?" asked Hannah.

"I just wanted to be with you."

She believed him, and swore her heart skipped a beat as he said it.

They left the restaurant at one thirty and were stunned to see Simon walking towards them.

"Well, hello you two," he said. "Did you just have lunch here?"

"We did," said Hannah, as she gave him a hug.

"This is my favorite restaurant," said Simon. "I'm so delighted to see you two together. I take it you're both happy that my little plan worked?"

"That would be a yes," said Hannah, and Hollis nodded his agreement.

"Well then, I'm not going to interrupt you. Besides, I'm famished. Enjoy your day," said Simon, and he turned to enter the restaurant.

They had both noticed the glow in his eyes and the smile on his face, and as he walked away Hollis said, "He looks like a proud parent at a graduation ceremony."

They drove to the beach and walked along the water's edge as they continued to get to know each other. Later that afternoon they shared an ice cream cone and found their tastes in ice cream were the same. When Hollis suggested they go to a carnival that was only in town for the weekend Hannah agreed, but only if he promised to come back to the beach in time to watch the sunset.

"Deal," he said.

The carnival was crowded, but they managed to ride the Ferris wheel four times and the merry-go-round twice. By six o'clock all the walking they had done made them hungry again, so they found a food stand, where they ate hot dogs and fries and washed it all down with lemonade.

Finally, Hannah pointed at the receding sun and said,

"We'd better go."

The traffic was brutal, and it took twenty minutes to make the mile ride back to the beach. They caught the sunset with about five minutes to spare.

"Good thing we made it," said Hannah, "or else I might have had to break up with you." She was joking, of course, and they both knew it.

He held her close as they watched the sun disappear from the horizon. Ten minutes later the westerly sky shone a bright red with clouds of pink dancing in it.

"The sunsets here are just beautiful," said Hannah. "I never get tired of them."

Hollis was gazing at her. "You're beautiful," he said, and they kissed for the first time that day. As the sky eventually darkened, he said, "I'd better get you home; work day tomorrow."

She had said she wanted to take it slow and that was fine with him. He knew there would be no jumping in bed right away as he had done with Amy. He just wanted to spend as much time as possible with this amazing young lady he had apparently known for lifetimes.

"I hope you don't have any plans for Saturday," said Hollis, as they drove to Hannah's apartment.

"I can be free on Saturday," she replied, "although I hope you're not going to wait until then to see me again."

He glanced over at her as he drove. "I want to see you every day."

"So what do you have in mind for Saturday?"

"There's an awards ceremony in Orlando. I'm up for teacher of the year."

"Oh my, that's fantastic," said Hannah. "I'd be honored to go with you."

When they pulled up to her driveway they kissed again in the car, and then he watched as she walked to the front door and waved from the steps.

The next few days flew by, although the time Hollis spent

at the school proved difficult. The ladies in the office were cool to him, and he could only imagine what Amy had told them. However, he was pleased that she seemed to be avoiding him and was not causing any scenes.

Hannah made supper for him at her place on Monday night, and Hollis returned the favor the next day. Wednesday night they went to a movie and held hands the entire time. The next night he was back at her place, where a night of watching television turned into a make-out session that was hot and heavy but, as the old folks would say, never reached second base.

Hollis wanted to just pick her up, carry her to the bedroom and make love to her, but she had said that she wanted to go slow, and he was trying to be respectful of her wishes.

He was getting ready to go home when Hannah suddenly said, "I have an idea."

"What's that?" he asked.

"Why don't we make a weekend of it in Orlando?"

He gazed into her eyes as the smile on his face slowly grew.

"We could leave tomorrow night after work and come home Sunday. I'll go online tonight and make the reservations. Tell me again where the ceremony is."

"Are you sure?" he asked, and they both knew what he was really asking.

"I'm sure," said Hannah, "that I'm going to make you wait one more night before you take me to bed."

His smile only grew as he gazed at the lovely lady before him. "It may be the longest twenty-four hours of my life," he said. "The event is at the Marriott. I'll send you the address when I get home."

"I know it's the 21st century and all, but perhaps we should stay someplace else," said Hannah. "After all, you have a teacher's reputation to uphold."

"I'll leave that up to you," said Hollis. He gave her a big hug and a long, sweet kiss before leaving.

The next night they checked in to the Gatewood Hotel, a small but cozy place just a mile from the Marriott. They brought their bags to the room and quickly unpacked before heading to the dining room. They were both hungry after the long ride, but neither one wanted to linger too long over dinner

When they returned to the room Hollis said, "I have a surprise." He pulled out a bottle of wine from one of his bags and showed it to her.

"It's French," she said with a smile.

"Look closer," said Hollis.

Hannah took the bottle from him and slowly read the label. She found what he was getting at after a few moments. "Bottled in Colmar," she said. "Oh my goodness, this could be one of ours!"

"It took a bit of searching, but I found out that they still make wine in Colmar. A little more searching and I found a brand name; had to go to three stores before I found one that carried it."

"Unbelievable," she said.

He opened the bottle and poured two glasses, which he had also brought. "To us," he said.

They clinked their glasses together, and then Hannah took a sip. "Not bad," she said, "not bad at all. Now, what shall we do with the rest of the night?"

He set down his glass and she did the same, and then he took her in his arms and kissed her. "I have an idea," he said.

"Show me."

They undressed each other slowly at first, then at a more rapid pace as their passion grew. Her nipples were already hard before he placed his mouth over them. The smallness of her breasts compared to Amy's didn't bother him a bit.

They wanted to make it last, but the moment had been building for a week now and in no time he was inside her. He was embarrassed that it ended so quickly, but Hannah brushed it off.

"The first time is always awkward," she said. "Let's take a quick shower and then do it right."

Twenty minutes later they began again. "Now show me what you've really got," said Hannah.

He started at her toes this time and slowly made his way to the sweet spot between her legs. After five minutes of pleasuring her, he started towards her navel.

"Not yet," said Hannah, and she moved him back down again.

Ten minutes later it was her turn to pleasure him. She brought him to the edge, backed off, and then did it again. Finally, she guided him back into her. They took their time and enjoyed the moment as they slowly moved in rhythm with each other. Then, when they both realized the end was in sight, Hannah said, "Now do it hard,'" and Hollis complied.

The award ceremony the next night was almost anti-climatic. Hannah watched from the audience as Hollis and four other nominees sat on the stage. All of them were amazing teachers, and Hollis was not the least bit disappointed when he was announced as the second runner up.

When they arrived back at the hotel, Hannah said, "Poor Hollis, you must be so disappointed."

He was about to pour two glasses of their Colmar wine and had not seen the smile on her face as she spoke. "No, I'm fine," he said. "Just being on the stage and having my name mentioned was enough for me."

She walked up to him, her smile now obvious, and said, "Oh no, I'm sure you must need someone to console you. Why don't you let me make you feel better?"

This time he caught on at once. "Yes," he said, "I could use some consoling. You know, to make me feel better."

"This way, please," said Hannah, pointing to the bedroom. They made love that night and then once more the next morning before checking out of the hotel.

Their love took off from there.

Barry Homan

NINETEEN

Maria waited three weeks after Simon's party and then decided she couldn't wait any longer. She took out his business card and called his cell phone.

Simon had just finished washing the few dishes he had when he heard his phone buzzing on the kitchen counter. He reached it in three quick steps and noted the caller ID. He wondered why Maria Vasquez would be calling him on a Sunday morning.

"Maria, hello," he said upon answering. "To what do I owe the pleasure?"

"Good morning, Simon," said Maria. "I hope I'm not disturbing you on your day off."

"Not at all," he replied. "What can I do for you?"

He heard a momentary catch in her throat that his patients often had when they were debating what to tell him. "If you have some free time today, I would like to stop by and talk with you," said Maria.

Simon couldn't imagine what she might want to talk about, but he had always enjoyed her company and he had no plans for the day. "Perhaps we could meet for lunch somewhere," he said.

Maria quickly blurted out "No" a bit harshly, then drew in a breath and in a calmer manner said, "This is something that needs to be done in private."

"Okay then," said a totally confused Simon, "why don't you come over around two o'clock."

"That would be fine," she said. "I'll see you then."

Over the next few hours Maria debated what she would say to the doctor. She walked around her room trying out different lines, from soft to blunt, before eventually giving up. She knew when the time came she would remember none of them. She would just have to be spontaneous and let the moment happen.

Simon had no clue what the afternoon meeting would be about. He had seen her at the party and they had talked for a bit, but it had never seemed to him that she had something pressing she wanted to discuss at that time. She had spent most of the night by the side of Wil Stevens. Perhaps the two of them were getting close and she wanted Simon's opinion of the shaman. He thought that was a stretch, but it was all he could come up with. He even wondered if Wil might show up with her.

Maria arrived on time and alone. Although she was dressed casually, Simon was once again amazed by how beautiful she looked. *She could wear tattered rags and carry it off*, he thought.

"Welcome," he said. "Please come in and make yourself comfortable." He noticed she was carrying an umbrella and added, "You can just leave that by the door, if you like."

"I thought it was going to rain," said Maria, "but it's held off so far."

He led her to the living room and suggested she sit on the couch. He took the chair opposite her after she had done so.

"Well," he began, "this is a nice surprise, although I must admit I am stumped as to why you are here."

Her emerald eyes were wide open as she looked at him, and he could tell by her body language that she was nervous about something. He couldn't imagine what.

"Oh my goodness, where are my manners?" he suddenly

said. "Could I get you something to drink?"

She didn't want anything to drink, yet she knew her mouth might become dry in the telling of her tale, so she asked for a glass of water.

He retrieved the drink for her and set it on a coaster on the coffee table. After sitting back down Simon said, "Now you seem a bit nervous, so whatever the reason you have asked to see me today must be important to you. Why don't we get to it?"

Maria rearranged herself on the couch, looked down at her hands which were fidgeting anxiously, and finally looked up and gazed directly at him. She took a sip of water and then began.

"I know in advance that you're not going to believe what I have to tell you," she said, and when Simon began to reply she held up a hand and stopped him. "Please, just let me get this out without interruption."

"Okay," he said, "the floor is yours."

"I know you're not going to believe what I have to tell you," she said again, "and that's okay. I understand. I just hope you will give it some consideration, and perhaps sometime down the road we can discuss it."

Simon, as confused now as he had been after her phone call, simply nodded his agreement. He had heard the phrase *you're not going to believe this, but ...* countless times over the years from his psychology patients. It usually turned out to be something he actually had heard before, although he never said that to them.

"I've always believed in the metaphysical," said Maria. "It makes sense to me and always has. I read a great deal about near death experiences when I was younger. I've read everything Moody has ever written. I've always been fascinated by the stories those people tell when they return to their bodies, and how nearly all of them appreciate life more and lose their fear of death."

This was not one of the openings she had practiced this morning, but she was speaking from her heart and this was where it had led her.

"I think a belief in reincarnation is an easy offshoot of that. If we can die and then return to this life, why can't we die and return to a new life? So when your book first came out I was immediately drawn to it. I remember the day I went to the bookstore and took it off the shelves. I turned it over and saw your picture on the back cover."

She paused for a moment as she stared into his eyes. *Here we go*, she thought.

"I was drawn to you in that moment. It was as though I knew you, like we were friends. I took the book home and read it all that same day. That night I put the book on my nightstand, with the cover facing the wall, so I could see your picture whenever I looked at it."

My goodness, she's come to ask me for a date, thought Simon. "I'm honored," he said.

She realized what he must be thinking, but ignored it and continued her story. "When I saw in the papers that you were moving to Sarasota I was thrilled at first, but after going online and seeing the stories of why you were moving I was horrified. It must have been an awful time for you."

She watched as his head lowered and a sudden look of sadness came over him, but he said nothing.

"When you opened your office here and started doing regressions again, I made my first appointment right away. In a way what happened was startling to me, and yet there was a piece of me that knew it was going to happen."

"That was your life as a Cherokee," said Simon.

"Yes."

"So what was it that you knew was going to happen?"

"My name was Leotie. I was married to the medicine man of the tribe."

"I recall that," said Simon.

"You were the medicine man," said Maria.

It took Simon a moment to process what she had said, and then he suddenly started chuckling and said, "What?"

It was obvious from the smile on his face that he didn't believe her. "You were the medicine man, Simon. You were my husband."

"That can't possibly be true," he said. "You must have just been projecting my image into your story."

"I don't believe that," said Maria, "but I will admit that I wasn't 100% convinced at that time. Yet when we met again at the psychic fair, I was sure it was the universe trying to get us back together again. That's the reason I made another appointment with you. I had to be certain before I said anything to you."

Simon had to butt in at this point, his mind spinning at these crazy allegations of hers. "Nora was my soul mate," he said. "Of that I'm sure."

"I know you want to believe that," she said, "and perhaps the truth is we have more than one soul mate; perhaps many. I've talked with Wil about it, and I know we tend to incarnate with the same people over and over. Perhaps they're all our soul mates. I don't know."

He considered her words for a moment before replying. Finally, he said, "My work has taught me that we do tend to return to the same core group of people, and I have received messages during my work that the idea of soul mates is much more complex than we here on earth can imagine. I have always found you to be an incredibly attractive woman, but I've never had the impression that we knew each other before. I've felt no tug in that manner towards you."

"Jill Palmer felt no tug towards Michael, yet he recognized her instantly. Perhaps that's the way it works most of the time."

"Perhaps," he agreed.

She took a sip of water, and then said, "Please let me finish my story."

"Continue," said Simon, his head nodding ever so slightly.

"I made the last appointment so I could know for sure if what I suspected were true. It was. You and I were thieves in our last life. This time we were brother and sister, as I'm sure you recall. You were my brother Randall. After that regression I knew for a fact that you were my soul mate. I have no doubt about it. I think I knew the moment I saw your picture on the book."

Simon looked at the beautiful lady sitting across from him. He did not believe her story for a minute, but it was obvious to him that she did. He scoffed at the idea that anyone other than Nora could be his soul mate. He wouldn't believe it.

"Well," he finally muttered, "you've certainly given me something to think about, although I have to admit I think you're barking up the wrong tree."

"As I suspected you would," said Maria. "I told you at the beginning you would not believe me."

"So you did."

"I don't know where we go from here," said Maria. "I have always found you to be an attractive man, and I hope someday soon you will ask me out … even if you don't believe me."

He just looked at her, lost for words.

His non-reply told her the visit was over. He needed time, as she knew he would. She arose from the couch and said, "Thank you for seeing me."

Simon began walking her to the door. "I will think about all that you've said. My regression work is important to me, and people are usually pretty accurate in picking out people from this life that they see in their past lives. I don't know why you saw me in yours, but I have to honor the thought that you believe you did."

"I guess that's all I can ask for," said Maria, "but please know that I am not crazy and I am not making this up. It was you I saw."

He handed her the umbrella as they reached the door, and pointing to the view of his balcony across the way he said, "You're going to need this. It's pouring outside."

She gave him one last look. Anyone looking at them

would think it was two sad people saying goodbye. She hoped that it wasn't.

Simon closed the door behind her and just shook his head. His mind was a jumble of thoughts as he walked to the kitchen and poured a glass of scotch over ice. Nora was his soul mate, of that he was sure. Perhaps Maria was also in his close circle of friends, but another soul mate? He doubted that, even though she obviously believed it.

He took his drink out to the balcony. The rain was coming down hard, slanting in from the west. Both seats were wet, so Simon just stood there. He looked out over the waters of the bay, which were rougher than normal. He thought the storm might get worse before it calmed down.

He moved back inside when the spray of water became too much for him. He slipped into his bedroom, looked around, and then wandered back into the living room. He was lost in a world of conflicting thoughts and he didn't know what to do.

He turned on the television, hoping to take his mind off things. Ten minutes later, finding nothing of interest, he turned it off.

He replayed everything that Maria had said over and over in his mind. Was she telling the truth? He was certain that she was, at least as she saw it. But Nora; what about Nora?

In all his years of doing regressions he had never had one of his own. He had never seen the need. He and Nora had been two peas in a pod, in love with each other and in love with their work. They spent a great deal of time apart due to their jobs, yet when they were together it was bliss. They never fought, rarely argued at all. He had no reason to believe that she was anything other than his soul mate. In fact, he was pretty sure he would never stop believing it.

As he sat on his couch, content in the knowledge that he was right, one final thing Maria had said to him popped into his head.

I hope someday soon you will ask me out, even if you don't believe me.

The thought finally brought a smile back to his face. She was a gorgeous woman, no doubt about it, and he had to admit he was attracted to her. Nora had been gone nearly eighteen months now. She loved him dearly, but she would want him to move on with his life.

Perhaps it was time.

Noticing that the rain had stopped as fast as it had started, Simon walked back onto the balcony. The air felt cleaner, crisper than it had before. The storm had temporarily cut through the humidity that had hung in the air all day.

"So what do I do, Nora?" he asked. "Is it time for me to move on?"

There was no breeze at all as he gazed at the heavens, but suddenly a chill ran through his body.

The wind chimes were ringing.

EPILOGUE

Hannah fidgeted in her seat, her stomach doing flip-flops, as Hollis carefully monitored the GPS while he drove. They had crossed the border into Alabama an hour ago and knew their destination was near.

"Nervous?" he asked.

"Petrified," she replied, "but also extremely excited."

"We should be there soon," said Hollis. "The town is just up ahead." He glanced at the GPS once more and noted their arrival time was six minutes away.

The air conditioner was keeping the car at a cool 67 degrees in the hot July sun, yet Hannah was so nervous she was sure her clothes were drenched with sweat. She looked at her husband as he drove and said, "I can't believe this is happening."

He gave her a reassuring smile. He had worried off and on whether his timing had been poor, all things considered, but there was no turning back now. "Everything's going to be fine," he said.

They had married on New Year's Eve, less than four months after meeting at Simon's party. Hannah had moved out of her apartment and into Hollis' condo two weeks earlier. They both knew it was right and neither one wished to wait any longer. His two sisters, Vivian and Terry, had taken to Hannah immediately, and were thrilled that their brother had finally found someone special.

Hollis returned to work after the Christmas vacation to find that Amy had quit her job. According to the gossip in the office, she had been dating someone new since November and no longer wished to work where her old flame worked. The office secretaries, stunned by the news that Hollis had married but noting how happy he was, began to lighten up on him, and eventually things returned to normal.

January turned into February, and as Valentine's Day approached Hollis wanted to do something nice for the woman he loved. He made reservations at Antonio's, a high class restaurant on the bay with a piano bar.

"Wow," said Hannah as they were shown to their table, "what a spectacular view."

They had a window seat overlooking the dock below, where half a dozen yachts bobbed in the water.

"A woman could get used to this," she said. However, after opening the menu and seeing the prices, she looked at him and said, "Can we afford to eat here?"

"Once a year, every year," Hollis replied, and they both smiled.

The dinner was fabulous, as they expected it would be, and neither had room for dessert. They ordered coffee after the dishes were cleared away, and when the waiter left Hollis said, "I have something for you."

"Don't you think the dinner was enough?" said Hannah.

"Not tonight." He pulled a small velvet box from his coat pocket and handed it to her. "For you, my love."

She surmised from the size of the box what would be inside, yet she was still stunned when she saw them. She was looking at a pair of two carat diamond earrings. "Hollis, these must have cost a fortune," she said.

"You're supposed to say 'Hollis, these are beautiful,'" he replied.

"They're gorgeous," she said. "You shouldn't have."

"Why don't you put them on?"

She took off the earrings she had been wearing and put her new ones on.

"They look fabulous on you," said Hollis.

Hannah took a compact out of her purse, opened it to use the mirror, and took a look for herself. "I've never owned anything this nice," she said. "Thank you."

The waiter arrived with their coffees and dropped off the bill. Hollis took a quick glance at the total and jokingly said, "Excuse me, I'll need one of those earrings back."

"No chance," she said. They took sips of their coffee, and then Hannah said, "Now I have a present for you."

"Okay," said Hollis, wondering where she could be hiding it, since her dress had no pockets and her purse could barely hold a wallet.

"It's in the form of news," she said. She saw the curious look on his face and knew she had his attention. "Do you remember those large breasts you had in our last lifetime together; the ones that made me instantly attracted to you?"

"I do," he said, wondering where this was going.

"Well, pretty soon I'm going to have breasts like that."

"What? Honey, I like your boobs just the way they are. I don't want you having any breast enhancement surgery."

Hannah smiled at him. "I'd never do that," she said. "What I meant was, a woman's breasts naturally get much larger … when she's pregnant."

He was stunned, speechless for a moment, and then he yelled, "Oh my God, we're having a baby!" loud enough for the whole restaurant to hear. Immediately all the other patrons in the room started clapping.

Hollis gave a wave to the other diners in acknowledgment as a dozen questions zoomed through his mind. He finally managed to say, "When did you find out?"

"Just this morning," said Hannah. "Apparently our honeymoon was very productive, because I'm about six weeks along."

The next few months flew by. They turned the second bedroom in their condo into a nursery room, and Hollis painted the walls a soft pink once they learned they were having a girl. They quickly decided to name her Anne.

"I wonder who it could be," said Hannah, "since all of our children from Colmar have already returned."

"I can't imagine," said Hollis. "Do you think it's too early for Pasha to return? I mean, it's been what, fifteen years or so since your adopted father passed?"

"Wouldn't that be something?" was all Hannah could think to say.

While they spent a great deal of their free time preparing for the birth of their first child, there was another project they were working together on. It had been Hollis' idea, and Hannah had been skeptical at first that they could succeed, but eventually he had convinced her to try. Their progress was slow in the beginning, and extremely frustrating at times, but it had paid off in the end.

"Spruce Street is just up ahead," said Hollis. "Are you ready?"

Hannah was too nervous to speak, and the baby was moving around in her womb as if she were excited too.

He turned onto the street, found the house up ahead on the right, and pulled into the driveway. The home had definitely been built a long time ago, yet it appeared to be well maintained. The grass in the front yard had obviously just been cut, and it was apparent the sidewalk leading to the front door had recently been swept in anticipation of their arrival.

Hollis helped his wife out of the car and they walked slowly to the front door. He pointed to the doorbell and said, "You should have the honors."

Hannah pressed the button, and they both heard the sound of chimes inside the home.

The lady who opened the door still looked young for her age. She seemed uneasy in that first instant, yet a look of hopefulness soon overtook her. After a quick glance at Hollis, she turned to gaze at his obviously pregnant wife. "Hannah?" she asked.

"It's me, mom," said Hannah.

The reunion with the mother who had been forced to give her up for adoption lasted through the afternoon and late into the evening. By the time they were ready to leave the next morning, Hannah and Hollis knew that Anne would have a grandmother who would love her unconditionally.

Tears were shed all around as the couple prepared to head home. The trio walked slowly to the car, and this time it was Hannah's mother who gently guided her pregnant daughter into the passenger seat. A moment later Hannah and Hollis drove away from the house on Spruce Street. Two people who had known each other for just ten months now.

Yet it felt like they'd know each other forever.

Barry Homan

About the Author

Barry Homan has been a spiritualist for many years and has believed in reincarnation ever since he was a young child. He is currently working on his third metaphysical novel, about a man who sees auras and a 50 year old murder mystery.

The third Simon Taylor novel is on the drawing board.

He lives in Florida with his wife Karen and their cat Gizmo.